Acquisition

by

Renee Canter Johnson

Acquisition

Cover Art by *Rae Monet, Inc. Design*

The Wild Rose Press, Inc.
PO Box 708
Adams Basin, NY 14410-0708
Visit us at www.thewildrosepress.com

Publishing History
First *Last Rose of Summer* Edition, 2014
Print ISBN 978-1-62830-583-8
Digital ISBN 978-1-62830-584-5

Published in the United States of America

...his lips didn't pause at her cheekbone.

They continued to her ear where his breath stoked a fire within her as he whispered, "I never make promises I don't intend to keep." Each "p" sound brought with it a wisp of superheated air that ran the length of her body and circled inward.

The flesh of his face all but brushed her cheek as he pulled away. She couldn't resist looking at him, into his prismatic blue eyes, flashing like a spring in the Yellowstone geysers.

Amanda stalled at a precipice of confusion, deeply drawn to him from a sexual perspective while deeply repulsed by the business at hand. How long they stood there she couldn't say. It could have been seconds, minutes even. But it seemed an eternity. Two opposing rods, they kept each other near and yet far.

She licked her lips, a Freudian slip to be sure, and she knew he would gather its meaning and store it in a cup to be returned to her when she least desired it.

His mouth opened slightly, as though he intended to make the most of the moment, but somehow he managed to pull away and turn for the door.

Amanda didn't stop him. She wanted him to leave. Another minute and she would have been powerless to prevent him from pursuing her promising mouth.

She remained standing until the door shut behind him. Then she collapsed in the chair, wishing the leather indentations in it were his body, caressing hers. She wondered how in the world a man had managed to get under her skin in this way—especially one she despised as much as he.

Praise for *ACQUISITION*

"Renee Johnson is a natural storyteller with a graceful elegance of style."

~*Janet Hulstrand,*
Writing from the Heart, Reading for the Road
~*~

"The beginning of *ACQUISITION* masquerades as a possible whirlwind office romance, but it blossoms into so much more. There's mystery, action, even a bit of cloak and dagger mixed into this sweet romance. A man with a secret, a woman with a past, and both have good reason not to like each other. I like that they're an older couple with a work ethic in common, and the romance grows at a natural pace. Love scenes are clean and proper. I also loved watching Amanda's eyes slowly open as she discovered a life outside of work. Bravo to the author."

~*Lisa Rayns, author of Wanted: Vampire—Free Blood*
~*~

"Renee Johnson's *ACQUISITION* is a delightful debut novel. I hope to read more from Ms. Johnson—soon! What these two discover about each other and themselves will turn the saying "it's not personal, it's business" on its ear. If you enjoy a fast-paced, multi-level romance, *ACQUISITION* is for you."

~*Denise Golinowski, author of Collector's Item*

Dedications

To my husband and son—Tony and Caleb Johnson—
for giving me love, and time to write.

~*~

To my teacher and mentor—Janet Hulstrand—
for helping me achieve confidence in my words,
and encouraging me to keep writing.

~*~

And to my editor—Maggie Johnson—for providing me
with guidance and the opportunity to become published.

Chapter 1

Amanda Lassiter pushed her spine into the back of the seat on the aircraft bound for Charlotte, trying to relax. *Anyone would be nervous about their first solo career adventure*, she assured herself. Yet she knew it was more than that. *Why couldn't he have sent me to Alaska? Why did it have to be North Carolina?*

"Would you like something to drink?" the flight attendant asked the lady seated next to her. He looked directly at Amanda while scooping ice into squat plastic cups. "And you?"

"Just a water, please."

He poured their drinks and continued to inch his way up the tight aisle with the rolling cart of beverages.

Amanda sipped the water slowly while reviewing her notes on Dixie Millwork and Building Supply, the company her Chicago-based Builders Tech had recently acquired. A red asterisk designated Reece Jordan as its Chief Executive Officer.

Reece Jordan. He might be difficult. She hadn't met him yet, but had been forewarned of his highly vocal opposition to the merger. If what she had been told was true, he would likely make her job of assessing their staff and determining the profitability of keeping their doors open as difficult as possible.

She needed to remain firm and never let him have the upper hand on anything. It would have to be *her way* right from the start.

The rest of the flight was a maze of broken concentration. The aisles filled with passengers going back and forth to the bathrooms and the flight attendant returning for the empty cups and napkins. Amanda could barely focus on the itinerary she planned to initiate as early as this afternoon, and was relieved when the "fasten seat belt" warnings were given. She stowed her briefcase beneath her seat and took a few deep breaths. *This is my big chance.*

Amanda jumped up as soon as the plane landed, briefcase firmly back in hand. She snagged her carry-on from the overhead compartment, and surged forward to the exit. A driver was supposed to be waiting for her at the arrivals gate. She paused to check out the faces anxiously awaiting their loved ones, imagining for a brief moment how nice it might be to have someone waiting to embrace her.

"Excuse me!" a man barked.

She turned toward his voice, taking in his height of more than six feet. A swath of blond hair swept across eyes the color of the Carolina sky—eyes failing to share the smile on his chiseled, angular face. Enough wrinkles feathered their corners to indicate middle age, though his body was fit and lean.

"I'm looking for Amanda Lassiter, and you match the photo I was given." He presented a color printed image of her from the company's website with a crease down the center of her face where it had been folded.

She glanced at the rendering. Her auburn hair looked a bit darker in the picture, but her hazel eyes really popped. And she thought she appeared to be about thirty-five, a good decade younger than her actual age.

"Oh, you must be my driver." She released the handle of her carry-on bag and extended a well-manicured hand. "I *am* Amanda Lassiter."

He took the luggage handle instead of her proffered hand, snapping, "Guess we'd better get going." His swift stride immediately left a gap of distance between them as he crossed the floor and headed for the door, rolling her bag behind him.

She had no choice but to nearly run in heels clicking noisily against the floor.

Outside, the Carolina warmth washed over her. It was the one thing she missed about the south. Chicago's climate left a lot to be desired, but Charlotte felt especially hot to her for early June. She began to perspire in her business suit jacket and sighed with relief when her driver ducked beneath the shade of the parking garage.

She still didn't know his name, but only someone with the company would have access to her identity and which flight she would be arriving on. Perhaps all of the employees of Dixie Millwork would resent her similarly.

She watched the muscular back of her driver. He reminded her of a tiger with barely controlled physical strength echoing from his strong arms and sharp features. When he reached the large four-wheel drive utility vehicle with magnetic signs advertising Dixie Millwork and Building Supply on the side, he threw her bag in the back and motioned for her to get in.

The overhead stream of planes becoming airborne or descending for landing made Amanda nervous. And the rush of taxi cabs and other vehicles trying to merge into each other's lanes of traffic only added to it. She made no effort to suggest conversation until they were out of the airport traffic. "I didn't catch your name," she said with an inflection in her voice which turned the comment into a question.

"Yeah, well, I didn't throw it," he said dismissively. He drove steadily ahead, clearly on a mission.

"Are you always this friendly?" She winced, knowing better than to banter with the employees, though she hadn't expected open hostility in the first five minutes of arrival.

"I'm just doing my job. Conversation wasn't part of the requirement."

"Fair enough! I'll be retaining my own vehicle as soon as I have my bearings and an idea of how long the company will need my services. So I suppose it isn't necessary for us to become acquainted. It could turn out we may not even require the position you currently fill."

She saw his jaw clench. He seemed more angry than nervous, as he whipped the car off an exit. Barely slowing, he proceeded with intent into the hotel parking lot, and underneath the parapet where limited parking was permitted for loading and unloading. He jumped out, grabbed her bag and set it at the door.

Motioning for her to follow, he said, "I understand your reservation is here."

"Well, yes, but—"

"Get checked in. A car will be delivered to you in one hour." He didn't wait for her to object. He simply jumped back into the SUV and sped out of the parking lot while she stood at the hotel entrance staring after him.

Geez! He never even gave me his name, she thought. *Whatever it is, he'll definitely be the first to go!*

It didn't take long for her to unpack the small, simple bag she traveled with. Then, short of describing the undesirable greeting, she checked in with her superior in Chicago, Judson Matheny.

"Yes sir," she answered politely. "The flight was on time, and I have a map of Charlotte in front of me."

"That's good," he said.

She smiled as the smooth timbre of his voice indicated his pleasure in things operating on schedule. Amanda knew it wouldn't remain so at the first sign of trouble.

He continued. "I understand you have a meeting with the CEO this afternoon. Keep me posted." The phone clicked. Judson Matheney's parting words were normally "keep me posted." He rarely said anything such as "goodbye" when he ended a conversation. In person, he might just look away and cease talking full stop. That was the signal you were being dismissed.

The front desk buzzed with news her car had arrived. Not wishing to be late for her first meeting at Dixie, she picked up her briefcase, and headed off for the company she would likely be dismantling in the next few weeks.

****

Amanda liked the area surrounding the building supply operation. She had done her homework before arriving and had a lot of information on the city and the surrounding county of Mecklenburg. Steady growth in the region indicated future viability in maintaining a

Builders Tech branch in Charlotte.

She made several voice recordings into a tiny recorder as she drove, noting pros and cons as she saw them. There was easy access to interstate highways, over the road trucks, and airport. Unemployment, though high in the state of North Carolina, seemed relatively low in Charlotte. And a cheaper work force could be maintained as they were not unionized. These were all pluses for maintaining the business.

However, there were several cons. Super Builders Mart, a giant box chain which often competed against Builders Tech, had their headquarters here. They already had a satellite store in Rock Hill, South Carolina, just thirty miles southwest of Charlotte—both cities being close to their respective state's borders. Personally, its biggest disadvantage was being located in North Carolina, which would add another yearly—at least—trip south for her.

She switched off the recorder and pulled into the parking lot which appeared to have plenty of room as it was, yet, could be expanded if necessary. She quickly added it to her list of pros.

Amanda walked through the front entrance, barely looking at the receptionist. She didn't even try to keep the tone of her voice from indicating the kind of authority she had grown accustomed to having. "I have an appointment with Reece Jordan," she declared.

"I'm so sorry," the lady said. Although her words were apologetic, her smugness indicated otherwise. "Reece had to go out to a job site. A sudden and important issue had to be resolved. Our customers' needs come before anything else."

She seemed to be exaggerating a southern drawl,

but then again, Amanda had grown used to not hearing the twang she had relegated to her own past.

Irritation swelled in her throat, but she remained professional. "And when do you expect him to return?"

The receptionist lounged backward in her oversized chair.

Amanda met her stare, looking into green eyes. Her red hair and pointy chin gave her a sinister, although not altogether unattractive, appearance.

"Can't say. I never know what he's up to or how long things will take him to finish."

Something about the woman reminded Amanda of a cat—one having just destroyed a down comforter and daring you not to like it. And she had the distinct impression the lady was implying a close relationship with her boss.

"What is your name?" she asked the redhead, drumming her fingers on the alcove shelf with the blank visitor's sign-in sheet glaring at her.

She answered in long segments, making it sound similar to the name for a drag queen. "Ver-nel-la."

"Well, Vernella, here's what we can do." She put on her best, straightforward game face and leaned in close to the receptionist. "I have been sent by the new owners of this company to assess many different areas of this business. It isn't necessary that I begin with a cohesive plan everyone understands, as was my desire and reason for scheduling this appointment in advance."

Amanda tilted her head and forced a smile before continuing. "If Mr. Jordan is unable to make our prearranged engagement, then I will simply proceed without him. Just direct me to the accounting department, and I will get busy doing my job."

"Oh, I can't do that," Vernella said, shaking her mop of hair.

"Then I'll find it myself." Amanda jerked the door leading from the reception area to the back offices open.

"Suit yourself, but nobody's back there."

"What do you mean? They didn't have to accompany Mr. Jordan on his field trip, did they?"

"No, but he gave them the day off. They worked overtime last week finalizing reports for DMBS, as we refer to the company. He wanted to make sure all of Dixie Millwork and Building Supply's records were documented properly before the head-chopping people descended upon us." With that she added a sneer and sniffed.

Amanda's jaw jerked but she was determined not to reveal her displeasure. "And your sales department? Perhaps I could work with the inventory."

Vernella shook her head back and forth, punctuating her words. "They aren't here either."

"So who, besides you, is here?"

"Nobody."

Rage billowed beneath Amanda's outwardly calm demeanor. "Then why are you here?"

"To relay a message to you." The grin curling along the receptionist's lips dispelled any assumption she lacked intelligence. She had enjoyed the game play, and Amanda wouldn't have been surprised if the next word out of her mouth was "checkmate."

She bit her tongue and returned to the window framing the red-head like a portrait. "And what is that message exactly?"

"Reece is taking care of his business. He'll meet

you tonight at seven o'clock in the lobby of your hotel. He'll have some records for you and the two of you can discuss the future over dinner in the hotel's restaurant."

"And if this isn't agreeable to me?" Amanda snapped.

"Tell him so tonight." She lifted her shoulders, suggesting "whatever," but the mischievous smile said so much more. He was still calling the shots and making it known. She wouldn't just come in from the corporation she represented and take over. He was initiating an offensive.

"Guess I have no choice."

"Guess not."

****

Amanda seethed.

Judson Matheney would be expecting some kind of report today. He knew her schedule.

She imagined him in his ubiquitous black suit and tie, wrinkleless white shirt, and shiny black shoes. *He must have them lined up in his closet labeled for the days of the week*, she thought.

He would likely be waiting for news from an insider on another company seeking loans in this latest economic downturn. His method of finding businesses in financial trouble was a specific prescription. And it worked every time.

Pacing the floor in the high rise above Chicago, android phone snapped to his ear, mini-computer in his hand, the sixty-eight-year-old Judson set the pace. He would not abide a slacker, and she feared he would receive the news she had been unable to secure her initial meeting with Reece Jordan as a failure.

A familiar gnawing tore at her stomach—stress,

acid, hunger. She tried to remember when she had last eaten. *Definitely not today,* she decided, thinking back to the numerous cups of coffee and water she had consumed, but unable to find anything resembling a food group.

Amanda remembered passing a strip mall with a sports store and stopped in on the way back to the hotel to purchase running shoes, workout clothes, and a bathing suit. The hotel had a fitness facility and an indoor pool, but not having anticipated the extra time on her hands, she had packed nothing for such activities.

If she had to kill a day, she might as well use it to work off some stress. After the flight in, the rude driver, the sly receptionist, and the absent CEO, she felt as tight as a rusty bolt against metal.

The workout helped, especially since she normally got a strenuous one daily. Sweating always relieved her stress. She felt prepared now to face Reece Jordan as the evening rolled around to seven o'clock. She rehearsed a couple of versions of what she intended to say to him.

The desk clerk alerted her she had a visitor in the lobby. Expecting it to be Reece Jordan, she slipped down only to see this morning's driver standing there.

Her heart sank. This was likely another attempt at dodging her. She dispensed with any niceties since his behavior earlier in the day suggested he didn't operate within the laws of civility. "Don't tell me Mr. Jordan has been called away on some other mission."

He grinned slyly at her, looking as though he knew a secret.

The desk clerk waved them toward the dining

room. "Your table is ready, Mr. Jordan. The hostess will seat you now."

The realization of his identity hit Amanda with the force of a jet-propelled engine. She was incensed.

Reece Jordan took her firmly by the elbow, obviously relishing in her surprise, and led her into the stately old dining room. An elderly pianist in a pink chiffon gown played softly as they entered, and a young woman stepped forward to greet them.

"Right this way, Mr. Jordan. I have the table you requested ready for you."

He retained his grip on Amanda's arm as they followed the hostess to a table in the rear. He pulled out the chair for her before settling into the one on the opposite side.

It could have been a lovely place to have dinner; crisp white linen napkins and table cloth, large comfortable mahogany chairs with red tapestry seat covers, candles lit behind hurricane globes on every table. It almost seemed a shame it had to be wasted on such vile behavior.

Amanda managed to retain her composure until the hostess walked out of ear shot. "So what is up with your masquerading as a chauffeur, then failing to appear for our meeting? Let me tell you right now, Mr. Jordan, these shenanigans will not make it easy for you." She hit the table with her finger to emphasize the word: not.

His jaw clenched, and he looked at her with cool eyes, dispelling any sign of cooperation. "I know why you are here, Ms. Lassiter, and I have absolutely no intentions on making it easy for you. You can go back to Chicago and tell your little Napoleon this could be his Waterloo."

"It really isn't for you to decide how this will be handled. If you would like, I could shut the doors on the business today. I really must impress on you the importance of cooperation if you wish to retain any semblance of your company here in the south."

A waiter arrived with champagne and menus. Standing at attention, he waited patiently for them to order. Reece dismissed him. "We'll need a few minutes to decide."

When they were alone again, Reece said, "You see, that is where you are wrong. You cannot *own* me, my clients, my employees, or my business philosophy. So you took over a building, an identification of DMBS; but you can't stop me from taking what I know and who I know and becoming your competition."

"I believe you will see a non-compete clause in the agreement you signed," she countered.

He lifted an eyebrow. "I didn't say it would be in my name."

They glared at each other across the table, her hazel eyes locked onto his icy blue ones. "Are you sure you want to spend the rest of your life and money fighting our corporate office in lawsuits?"

He threw his hands open, palms upward on the table. "Won't happen. Silent partners are just that, silent. You wouldn't be able to prove anything. So let's get something straight. I am calling the shots of this little arrangement. And if at any time I am less than satisfied with the negotiations, I will simply vacate the premises and you can have empty warehouses and blank computer screens."

"I didn't come here to negotiate, Mr. Jordan."

"Well, then, you'd better go back and send

someone who can."

The waiter started back to the table and Amanda waved him away. "So you want it to get ugly?"

His face distorted into a sneer. "From my perspective it's already about as ugly as it can get."

"You received a great deal of money with the expectations of your cooperation and ease of transition."

"Wrong again. That money has not made its way to me. And there is still the issue of dignity."

Her voice raised an octave. "Dignity? I'm surprised your vocabulary includes such a word. You most certainly have not demonstrated it to me."

"Didn't think you deserved it."

Amanda's face flushed. All of the blood in her body seemed to be gathering in her cheeks as they pulsed with the heat of the sudden surge. She stood, pushing the chair across the polished floor with a pronounced scrape. "I believe this dinner is over. I will be at your office at eight o'clock sharp in the morning. And you and all of your employees had better be there."

She heard him chuckle behind her as she stormed out of the restaurant, probably knowing she had nowhere to go except up the stairs.

Chapter 2

The following morning Amanda pulled into Dixie Millwork and Building Supply, or DMBS as it was on their logo, at ten of eight.

The parking lot, already half full, indicated at least some of the employees were back at work. She counted the cars and made a note of how many there were, assuming at least that many people should be somewhere in the building.

Her heels clicked on the concrete as she crossed the lot, head high, briefcase gripped in one hand. She understood the importance of appearing poised. In fact it accounted for half of the equation. If they perceived her as confident, then there was a better chance they would feel as though she had a reason to be sure of herself.

Amanda opened the side door, an entrance away from the one leading straight to Vernella's throne room, to what seemed a beehive. Loud voices called out to one another. Apparently no one had even noticed the way she strutted across the lot. The conversation indicated they were busy trying to find an order for a major customer.

She listened as they lamented over a string of complaints. It seemed yesterday's little game of hide-and-seek had backfired on Reece Jordan. All of the trucks bearing inventory for orders yet to be delivered, had been sent to other lots around the area in order to throw her off. But apparently it meant the deliveries weren't assembled and dispatched as promised and the repercussions ricocheted to sting both Reece and the sales department.

She found Jordan in his office, easily tracked down the hall by the sound of his voice booming above the rest of the din. She stood for a moment, enjoying the panicked state he seemed to be in, knowing he deserved it and had brought it upon himself.

The smile vanished from her face though as she heard herself mentioned in the conversation he engaged in over the phone.

****

"Yeah, I know. I'm sorry. It isn't like us, you know that." Reece paused, telephone receiver pushed against his ear by his upwardly hunched shoulder. "Well, if it hadn't been for that damned woman Builders Tech sent down here." Another pause as he listened to the voice from the other end of the line, breathing hard as he took rebuke from the customer.

"Right. Can you believe it? As if I'm going to…" He looked up and saw Amanda Lassiter standing in the doorway, framed by the solid oak jamb of his dad's old office, and lost his train of thought.

He let his eyes roam down her body, from her sleek auburn hair, to the tailored jacket, down the length of her pencil skirt, along shapely calves and even taking in the shoes—tall, pointed pumps making her calf muscles pop and his mind go to places it definitely shouldn't.

The voice on the other end of the line pulled him back into the conversation. "Yeah, I'm here, just a bit distracted." He shot her a look before swiveling his chair around so he wouldn't have to see her while he tried to deflate the angry customer on the other end of the phone. "We'll talk about it over beers when you stop by." He paused. "Right. Heavy discounts? You got it!"

He swiveled back around to face his nemesis. "You're early," he scowled.

"Barely," she replied.

"It will be a few more minutes. I have some things to attend to since the office was closed yesterday."

"An unnecessary delay of your own choosing."

"Be that as it may…"

"I am in no mood for games." She snagged a document from the outer pocket of her briefcase, obviously placed there for just such a moment, and slapped it down on the desk in front of him. "Do you know what this is?"

"Why should I waste time guessing when you are obviously dying to tell me yourself?"

His phone beeped. He reached out to it and Amanda disconnected the cord from the base of the phone, immediately ceasing the intercom.

"What the hell…?" He could feel his face reddening at her display of authority.

She continued as though he had said nothing. "This is a copy of the legal document outlining your participation in our requests."

He opened his mouth to speak.

She held up a hand, stopping him. "If you wish to influence the outcome of this endeavor, then your cooperation is essential. If you try another tactic such as yesterday's little diversion, I will invoke the clause I have highlighted. Would you like to read it out loud for us, so I know we are on the same page?"

He tossed the document back across the desk. "I don't need to read another damned thing. I know what it says." His jaw clenched and his blue eyes were glaciers, cold and dangerous.

"Well then, if your removal from the premises isn't necessary, and you are ready to cooperate, I think both of us can begin with our day. Here's how I see this unfolding..." She produced another document outlining the order in which she would gather data and make assessments.

He read over it, face growing hotter by the minute. "I'm supposed to cooperate in my own demise?" Reece ground his teeth. He thought he might be having an aneurism as a pain shot into his forehead and pulsed like a ticking bomb.

"Not exactly. There could be a last minute reprieve."

"Reprieve? What's that supposed to mean?"

"Super Builders Mart wants your demise badly enough to make a generous offer to Builders Tech if we agree to shut you down."

He lowered his voice. "Yeah, they've wanted me out of business for years. Their home office is here." He didn't understand where she was going with this, but he felt like it had something to do with what she referred to as *a reprieve*. That could only mean a continuation of the business.

"The head of our company, Judson Matheney..."

"Yes. I am familiar with him," Reece scoffed.

"You see, Matheney doesn't really care whether we save DMBS or start dismantling it. But my feeling is that Super Builders Mart wouldn't be interested in placing such a high ante on you if you weren't doing something right. Apparently they don't want us to open a Builders Tech any more than they want you to remain in business. And they are willing to pay quite well to assure this end."

"What are you saying?" He calmed a little, sensing a game changer, though he had no idea how.

"Well, it just means the problems leading us to this buyout were not within the business structure itself. Might you know wherein they lie?" She cocked her head to the side, raising an eyebrow.

He knew exactly what the problem was, but he'd be damned before he would ever tell her. "I suppose you'll just have to use your expensive education and clever mystery-solving techniques to figure it out."

"That's fine. I intend to do exactly that."

"Reece?" Vernella's voice burned through the atmosphere of the heated office like a detonator. She had briefly rapped her knuckles across the door as she called his name, then proceeded into the office stepping between the two of them as though Amanda wasn't even there. "I have a whole panel of calls waiting for you. Is something wrong with your phone?"

Before he could answer, Vernella saw the cord end dangling from his phone. "Oh, here's the problem."

As she attempted to reinsert the life line to its base, Amanda stopped her. She stepped in front of Vernella, pushing the phone out of reach of the cord end with one carefully manicured finger giving his receptionist a steady, dismissive look. "We know what the phone cord is for and will resume taking calls when we are finished."

Reece's mind jangled along with the never-ending

panel of calls. Vernella and her phone calls ceased to exist as he played out scenarios in his mind. He quickly began to grasp that a lifeline had been extended. Yet he didn't know what the ramifications of the Lassiter woman's resulting research would bring.

Amanda turned to Vernie. "You need to return to the switchboard, Vernella. And tell all who call that Mr. Jordan will get back with them shortly. He'll let you know when he's ready to have the list. Understand?"

"Reece?" Her one word question lasted for three syllables, indicating her displeasure with the dressing down. He nodded, and she shot another look at Amanda before leaving.

After her footsteps fell away, Reece turned to Amanda. "So are you telling me we might be able to maintain a presence here, keep our employees and our customers?"

She raised a hand indicating he shouldn't jump to conclusions. "It's only a possibility. I'll need to crunch some numbers, evaluate staff, and gather a little marketing research on the area—things like that. But if you continue to fight me at every angle, I see no point in attempting to rescue this business. I'll simply have you removed from the premises, take over this office, and begin to remove anyone else standing in my way."

His jaw clenched again. But he felt the pressure behind his eyes dissipate. Whatever pride he had worn as a shield and a sword lay completely deflected in the light of saving the beloved company, his employees, and his own reputation. "So what do I need to do?"

Of course, he had covered up as much as he could in the way of dollars flowing out of the accounts— something he knew this woman would eventually find.

One thing at a time, he thought.

"That's the beauty. You don't have to do much. I can take care of this and you can take care of your business." She reconnected the telephone to the jack plug.

"Fair enough I suppose," he agreed.

"I'll just begin, and you can take phone calls around me." Amanda moved toward him and the side of the desk he occupied.

Reece stood as she moved toward him, not sure about the amount of space she needed, or even what she intended on doing. His emotions had taken a wild ride over the past few minutes. She had stormed into his office like a battering ram and then offered an olive branch. He was wrung out, and it wasn't even nine o'clock yet.

She brushed up against him as she joined him behind the desk. A wisp of lavender wafted underneath his nose, making him soften toward her. In an instant, somehow he had gone from intolerance of her to gratefulness. Would she really be able to prevent Builders Tech from shutting him down and selling pieces off one by one?

He was aware of her presence, insanely so, though he would never admit it. He attributed the situation's tension for causing her to emit such chemistry before snapping back to his senses. "Wait a minute. You can't work in here."

"Oh, yes, I can...and will." She set her briefcase down on the desk and began to unpack a few things, a laptop computer, a flash drive, and some sort of connector that reminded him of an umbilical cord.

"What is all of this? What are you doing?"

"This will transfer your computer's data to my machine." Before he could object, she hit a few keystrokes and a flashing green light indicated the computers were talking to each other.

He tried to stop the transfer, reaching across her in an effort to escape the program.

Amanda intercepted his reach, taking his hand in hers and setting it gently onto the desktop.

For a brief moment he was as connected to her as her computer was to his. Electricity filled him, her eyes met his, and he wondered if she felt the jolt of their chemistry. It lasted long enough for the program to begin the uninterruptable transfer. File after file of their sensitive data clicked along the bottom of her screen.

She took a deep breath and stepped away from the desk.

His attention span broke, thwarted by Dan, the millwork supervisor who gave a little cough before attempting to knock on the open door.

Reece jerked at the interruption, acutely aware of his racing heart. In typical male fashion, his brain was at odds with his desires.

"Yes, what is it?" Although he asked the question of Dan, his eyes kept contact with Amanda's. His hand opened and closed in an effort to stop the tingling. She was tough, and determined, and way too damned sexy.

After taking his ranting the previous evening, she still wore a mantle of self-assurance, intriguing him beyond belief. He needed to get away from her, and used Dan's interruption as an opportunity to take off to the shop area.

****

Amanda released the long, deep breath she had

been holding since touching Reece's hand. If he had slapped her across the face, it wouldn't have been more jarring.

Her hand still burned from the contact with his strong electric grip. Had it been so long since she had been with a man that even the slightest touch from one she could never be interested in confused her body with carnal desire?

The back of one hand swept across her forehead. The heels of her feet began to burn. She sat in the large leather chair warmed by Reece just moments before, feeling the indentations his long muscular legs had made in the leather. She tried to concentrate on the data fields, watching the blocks fill in on her computer.

At least I'll have the company's files before the day ends. She considered contacting Judson while things were on a good note. He had—thankfully—been at dinner the previous evening when she phoned about the initial meeting with Reece Jordan.

Mary, his assistant, had suggested sending a quick text as he had appeared anxious to receive word from her. She had typed—*on schedule*—into the text box and hit send with the hopes he would be too busy to ask questions and might interpret her brevity as a good sign.

Amanda had paid attention to all of the minuscule giveaways where Judson was concerned. Too much information was interpreted by him as a sign of weakness or an attempt to convince where facts were thin. Where others might have taken her brief message as too vague, she had been willing to bet he would give a quick, nearly imperceptible nod and continue with his evening without even responding.

Apparently she had been correct.

She looked at her watch. Chicago was an hour behind Charlotte. If it was nine o'clock here, it was eight there. Judson was probably already at the office, but not at his desk. He had an apartment connecting with his office in the complex. But instead of using it as living quarters, it housed his private gym.

His custom was to be delivered by his driver at seven every morning. He would spend thirty minutes going through a weight training routine and another thirty on his treadmill with a laptop attachment. While he climbed mountains and ran along the beach—via his fitness applications—he busily scrolled through his e-mails and caught up with the news of the morning.

He would be in the shower at eight, have a quick breakfast on the sunny balcony—weather permitting—and be ready to face the onslaught of multimillion-dollar deals by nine o'clock. Judson never broke with the routine. Even sick, he continued with the schedule, whether or not he could push himself as hard as normal on the treadmill.

At sixty-eight, he was amazingly fit. He said it was the one thing everyone could control, as opposed to hair loss, height, and wrinkles.

That philosophy caused every employee at Builders Tech to respect their bodies, work out fiendishly, and eat sparse meals. They had even been voted "most physically fit" by their insurance provider, who gave them heavy discounts for their attention and devotion to health maintenance.

Thinking about that made Amanda proud of the decision to seek a workout instead of indulging in a frozen yogurt, much less the southern cuisine—fried green tomatoes, chicken-fried steak, cornbread—

beckoning for her to sample them.

Amanda's stomach growled at the memory of the succulent dishes. It didn't help that she had skipped breakfast in favor of a quick cup of coffee. She lived on green salads and energy bars. It was best to stay away from anything that might entice her to overeat.

The ping of her computer erased mental images of rounded bowls of mashed potatoes. The download was complete. She pulled up the income statements, assets and liabilities chart, and bank statements—all from the date of acquisition. Then she pulled up identical ones from then to the current point in time which she had just downloaded, placing them on a split side-by-side screen in order to compare them more easily.

Something wasn't right. Large disbursements had been drawn on the bank account without a corresponding column of assets or services rendered. They had all gone to J & S Consulting. She wasn't familiar with this firm and made a note to check them out while continuing to comb through the reports looking for any other discrepancies in their numbers.

****

Reece returned to his office as his old self. The testosterone in the mill shop—mixed with its sounds, smells, and agitation—relieved him of any lingering desire for the stranger who had shown up to turn his world upside down. He paused for a moment outside of the open door, watching the intensity with which Amanda worked.

He would have respected her tenacity if it wasn't likely to be used against him. She had the focus of a fighter pilot and the body of a dancer. He heard her whisper, "J & S Consulting," as she scribbled it down on a notepad.

His heart practically stopped. She hadn't been there a full day yet and had already found something he wished she hadn't. His jaw clenched and he burst into the office which had been his until an hour ago.

"Come on up and out of that chair," he said as he grabbed it and twirled it around to face him.

She turned confused eyes up to him at the sound of the irritation in his voice.

"Up, up, up," he repeated, using a hand signal to indicate rising.

"What is so urgent? Maybe you could practice some manners," she shot back at him as she vacated the chair in question.

"Look, this isn't going to work. You can't remain in my office. I have things to do, a business to run. And I can't do that if you're going to interfere."

She started to speak and he held up a hand interrupting her, "I know, I know...it technically isn't my business anymore. But these are accounts I opened, I serviced, and I have my own reputation on the line for. So, as long as my name is still on this door, I need you to find someplace else to crash."

"And what if I need your assistance around the shop?"

"Give me an hour, two at the most. Maybe I could get Vernie to show you around while you wait."

"Vernie? As in Vernella?" She asked it as if it was the worst possible scenario she could imagine, causing him to grin.

"Yeah, she's a great gal. You should get to know her."

Amanda interrupted him this time. "No, thanks. I'd

rather wing it on my own. I'll be back in one hour." She disconnected the computer cords and repacked her briefcase, disappearing in the direction of the accounting office.

****

The accountants were easy to work with. Having a background in balance sheets, credits, and debits made it less difficult for them to understand the principle of business mergers and acquisitions. And, except for their jobs, they had no stake in the company. They seemed to get the bigger picture. Cooperating with the new owners—and her as their representative—would make it much more likely they would retain those jobs.

Reece Jordan had a personal interest in what had once belonged to him. He couldn't be detached. Amanda understood that. But her future at Builders Tech was on the line, and she would not sacrifice it for a ship already sunk. If this transition went smoothly, she might be awarded the title of Vice-President of Acquisitions.

She liked the sound of it. *Amanda Lassiter, Vice-President of Acquisitions.* It rolled off the tongue as smooth as a fine sewing machine's motor. It sounded delicious even in the silence of her mind as she sat in the back chambers of the long hallway of DMBS amidst the quiet accountants with noses to their computer screens. Along with that promotion would be a larger office, a seat at the table when the inner circle met with Judson Matheney, and a nice, fat raise.

Two hours later, she had everything she needed from the efficient accounting department. She made an extra copy of the last two months' bank statements, and the accounts payable ledger, storing them in her computer for further comparison to those in Reece Jordan's. From there she moved on to inventory.

At some junction between accounting and inventory, she landed in a foreign country. At least the language spoken was foreign to her. Few of the small building supply stores they had acquired actually had their own millwork shops. And those who had, had been assessed by members of the group with backgrounds in the nuts and bolts—literally—of construction.

Amanda's specialty within her teams at Builders Tech had been in finance. She had not been warned about the odd-sounding words flashing across her screen as part of inventory—shims, casements, double-hung, diamond-lite, finger-jointed.

Some items were listed as linear feet while others were counted as pieces. Many were listed as pairs or sets. Amanda wanted to have an accurate account of every possible inch of lumber and glass, but was lost in a sea of confusing terminology.

She walked back to Reece Jordan's office and entered without bothering to knock.

He had asked for an hour and she had already given him more than two. He was on the phone again, and a number of lights blinked on the telephone base.

Reece indicated them with a sweep of his hand and she threw up her arms. "I'll be back later," she said before strolling out to the construction area where the millwork shop took the odd-sounding parts and turned them into entryways and window units.

The insulated door slammed behind her as she left the quiet of the office space for the din of the shop. Dust billowed as the table saws sliced into wood objects, nail guns pinged, and forklifts beeped as they hauled pallets of items unidentifiable to her.

Amanda continued to the production line marked "Interior and Exterior Door Units" and "Window Frames." Crossing the thick-with-sawdust concrete floor, her heel caught on something, pitching her forward. She fell against a machine with an overhead sign reading "Router," narrowly missing the moving parts with her hand.

As she made apologies, Reece burst through the door. The giant slam was not to be missed. "What do you think you are doing?" he asked, before grasping her by the arm and dragging her back into the office area.

"Remove your hands from me this instant!"

He did as she demanded, but not before snatching her around to face him. He pointed to the sign above the door.

"Do you know what *that* is?" His voice, sharp and angry, punctuated his frustration in dealing with her.

She saw the yellow hard hat and the words beneath it spelling "*Required beyond this point*" which she had missed in her eagerness to get to the millwork shop. "Oh, sorry. Must have missed that."

"Do you have any idea what the Occupational Safety and Health Association would do to me if they caught you out there like this?" He motioned up and down her body with one hand.

Feeling chastised, her face flushed. Amanda felt the surge of heat in her cheeks. It put her on the defensive. She pointed to her watch before straightening her skirt and sweeping particles of sawdust from her hair. "Well, if you had met with me as planned, I wouldn't have been out there in the first place."

His jaw clenched. She already recognized it as his trademark signal of duress. His voice went up several octaves higher than normal. "I asked for one hour." He pointed at her with his index finger. "One!" he reiterated.

She held up two fingers. "It's already been more than two!"

"One, two; what's the difference? Don't you have something to do that doesn't require me to hold your hand?"

"I was doing just fine before you showed up with your ramped up machismo, and if you will move away from the door, I will continue what I started."

"Oh no! I don't intend to have an OSHA charge against me. You apparently don't have any idea how hard it is to run a complex of this size and structure."

She composed herself and tried to convey strength and determination through her voice. "If you had shown up yesterday, this conundrum wouldn't even be a topic of conversation."

He loomed over her, completely unfazed by her comments. "What is it with women and their complete failure to let go of the past?"

She stood tall facing the building giant. "That sounds like a sexist remark to me. What happened to our agreement of a joint venture?"

His voice boomed over hers. "Joint venture?"

"It's the best way to look at this. My company has made you a very wealthy man, Mr. Jordan."

"Do you think this is about the money?"

"Isn't everything?"

****

Reece Jordan and Amanda Lassiter were in a sparring match. Office doors down the hallway had opened to hear the two of them in the rare toe-to-toe exchange. Nobody had talked to Reece in such a manner before now.

He felt his jaw tightening, his teeth grinding. She was fire and ice, hot and cold. Or maybe that was just him around her. Moments passed, the loudest silent moments he had ever heard, the soundlessness taking on an audible buzz. Thoughts formed the words he wanted to say, but professional dignity held them back.

Amanda finally broke the barrier. "You might as well surrender to me…"

There was a pause after the first part of her sentence, one lapping a fire into Reece's body once again. The heat between them was palpable; to surrender to her would be a joy, but not here. Not in the office, not in the hard hat zone, and not in front of his employees.

"…and to this process," she continued. "It will make it much easier in the long run."

The sudden flash of desire had burned off his white-hot anger. "Well then, we had better start by fitting you with an appropriate hat! Stay right here."

He burst back into the shop, bare-headed himself, pilfering through the hats in the bin. He finally found one that seemed small enough to fit her and returned, plopping it onto her head.

"If you are so damned interested in how this all works, come with me." He opened the door and she followed him back into the noisy shop. He grabbed a hat for himself and began to talk over the sounds of the machines.

Reece had only given her the basic floor plan of the millwork shop when a whistle blew. It was loud enough to pierce through the whirring noise of the machinery and drown out the racket of the various power tools. Everything ceased moving by the time the whistle died. Up and down the lines with air compressor cords dangling from the ceiling, the pumping ceased. The humming and droning of engines halted; conveyor belts were at a standstill.

The men and women around the work tables removed their hats and laid them alongside their heavy gloves, ear plugs, and thick goggles. They were walking away, moving in an orderly fashion to a space beyond the furthest wall.

"Lunch time," Reece explained.

"You don't keep half of them working while the other half has lunch and then vice-versa?"

"What purpose would that serve? If one person is missing from a station it slows production. My electrical cost is the same, but the output isn't. I may as well shut down for an hour and let them all have a chance for a nice quiet meal. And speaking of which, would you care to have lunch with me and one of my customers? He's due to be here at any time."

"No, thank you."

She looked at him as though he were weak for desiring a break in the middle of the day. Or was it the chastising tone of her voice? Either way, it had the effect of irritating him.

"Have it your way. But don't try to inflict your northern, I'm-better-than-you-because-I-never-eat attitude onto the rest of us. We believe there is just a little more to life than work."

He pushed past her, not allowing her a chance to respond. He didn't want her to change her mind either. The very last thing he needed was to have to look across a table at this woman over a sandwich.

****

Amanda fumed and scowled. She retreated to the breakroom and poured herself an as-old-as-the-work-day cup of coffee. Thick and darkest black, it looked about as appetizing as it tasted. She made a face and dumped it out in the sink.

A mousy, overweight young woman from the accounting department walked into the breakroom and quietly retrieved a plastic bowl from a neoprene container with a name scrolled across it in permanent ink.

Amanda recalled having seen her during the small space of time she had spent there looking over the accounts. "Hello," she said to the young woman.

She responded with the flat "i" that lasted for three syllables and seemed to have an "e" on the end. "Hi."

It ran through Amanda with the same sharpness as the whistle that had just blown through the building. She took a deep breath and rinsed out the coffee pot. "Do you know where the coffee is so I can make a fresh pot? This one was beyond drinkability."

"Yes, ma'am, I do. I'll make it for ya, if ya like." She reached a chubby hand for the pot and Amanda relinquished it to her.

"Thank you. That would be nice."

Amanda watched her lumber about the small area, reaching up for a fresh filter and immediately grabbing the hem of her blouse to yank it back over the newly exposed roll topping the waistband of her pants. She looked away, trying not to let the accountant see she had witnessed the uncomfortable moment.

It hadn't worked. She caught her mid-stare. "How do you stay so skinny?" the woman asked.

"What's your name again?" Amanda asked

She blushed and started shaking. "Oh, I didn't mean to be rude."

"No, I didn't think you were being rude," she corrected, realizing she had made the young woman nervous. "I just want to learn as many names as possible. Especially of the people I think are the most helpful."

The woman relaxed. She spooned the last necessary bit of grounds into the filter and hit the start button. The coffee pot began to hiss and gurgle as it heated the water and pushed it through the dark chocolate-colored grains. "My name is Susan."

"Hello again, Susan." Amanda offered her hand. "I remember seeing you in accounting this morning. Have you worked here long?"

Susan took Amanda's hand in her clammy one, the shake more a jiggle than an appropriate firm handshake. "No, not when compared to most of the other employees."

"I'll make you a deal," Amanda said.

Susan raised her eyebrows. "Oh? What kind of deal?"

"I'll tell you how I stay thin if you'll work on that limp Southern handshake." Amanda smiled and Susan did the same.

"It's how we are taught here," she explained.

"I know, Susan. And it is a fine thing for a cotillion, but not for a corporation."

As the coffee brewed, Amanda instructed Susan on the mechanics of a proper business handshake. By the time it was finished, she thought the girl had the basics.

"You keep working on that." Amanda started to leave.

"Ms. Lassiter, you forgot something."

"Oh?" Amanda scanned the six tiny tables and the open counter. She could see nothing belonging to her she might have left behind.

"You forgot to tell me how you stay so thin." Susan smiled and the force of her lips pulling backward forced her chubby cheeks to squeeze against the corners of her eyes.

"I eat little and exercise much. And I drink a lot of coffee." She raised the mug to punctuate her last sentence. "If you want to be thin, you have to realize food is the enemy. Stop looking at it as a friend. Stay away from anything that tastes good. You are sorry you asked now, aren't you?"

Susan frowned. "I was hoping for an easy answer—something more along the lines of drinking a certain tea after meals, not drinking coffee instead of having them altogether."

"We all hope for an easy answer. Sadly, it isn't available, Susan. If it was, *I* would have found it years ago."

Susan squinted at her.

Amanda could tell Susan would never believe how much she struggled with her weight. Nobody would. She didn't have the extra rolls of flesh that were tell-tale signs. And where there had been indications, such as the underside of her arms, she simply built up the muscles beneath to fill in the skin.

Amanda retreated to Reece's office, grabbing the knob with one hand while continuing to walk. She hadn't expected that the inward-opening door would be locked and ran into it, sloshing her freshly brewed coffee all over her suit.

"Damn it!" She returned to the break room, grabbing paper towels that she immediately swiped at her skirt with.

"Here. Let me help." Susan was still there, her plate of food sitting on the table, untouched. "I may not know how to shake hands properly, but a stain can't last a minute around me."

"Certainly," Amanda handed her the towels.

Susan offered her own jacket. "Slip that skirt off and cover up with this. I'll get the stain out, but I need to have it over the sink."

Amanda glanced at the door.

Susan followed her gaze. "Don't worry. Nobody will bother us. They usually go out for lunch, especially now that they all wanted to talk about you."

Amanda chuckled, slipping out of the skirt and draping the jacket over her lap as she sat at the table finishing what was left of her coffee.

Susan pulled the expensive linen/wool blend away from its even more precious silk lining. The coffee had washed down the front, not making its way through to the lining beneath. She then stuffed wads of paper towels behind the stain and began to flush it with club soda she pulled from the refrigerator.

"And you didn't want to join in the gossip about the evil—what was it Vernella called me yesterday— oh, yes, the 'head-chopping' person?"

"I'm not really comfortable having people watch

me eat. And I suppose I suspected something like this would eventually happen."

"You mean you suspected the company might be headed for trouble?"

Susan gave a little gasp. "I've probably said too much. It's just…I…well…I work in accounting. There's not a lot that slips by me." She became intent on the stain, dabbing and dampening, and repeating. Amanda let the conversation drop. There was definitely something going on with management which at least one of the employees had noticed.

Maybe she *should* have Reece Jordan removed immediately. It might be best to shut the doors, sell off the property, and take the incentive from Super Builders Mart just as Judson expected her to do.

Susan handed her skirt back to her. "Good as new. Just needs a little more drying time, but that won't take long in a North Caroline June. A walk around the parking lot oughta do it."

"Thank you, Susan." Amanda handed her the borrowed jacket and slipped the skirt back over her hips. "I've got to make a couple of phone calls before Mr. Jordan gets back from lunch."

Amanda grabbed her cell phone and headed out to the parking lot. The heat of the afternoon sun reflecting off the asphalt would dry her skirt in no time. She leaned against her car door, waiting for Judson's assistant to put her through to him.

Mary picked up the line again. "I'm sorry, Amanda, but Mr. Matheney is on a conference call. Can I take a message?"

Amanda paused. If he were in the middle of a conference call, why hadn't his assistant just said so in the first place? Why put her on hold and come back to her with that information? She almost asked, but then thought better of it. "Tell him all is well. I'll be in touch later."

"He'll be glad to hear it. Thank you, Amanda." The line died.

Feelings of self-doubt crept into Amanda's psyche. Why hadn't Judson taken her call? Why the subterfuge with the sudden *conference call* that his assistant would have arranged and therefore would have known about the instant she rang his office? Why would he be glad to hear that all was well? Why hadn't she said, "He expected nothing less from you?"

Suspicion tingled where she had once been confident. Did they all *expect* her to fail? Was this a set-up to get rid of her?

Wheels turned into the parking lot. The SUV that had taxied her to the hotel from the airport swung wide into a parking space by the side door, and Reece Jordan exited the vehicle. He grabbed the door and held it for a man and a woman getting out of the back seat.

That hit her wrong, too. He certainly hadn't held the door for her yesterday. Yet he expected her to hold the door to this building supply open for him and his employees.

She felt the spot where the coffee had spilled. It was dry.

Amanda straightened and marched back into the office, entering the door behind Reece. "Aren't you going to introduce me to our customers?" she asked.

Reece reddened.

The couple looked from Reece to Amanda, and back to Reece again.

"Mr. and Mrs. Patrick, this is…" He flapped his hand back and forth as though he had forgotten her name.

She stepped forward, right hand extended. "Amanda Lassiter, from Builders Tech."

They each shook her hand politely, nodding and exchanging greetings.

Reece gave her a look of warning to say no more.

She ignored it. "I hope we can count on your loyalty once we decide what to do with this location. Builders Tech has a branch in Rock Hill should we decide to close DMBS."

They mumbled something.

Reece grabbed her arm, pulling her along with him. "Please excuse us," he threw over his shoulder as he hauled her to his office.

She pointed a red-tipped finger at him. "If you lay a hand on me again, so help me God, I will—"

He had the door unlocked and swung open before she could finish, grabbing her once again and tugging her in behind him. "You'll do what? Embarrass me in front of some of the best customers we have? Oh wait, you've already done that! Thank God you didn't take me up on the offer to join us for lunch!"

She shook free of his grasp. "I intended to do a little work in here. Imagine my surprise when I found the door was locked. Next time it happens I'll have it removed from the hinges."

"I always lock my door when I am away. Who knows what riff-raff will wander into the offices? What was so damned urgent you couldn't wait until I returned to get in here?"

"Listen, you warned me about trying to turn you

into some version of us Northern workaholics. Now I am setting you straight on something. I don't lunch. I don't siesta. I work. It's who I am! Don't try to shove your loosey-goosey, devil-may-care attitude onto me either. That's likely what caused your company's vulnerability and is the reason I'm standing here."

She saw Reece grip and flex his hands. If she had been a man, he might have hit her. For a moment she thought he was considering it anyway.

"Get what you want and then get the hell out."

"What I want is to finish the tour of the millwork shop. Can I take it they will be back to work this afternoon?"

"They should be there shortly."

Reece snatched the phone and hit the button for the front desk. "Vernie, send someone to take care of the Patricks."

Amanda watched his face redden even more as he appeared to be hearing something from Vernella he didn't like.

"What?" he shouted. "I *am* calm." He turned to glare at Amanda. "I see." He slammed the phone back into its cradle. "Congratulations. It seems our little shouting match was overheard by everyone within the walls of this complex."

"Including the Patricks?" she asked.

"God, I hope not." He pressed his fingers against his eyelids. "Our salesman whisked them away when it became apparent they were about to overhear something which might cost him their loyalty."

"The salesman overheard us, too?"

He nodded.

"And they are elsewhere in the building now?"

"Apparently." He still looked as though he might have a meltdown.

"Well then, let's get started."

"After you," he said to Amanda through clenched teeth. He stood aside in the doorway.

The whistle blew again, and the crew piled in through the back door. Within a minute, the entire millwork shop was jumping and humming and slamming and banging.

Amanda strutted back to the spot where she had left her hard hat and placed it over her head.

Reece did the same and indicated the path they should follow across the sawdust-covered floor.

Her heels weren't the best choice for walking through the dusty shop, but she would have died before saying it was a mistake. Amanda could feel the grit slipping into her shoes, irritating her feet. But she kept walking.

****

Reece explained to her, in the same way he did to the sons and daughters of the elite construction company owners, how things were assembled, what routers were used for, and why shims were necessary on window units.

He explained door sizing for interior and exterior placement, window grids, half rounds, ornamental inserts, transoms, peep-site bores, decorative molding, and the way they figured out what made a unit right hand or left hand—opening in or out—hinge placement.

She watched as a door was prepped for the hinge and saw the two sides of it come together, one on the door and one on the frame, hinge pin sliding into place to lock the door to the frame.

Holes were bored for the knobs and kick-plates were attached to some of the exterior doors. He showed her the simplicity of the process, teaching what a 2-8 meant—two feet and eight inches—and what a six-panel door versus a flush looked like in a frame.

She displayed a true curiosity and desire to learn, which surprised him. Somehow he had envisioned her as being a northern big city snob, too self-absorbed into social ladder-climbing to care about the real business of building the products people used in their homes.

But she was connecting with his employees, not too haughty to speak directly to the dust-covered men running the saws and to ask questions about their lives. Reece couldn't tell whether she was genuinely interested in them, or just trying to win allies in the event the Chicago big-wigs decided to keep the shop going.

After the tour of the millwork shop, Amanda returned to Reece's office. "We need a place with connecting offices or we will to have those filing cabinets removed and another desk brought into this one for me." She pointed to the row of cabinets along the opposite wall of his office.

"Oh, absolutely *not* in here," he argued, though part of him tingled with the thought of it. This was business, not pleasure. He couldn't perform his work duties if he had to worry about her overhearing every comment. And he didn't need the constant titillation being around her seemed to inspire in him.

"Well, what are the other options?"

He held up a hand. "Give me a minute. I'll think of something."

Like a sleeping giant his head popped up, and he

yelled into the telephone's intercom, "Richard, step into my office please."

The sound of a chair sliding backward wafted through a connecting door from the side of the office. It peeled open and a man, close to sixty, entered.

"Yes, Reece?" He had salt and pepper hair and a thick mustache. Large curious eyes peeped over the rim of thick glasses.

"Richard Yates, I'd like you to meet Amanda Lassiter."

The man stepped forward and offered his hand, his head bobbing in the manner of saying "yes" to something.

"Hello, ma'am," he said as she took his hand and gave it the customary shake of greeting.

"Have a seat, Richard." Reece pushed a chair out with his foot, not bothering to stand, which he could tell by her sharp expression Amanda took offense to.

"Really?" she replied indignantly. She corrected the position of the chair, straightening it slightly before indicating with the sweep of her hand that Richard should sit.

He mumbled, "Thank you," and did as instructed.

Reece straightened a little and faced the man. Then he pushed another chair over to Amanda, again with a pointed foot, and motioned for her to sit. She raised an eyebrow and crossed her arms over her chest.

"Sit please," he managed through a slit of his mouth.

She pulled a chair from the other side of the room and sat it down with a thud beside Richard. The man kept looking at them as if he didn't know who he should be the most frightened of.

"I used to have more charm," Reece sneered.

"Pity it has deserted you," she replied, appearing determined to have the last word.

His jaw clenched. "Well, be that as it may…" He let the sentence drop while he struggled to remember what it was he started to suggest before entering into the match of wits with his opponent.

The worst thing he could imagine was seeing his company torn apart by a woman who caused him such mental and physical anguish. He hated her and desired her at the same time. Maybe if he pushed her to the brink she might go back to Chicago and they would send someone he wouldn't have to resist desiring physically.

"Oh, yes," he continued, finding his stream of thought again. "Ms. Lassiter has need of an office space either inside of mine, which I believe would be an unworkable situation for me, or I could simply have you find another place to set up temporarily and I can move her into your digs."

Reece understood it was clear to all of them this was not a debate, nor a discussion. The marketing director had just been expelled from his office.

"Well," he said slowly. "I could go down to accounting. There's probably some room in there. But they need quiet in order to think and run numbers and I need to be on the phone most of the day. That could be a problem."

"I see," Reece commented.

"I'll tell you what I think we should do," Amanda interjected, clearly unimpressed with the theatrics. "I think we should move out the filing cabinets as I originally suggested."

"No, that will not work for me," Reece argued.

"Why don't we look around? Maybe there is something upstairs. I don't really need to be in the hub of the daily activity down here, so being upstairs would be all right with me," Richard suggested.

"That's an excellent idea. But are you sure you won't get lonely up there by yourself?" Reece was glad Richard had reached the solution. It was always a better idea to allow employee input rather than simply exiling someone else to a lonely corner of the business. "Why don't you select the spot, and I'll have some of the shop hands carry your things up there. We can get a new desk delivered for Ms. Lassiter."

Amanda sat opposite him, arms folded over her chest, legs crossed at both the knees and the ankles. She shot looks at him that would have caused a weaker man to shrivel.

The uneasy gentleman quickly left the hornets' nest, headed for the stairs leading to the attic, and put distance between himself and the pair of chiefs that had squared off in Reece's office.

When Richard was out of earshot, Amanda closed the door and began to chatter about something. Reece heard her but wasn't paying attention. He started scrolling through an internet site, furiously looking up something of interest only to him.

The item he had been seeking presented itself and he grabbed the telephone. She snatched it from his hand. "Do you mind?"

"What?" He had no idea what she was frustrated about.

She lifted her shoulders and said, "You're kidding me, right?"

"No, I'm getting your desk ordered." He turned the monitor toward her so she could see the desk he had in mind for her. It was a Louis XVI gold-trimmed monstrosity that no one except royalty could pull off. She blushed, and he suppressed a grin.

He escaped that screen into another with a reasonable match to the other desk styles in the offices and placed the order. "It will be here tomorrow and we'll have you set up and ready to go by day's end."

"Was all of the drama necessary?"

"Probably not," he admitted. "I'm not an expert at this *buyout* thing. I have a mixture of emotions about it and I can't be charming *and* efficient all of the time."

"I'll settle for *some of the time* and a place to set up temporarily."

"Here"—he rose to offer her his seat again—"I think I can manage for the rest of the day."

"You won't run back in within five minutes ordering me *up and out* will you?"

"Probably. It's a chance you'll have to take." He grinned at her in spite of himself. He had never met a woman so much like himself before.

****

Reece found Richard wandering around in the old catalogue-pulling room that sometimes served as a meeting room. A long table punctuated the bowling alley-shaped space. "Hey, sorry about all the drama downstairs, Richard," He clapped the man on the back. "That woman is impossible!"

"It's all right. Do you suppose we'll still have a job next week?"

The two men had known each other for all Reece's adult life. Richard had worked for his father and now for him. To see the concern on the man's obviously worried face regarding his family's finances made Reece want to gnash his teeth. And all because of the unaccounted-for cash disbursements he knew still waited for some explanation.

"I don't know, and that is the truth. I can't read the tea leaves on this one. You know what I mean, of course."

The older man nodded. Richard was aware of where the funds had gone. He had worked hard to downplay any rumors and present the image of Dixie Millwork and Building Supply as the pride of the south. But he wasn't a magician then, and he could do nothing now.

"I should be retiring in a few more years," he said with regret. "If this goes badly, who will hire me?"

"Keep your chin up. Maybe I can stall her for a few weeks or months." He winked at the older man.

They expelled nervous laughter. "Well, if anyone can, it's you," he agreed.

Footsteps groaned on the stairs. A thin, high-pitched voice called out into the darkness. "Reece? Reece, are you up here?"

"I swear that woman is like a magnet, and your butt a sheet of steel," Richard mused.

Reece was glad for something to smile about and returned the chuckle. "Yes, Vernie, come on up."

She pounced up the last few steps and into the dim light of the rarely-used space. "I've been looking for you."

"What's wrong?"

"A wall of calls, and I need to speak to you about *that woman*." Her face became even more pointed and vulture-like, as though biting into a persimmon, upon saying the word *woman*.

He teased her to ease the tension. "Come on Vernie, I can't believe you're letting a Yankee get the best of your southern sensibilities."

"She makes me writhe and my skin crawl. But I *had* her on that first day. I wish you two could have seen her face when I delivered your message." She laughed, appearing amused at the memory.

Reece didn't laugh. His face tightened. "That may have been a mistake. We ignited a fire, instead of extinguishing one."

Chapter 3

Downstairs, Amanda kept going over and over the numbers. She had missed something. Nobody would take this much money out of a company on a regular basis and not expect to get caught. Reece didn't strike her as the kind of man who would be stupid enough to do that himself, and he certainly wasn't the kind to put up with theft or fraud or incompetence.

No, she must have made a mistake, missed something, had a computer glitch. She put in a call to Gary, the computer technician at Builders Tech. One of the best things about working for such a powerful company was that they employed the best and the brightest in every field. Gary would be able to determine if her computer had a glitch by running an Internet program. It still amazed her how far technology had advanced in her forty-six years.

The diagnostic cleared the computer of any possible malfunction. The error belonged to her, the bookkeepers, accounting, shipping…or worse. *I'll just have to start over*, she assured herself and began again.

****

The noise of moving the marketing director out of his office seemed to be magnified just for her benefit. A constant barrage of loud voices made its way to Amanda along with squeals of the furniture legs scraping the floor, squeaky desk drawers, and banging for some reason that didn't quite seem necessary to her.

She didn't blame them for resenting her. She had arrived in a nice suit with a briefcase and an agenda which probably wasn't in their best interests. Not only did she hold their futures squarely in the palm of her hand, she had now displaced one of their own. And if she couldn't find the missing dollars, someone might be facing criminal charges as well.

Amanda couldn't bring this up to Reece though, until she was certain. The last thing she wanted to do was to make a fool of herself in front of him. She sensed he was waiting for just such an opportunity and she'd be damned if she would give it to him.

"Knock, knock," he said before striding into the office and straddling the chair she had sat in earlier. "So this is what it's like on this side of the desk," he mused, as though forgetting his reason for being in there.

"How do you find it?" she asked.

"I can't really concentrate on it for the noise. How do you work in this racket?"

Something didn't seem right. From the first moment she had observed Reece Jordan at DMBS, there had been nothing but noise and he seemed in his element at the center of the hub.

He waited for her answer. Finally she said, "I manage."

"Well, why don't you let me show you around the town this afternoon? And tomorrow, after we get everything set up for you, you can get that perky nose back to the old grindstone." He grinned.

She looked at him suspiciously. "Why the sudden interest in my ability to concentrate?"

"These are my figures you're tinkering with. If the

noise causes you to make mistakes, well, I'll be the one paying for it, right?"

His reasoning appeared logical. He almost seemed to know she had found errors on the page. She pushed the chair away from the desk, leaning back into the leathery suppleness caressing her body in the hollowed spaces formed over time around Reece's own weight and shape.

"What did you have in mind?" she asked.

"Uh...oh...yeah..." He seemed to have lost his train of thought. "Uhh...a job site. Maybe you would like to go out and see some of the projects we're supplying with our specialty mill-work items."

He had stuttered over the words enough for her to know he wasn't really trying to get her out to a job site. She extended one long, expensively hosed leg, pointing the toe of her designer heels. "Don't think I'm dressed for it."

Reece had followed her leg with his eyes, but quickly snapped backed into the conversation. "What?"

"You asked me if I wanted to visit a construction site, and I said I didn't think I was appropriately dressed for it."

"Oh, right, right," he acknowledged. "Maybe they should have sent someone from Chicago who knew how to dress for a construction crew."

His hot-and-cold personality infuriated Amanda. She never knew which Reece Jordan she was going to get when he opened his mouth. "For the record"—she sneered, her leg snapped to the floor in serious mode— "I didn't dress for a construction zone because I didn't come here with the intention of building houses."

"No, you arrived to do the opposite of building,

didn't you? You came to destroy." Whatever charm he had intended to flash had disappeared in a blaze of anger.

"Apparently this business has been in self-destruct mode for some time, Mr. Jordan. We're the only lifeline you have, and you know it. *That* is what is making you seethe. You are just a typical southern masochist who doesn't want to accept the fact that we have you by the balls."

Amanda had just lost her temper and knew she should feel badly about it, but somehow it felt good. She had at some point in her tirade leapt up from the chair, poised over the desk, and met his glare from the opposite side.

Reece leaned in close to her face. "When you have me by the balls, you will have more bull than you've ever had in your pasture," he retorted.

"Don't make promises you can't keep."

Their faces were close. She could see the pores on his face, the broken capillaries along his nose, the tiny pupils withered by the flash of the fluorescent lighting above their heads. His breath burned hot on her cheeks, escaping his tightly pursed lips in puffs. She could have kissed him by moving only an inch or two forward, and she was tempted to, if only to diffuse the tension.

He reached toward her with his index finger, letting it caress her brow bone as he slid a single strand of her hair away from her face and around the curve of her eyebrow. He leaned in as though to kiss her cheek and she expected it, breathing heavily and slightly confused.

But his lips didn't pause at her cheekbone. They continued to her ear where his breath stoked a fire within her as he whispered, "I never make promises I don't intend to keep." Each "p" sound brought with it a wisp of superheated air that ran the length of her body and circled inward.

The flesh of his face all but brushed her cheek as he pulled away. She couldn't resist looking at him, into his prismatic blue eyes, flashing like a spring in the Yellowstone geysers.

Amanda stalled at a precipice of confusion, deeply drawn to him from a sexual perspective while deeply repulsed by the business at hand. How long they stood there she couldn't say. It could have been seconds, minutes even. But it seemed an eternity. Two opposing rods, they kept each other near and yet far.

She licked her lips, a Freudian slip to be sure, and she knew he would gather its meaning and store it in a cup to be returned to her when she least desired it.

His mouth opened slightly, as though he intended to make the most of the moment, but somehow he managed to pull away and turn for the door.

Amanda didn't stop him. She wanted him to leave. Another minute and she would have been powerless to prevent him from pursuing her promising mouth.

She remained standing until the door shut behind him. Then she collapsed in the chair, wishing the leather indentations in it were his body, caressing hers. She wondered how in the world a man had managed to get under her skin in this way—especially one she despised as much as he.

Chapter 4

Amanda stayed at the office until five o'clock, only to appear professional. There was no further productivity from her, but she did see the value in making the employees all believe there had been.

After leaving DMBS, she headed for the only sporting goods store she could find in the GPS under shopping, and spent too much on boots and jeans she would probably never wear again. In fact, she doubted she would even take them back to Chicago. But, Reece Jordan needed to learn a lesson, and she intended to be the person to teach it to him.

She arrived at the office early the next morning in order to hide the gym bag housing the boots and jeans beneath her desk in the event another situation arose requiring them. When she entered Richard's former office, still unready for her, she heard voices emanating from Reece's side of the door.

A woman…in tears maybe? A little taken aback, Amanda stowed the bag inside of a cabinet and went about her business.

Later, making the trek back from the break room after attaining some much-needed coffee, she ran head-on into a disheveled and crumpled Reece. He was stumbling through the hallway rolling his shoulder around, suggesting it had a kink.

"What happened to you? It looks like you spent the

night here." She instantly wished she had said something else.

"Yeah, waiting on you," he quipped.

"Seems like you waited in vain." She turned to enter the office, and he caught up to her.

"Yeah, well, it's not too late."

She turned her back to him. "It certainly is. You might want to clean up before your employees arrive. That includes brushing your teeth."

Amanda proceeded into her office. She sat perfectly straight—in her crisp white shirt and hound's-tooth skirt—at the table she was using as a temporary desk. She had secured her hair in a fashion that would not necessitate his touch in order to straighten any part of her out.

Reece followed her into the doorway, staring at her without speaking.

"Are you waiting for something?"

"For you to finish slinging your insults! I thought we could get them out of the way all at once, so we could be free to take care of business for the rest of the day."

Even disheveled he resembled an Adonis and she hated him for it. Why couldn't he be seventy and hunched over?

"I'm sorry for...for..." She paused, searching for what it was she felt sorry for.

"That's enough. I don't need specifics. I'll take the 'I'm sorry,' and we can make up." He made a couple of strides and extended his hand.

She looked at it. It should be a minor thing, really. Yet, she knew the second she laid her hand into his the fireworks would reignite. "No way am I touching that hand until you've cleaned up. There's just no telling where it's been."

He half-sneered and half-laughed. "You are a hard ass, I'll give you that."

"Yeah, well, you wish you knew how hard it was." The words slipped out, words she typically never said and that were taboo in a workplace environment. Heat scorched her face.

He grinned, leaning over the table. "Yes, maybe I do."

His eyes glistened—sun on snow—the blue of the sky reflected in its surface of white. With the wall behind her and Reece in front barring an escape, Amanda felt trapped. She couldn't look into those eyes any longer. The reflection burned, searing her flesh. She knew he could see the red in her cheeks and hear the heaviness of her breath as her chest rose and fell.

She had an urge to voice the thought, *just do it and get it over with.* She feared a connection to this man. He was like too many southern men she had known before.

But he didn't take advantage of the situation. Instead, he turned, chuckled, and slipped away, leaving her with a shred of decency.

****

Workmen were still trying to move all of the marketing director's belongings upstairs, and Amanda's desk had not yet arrived. Every time she thought she had a hard surface to work upon, someone snatched it away.

As frustrating as all of the upheaval was, she resisted going back to Reece's office, not wanting to tangle with him while she still felt shaky from their last encounter. *How on earth does he get under my skin when I despise him so?*

And she was irritated with the home office. Judson had not returned her call, nor responded to the text message she had sent him.

Perhaps Gary had sent word of her computer diagnostics request and possible ineptitude. *No, not Gary*, she thought. Though he might as well tell them all she wasn't getting her work done. *Clearly, I am already behind.*

She thought about Judson's assistant, Mary McNeil. It used to be common practice to refer to people in the position she held as a secretary. Now everyone wanted a better-sounding title. Mary insisted on being known as Judson's assistant. It was surprising she didn't want to be called his *executive* assistant.

Amanda would rather blame Mary if she could. What Mary thought about her made no difference. If Judson thought ill of her, it could cost her the position she hoped to be in line for. While Amanda knew his assistant wouldn't dare go against Judson's authority, Mary wasn't above letting people stew a little. *Is that what's going on there?* she wondered.

She settled in over a short filing cabinet, opened her computer and began to work. Masculine voices washed forward and then hovered over her.

"I'm sorry, Ms. Lassiter," one of the workmen said, as he reached for the filing cabinet.

She was sitting with the laptop balanced on her knees—lack of hard surface altogether now—when she heard a familiar rumble. Reece had returned from somewhere looking immaculately fresh and sipping coffee from a mug that looked as though it could hold a full pot's worth.

He engaged in conversation with one of the workmen before turning his million-dollar smile on her. "You won't be getting much work done around here today, so let's find something interesting for you to learn about down here in the south," he suggested.

"Are you offering a truce?"

"Well, it *is* a bit like a war zone around here." He dodged as a corner of a book shelf came dangerously close to his chin.

Another workman took hold of the cabinet she had stored the gym bag in. "Wait a minute," she called out. He set the cabinet down for her.

Amanda reached inside and pulled the bag out. She opened it and revealed its contents to Reece. "I am ready for combat."

Surprise and delight flashed across Reece's face. He smiled and appeared to soften a bit toward her. "Well, go on and change, and we'll get started."

Amanda hesitated, struggling to decide the best place to change.

He noticed, and motioned toward a door at the back of his office that she had assumed was only a coat closet. "You can change back there. I keep a room here for late nights and early mornings." He leaned against the doorjamb with one foot propped up, watching her.

She raised her eyebrows. "That is about the last thing I want to be seen doing—coming out of your private quarters in different clothes."

He laughed. "Well, I hadn't thought about it like that. Ladies' room, then?"

"Much better."

****

While Amanda was gone, Reece returned to his

office. One look at his large, old chair and the image of her relaxed against it the day before flashed through his mind.

He had envied the chair as he imagined how she would feel pressed against him in a similar fashion. And when she had extended her foot, his focus had not been on the shoe she was trying to highlight. It had been along the curve of her leg, watching the calf muscle pop and wishing his hand could start at the tip of her toe and work its way along the silky undergarments beneath the smart skirt.

And he recalled mere moments before as he stood in Richard's office observing her from the back side. Reece had longed to yank the fancy clip from her twisted hair and watch it waterfall down her back. Then he wanted to pull the hem of her skirt up to the waistband, unbutton her blouse and drop kisses in the valley of her cleavage.

Damn her, he thought, as he responded physically to the images in his mind.

Amanda returned, looking thirty despite his knowing she had to be at least in her forties.

It seemed to be getting harder to judge a woman's age, especially when that woman had taken the kind of care with her appearance as she.

Her slender body looked more voluptuous in the snug jeans and boots, and she had the white business shirt tied in a knot at the waist. Her hair had been loosed from its prison of clips and pulled into a high ponytail on the back of her head,. bouncing when she walked.

You're killing me. Grabbing his muck boots, he headed out for the company truck. Reece tried not to notice the delicate turn of her wrist or the slight scent of lavender trailing her as he helped her into the truck. It bothered him that she could reduce him to a quiver so easily. The mere act of taking her hand and supporting her back as she climbed up into the vehicle had a stomach-knotting effect.

Reece was happy to crawl behind the wheel. The oversized dually with its diesel engine always made him feel manly. It was the ultimate he-man truck, designed for working, hauling, digging through mud, and getting the work done. He loved its sound—the stroke of the pistons, the chatter muffling sounds from the outside. It often felt therapeutic to just ride above the traffic, get back out into the countryside, and put the troubles of the office behind him.

"This is a bit like a cockpit of a plane." Amanda pointed to the various indicators along the dashboard. "Feels like one, too," she added.

The exhilaration of the building pressure inside the giant truck as it wound up and surged forward caused her to press into the seat as if bracing for take-off.

Reece kept to the truck lanes until he hit the exit leading toward Lake Wylie. After a couple of turns they were on a two-lane country road surrounded by trees and plots of farmland.

"Where are we?" she asked as they whipped past fields dotted with older homes and full-of-character barns.

"We're still in Charlotte, just the outskirts. All of the area around Lake Wylie used to look like this. Part of it belonged to my family."

She glanced over at him just in time to catch his jaw grinding. "But it doesn't now?"

"Only a small section of it. My father sold the majority to developers about thirty years ago, during the building boom around here."

"You don't seem happy about that."

They continued along the scenic drive. "It's such a waste really."

"So which is the part you still own?"

"You're about to see for yourself." He had surprised himself by bringing her here. He didn't bring anybody out here. This was his place, his dream, his private piece of heaven nobody else in the world was privy to.

Although costing him dearly, he had purchased the strip of land from his dad to prevent its degradation as well as that of the rest of the old family farm. The price hadn't mattered. He had wanted the place more than he had ever wanted anything.

Perhaps because her time here was limited he thought it okay to share the spot with her. Or was it that he wanted to be seen as more than a number on one of her spreadsheets?

The road narrowed, making it hard to keep the monster truck within the lines. But it wasn't dangerous as there was no one else interested in this expanse of tar and gravel. They had long since left the smooth-surfaced asphalt. Soon the large, red cattle gate over the driveway loomed ahead. Reece pulled into the drive, down-shifted the truck, and grabbed a key from the ring he produced out of his pocket.

Aware of Amanda's eyes on him as he exited the truck, Reece leaned over the lock holding the chain ends together. After swinging the gate open, he hopped back inside of the truck and smiled at her. She blushed and averted her eyes from his.

What was that about? Had she been taking stock of him in a *nonbusinesslike* manner? Not likely. Amanda Lassiter was all business, all the time.

Reece felt unexpectedly vulnerable. He knew it made no difference what this northern woman thought of his piece of paradise, but he wasn't dealing in actual graphs. This was the place that meant more to him than any other in the world. "I hope you like it," he said, not knowing why.

When had the driveway become so overgrown? It was hardly wide enough for the truck to pass through. They were barely moving, rolling toward the wide-open field. "I must get this trimmed back," he commented as tips of the evergreens and laurels brushed against the back fenders.

He had actually delayed trimming them because he enjoyed saving the view until the last minute. Just as they exited the grove of trees, the large under-construction building appeared to the right atop the hill. Piles of dirt still sat in mounds where they had been dipped from the ground. At least it was under roof.

"What is it?" Amanda asked. "A house, hotel, or lodge?"

Reece looked ahead to the structure made entirely from logs with its huge window cut-outs. "This is my future home in the lovely Jordan's Valley," he answered.

"Jordan's Valley?"

"Named for my father's family," he explained.

"Thought as much," she admitted. "It's magnificent. Such a nice green valley surrounded by forest."

"Just wait until you see the view from up there." He shot a grin at her before turning the truck toward the hilltop.

"Is this one of the construction sites DMBS is working on?"

"Absolutely not! This is my personal project. I've been working on it for years, a labor of love really." He continued up the hill, bouncing over stones and rough patches as they climbed toward the heavens, as if headed into the clouds.

Reece kept the truck to the right of the drive until it leveled and then swung it sharply left. The view lying before them was too magnificent for words. A blue-green lake squatted beneath the hill. Sloping upward from its belly, the landscape was nothing but trees and outcroppings of rock.

"Wow!" she exclaimed, disconnecting the seat belt and leaning forward to get as good a view as possible.

"Wait," he said, "I'll help you down from the truck." He could move as swiftly as a jungle cat when he wanted to, and this was one of those times.

He scanned the horizon, the ridges of blue toward the mountains of the north catching his eye as he waited for her to step out onto the runner along the side of the truck. When she did, he reached up with firm hands taking her by the waist. His fingers wrapped easily around her midsection.

Amanda's shirt slid upward as he lifted her off the truck's edge. His fingertips brushed her bare flesh, immediately sparking goose bumps he could feel raising along the surface. They certainly weren't chill bumps in the warmth of the June sun. *She feels something too*, he reasoned.

Reece set her feet onto the solid ground beneath her. His fingers rested at the bottom of her ribs and he made no attempt to remove them. They could have been fused to her.

For the first time in Reece's life, he was more interested in the view of her expression-filled eyes than the one of the valley before him. He didn't flinch and he didn't stop looking at her, knowing she would glance back and he would catch that moment when, unguarded, he could tell if it was safe to move forward toward her.

When she did as he hoped, he leaned in. His thumbs slid across her ribcage and underneath the ridge of fabric of her blouse. He teased the nerve endings of the skin beneath and more goose pimples bubbled to the surface.

She lifted her chin, head back, eyes still in an eternal lock with his. Her lips spread apart ever so slightly and he lowered his head downward to taste the nectar her tongue left behind as it swept over her bottom lip.

A loud squawking noise broke their intense stare. Reece threw back his head, glancing upward. Another loud call issued from above as a hawk circled, gliding weightless on the breeze. It was enough to cause Amanda to look heavenward too, and escape the near mistake in the making.

Reece lowered his eyes, watching the expression on her face. Her lower lip was now caught in her teeth, making her appear nervous—whether caused by him or the sudden shrieking he couldn't determine. He dropped his hands from her body, and she pulled her shirt down over the waistband of her jeans.

"This is amazing," she managed to say.

Reece detected the slight quiver in her voice and knew she had been as affected by their near-kiss as he had been. "Yes, it is," he agreed, though he was looking at her instead of the long-range view. "Come on inside," he encouraged.

A sweep of his hand placed her squarely in front of him as she climbed the steps of rock onto the porch. He trailed behind, trying not to watch her hips as they engaged to pull her upward.

He reached for her hand, and she pulled it away. Oddly enough, he was relieved. The last thing he needed was to touch her again. What if he couldn't stop the onslaught of passions raging inside of him every time he got near her?

She might even file harassment charges, and she would be right to do so if he laid hands on her. Yet that was all he seemed to want to do, lay his hands *all* over her. Except when she began a tirade of one kind or another and then he just wanted to place a clamp over her lips.

Amanda moved forward as Reece indicated, through a massive entrance door and into a foyer spanning two floors. "This is fantastic!" she gasped. "It reminds me of a western lodge with the wide-open floor plan."

"I think so, too." He tried to look only at the insulated wall of glass piercing the logs like eyes into the soul. He walked slowly over and peered down into the lake. "You should see it when it snows; all is pristine and white for days. It is a piece of heaven like no other."

"How long have you been working on it?"

"About twenty years, I guess." He ran a hand over the logs framing the window, feeling their solid strength and hoping some of it would leak into him. "Although, I have to admit there has been nothing of consequence going on out here in the past few months."

"Twenty years? That's a long time to work on something which isn't finished, isn't it?"

"There is something you should know about building houses and structures of any kind. Those of us who do it for a living know how it should be done. We also know the corners that can be cut to get a project through to the end, and a resultant paycheck into the bank account. That's why we rarely build our own homes. The simplest house can take years and many thousands more to build than something comparable."

"So why did you start it?"

"This piece of land deserves the best. I'm in no hurry to finish this structure. Every product in it, up to this point, is the best available and there will be no corners cut, no expenses spared. I work on it myself and will only hire helpers when I can be here to assure everything is done right."

"I know I have a lot to learn about construction, but what is it that would concern you about hiring help? Surely you have connections with the best workmen."

"I can walk you through any house, even a new house and show you every single thing that is wrong with it. A wall may not be exactly plumb or a corner perfectly squared. The roof may not be precisely pitched or the sheetrock smooth. I can tell where inferior products have been introduced, windows aren't low energy, or doors aren't from solid wood. They stand out to me as clearly as a missing column of figures would to you."

She quickly made eye contact, and his heart sank. He knew she had found the slip, the thing he most wished to cover until he could correct it.

"Yes," she said, "and I'll never get my work finished if I stand out here all day enjoying this view." She walked toward the door, and he let her go. She couldn't leave without him, and he needed a minute to collect his thoughts.

Reece felt pulled in a hundred directions. He suddenly wanted her to approve of him more than anything. Of course, he also wanted to assure a presence in his own town of the company that had supplied building materials for generations. He wanted to protect his employees and their beloved jobs, never more so than in this bad economy. He wanted to provide for all of his family, even the extended members who may be no more than bad memories of worse marriages. He wanted to secure his own future—though less than he wanted those of the ones he cared about, assured.

And he wanted this stubborn, smart, beautiful, enticing, quick-witted woman in his bed, though he knew the combination would never work. She was married to her company; that much was obvious. There was a joke he and his colleagues used to pass between them about the only thing worse than a man married to his work was a company woman. And Amanda was just such a woman.

Reece collected himself and made his way back to the dually. Thankfully, she had managed to hoist herself back into the cab of the truck before he left the interior of the house. That way he didn't have to put his hands on her to help her up, and subject himself to the torturous longings that bloomed every time he did.

He knew he had to make himself stop desiring her so damned much, yet through the corner of his eye he could see the strands of her hair that had fallen away from her pony-tail holder. They danced around her neck and he longed to chase them with his fingertips, feel the goose bumps against her skin that would whelp beneath his touch, and see the fire blazing in her eyes as it had only moments before.

Keep your eyes on the road, he coached himself—refusing to look at her again, avoiding eye contact.

The tension in the truck on the way back to DMBS was palpable. He could tell she desired him too, if only in a carnal, lusty manner. He didn't care *how* she wanted him; the fact that she did at all, made him want to jerk the giant vehicle off the road and lift her naked and free onto his lap, to explore all he could offer her.

The grumbling of his stomach interrupted his thoughts and echoed in the cab of the truck.

"Hungry?" she asked.

His head snapped toward her, and she blushed.

"Your stomach growled...I...meant..." She stopped trying to explain and turned her head toward the landscape passing her window.

"There's a little family diner just ahead. Let's grab a bite of lunch before going back," he suggested.

She nodded agreement. "I could use a drink for sure."

Reece pulled the truck into the parking lot and Amanda quickly jumped from her seat onto the ground as he secured the brake and locked the door.

He took his time, allowing her the opportunity to

put a little distance between them, catching up with her at the restaurant's door. He held it open for her, careful not to brush against her as she strode past.

Amanda suggested the booth in the back and he nodded. They hadn't been seated for more than a moment when an older lady appeared with an old-fashioned order pad, no menu in sight.

"Hey there, Reece," Annie said happily. "I haven't been seeing much of you lately. 'S about time you dropped in. What'll you be havin' today?"

Reece saw Amanda wince as Annie talked to them. "I think we are in need of a couple of your cheeseburgers, Annie," he replied.

"You're eating *two* sandwiches?" Amanda asked. "I was thinking a green salad with vinaigrette dressing on the side."

"What kind of dressing is that? We only got ranch, Thousand Island, and Italian. But here's a tip"—she leaned forward as though about to give a secret stock tip—"our salads just aren't much good. Take it from Reece here and go with the cheeseburger. It's sort of a specialty, if you know what I mean."

Amanda appeared to be considering her options. She looked completely lost in thought.

Annie responded to her silence. "Of course if you're stuck on a salad, I can put some cheese on it, maybe a little macaroni salad, and some ground ham."

She gasped. "No, I'll take the burger, since you're known for it."

"And to drink?"

Reece spoke up again. "Two sweet iced teas!"

"House wine of the south," Amanda mumbled.

Something in the way she said that caused Reece to

glance up at her. Was it that she knew such a phrase about the popularity of southern sweet tea, or the twang of the "i" when she said "wine"? He couldn't put his finger on it, but something caused him to sense a southern connection in her.

After Annie disappeared with their orders, he asked, "Do you have relatives here in the south?"

"No," she said flatly. "Why do you ask?"

"I don't know. Just making conversation I guess." She wouldn't meet his gaze. He sensed she might be covering something up. Could it be their little northern fireball had southern roots she wasn't showing?

When it arrived, the ice in the glasses was already melting from the warmth of the recently brewed beverage. Amanda took a sip, winced, and immediately squeezed the lemon on the edge of the rim into the topaz liquid.

"Yeah, sweet tea," Reece said, "nothing like it." Then noticing the lemon she was reaming into the glass, he tilted his glass forward offering the yellow slice of tartness from his own glass. "Want mine too?"

"Actually, yes." She smiled as she accepted the proffered citrus and added its contents to her own glass. "Thanks."

"You're welcome."

Reece enjoyed the softer pace of the non-antagonizing, plain, civil conversation. He seemed to want to devour her, one way or the other.

Her face collapsed into an expression of ecstasy as she bit into the juicy burger. He stopped mid-bite to watch her. She caught him watching and wiped her mouth with a napkin. "Sweet Jesus, I don't remember the last time I had one of these."

He chuckled before chomping into his own again. A little sleeve of wax paper cuffed around the middle of the sandwich was supposed to catch drips, but it never did so effectively. "Annie told you they were good."

"It's huge though. If I eat the whole thing I may have to unbutton my pants."

He once again stopped mid-bite. "That's all right too," he encouraged, lifting an eyebrow.

His mind produced the image of her knotted shirt up around her breasts and the waistband of her jeans open as she unbuttoned them and laid them to the side. *Stop it now*, he said to himself. He felt himself growing as his desire for her returned along with the mental image of his hand sliding into the opened jeans, touching her and feeling the warmth beneath.

Reece glanced around the diner. He couldn't understand how the other patrons seemed to be having normal conversations with an ordinary tone. Couldn't everyone in the diner tell how much he ached for this woman? Did they all know how his pulse raced and his blood thundered beneath the surface?

His blood gushed through his veins, pooling in the area between his legs, seeming to signal his brain he needed satisfaction. His hunger was deeper than that of his stomach. He needed to plunge into the warmth she promised beneath the icy surface. He just knew a fire blazed there. He had seen evidence of it.

"Is everything okay?" She tapped him on the arm as he was frozen in a world of thoughts known only to him.

He attacked his sandwich with a vengeance. "It's perfect."

Chapter 5

Amanda insisted on paying for her own meal and Reece appeared to grow tired of arguing with her, finally giving in.

Although he offered a hand up to her as she took hold of the truck's door, she hoisted herself upward without his assistance. "Thanks, but I can handle it by myself."

Her words hung between them, their meaning possible to take in several forms. She watched Reece shake his head and walk around the front of the truck.

She looked away when he landed in the cab with her, careful not to get sucked back into the vortex of his charm. For a brief moment she had let herself slip, allowed herself to experience the sensation of his fingertips against her bare flesh. Droplets of fire had danced across her stomach and spread upward and downward simultaneously.

She didn't think she was strong enough to fend off the desires billowing beneath the surface, raging for this man who most of the time she found offensive. Why did she have to be physically attracted to the most infuriating men?

At least she had stopped herself—well, that was too strong a statement even to make to herself. The hawk had interrupted them. Had it not been for his sudden squawking out, she might have given in to her desire to know how Reece kissed. And if it was as wonderful as she suspected, then who knows what might have happened—two mature adults alone in the half-finished mountaintop home surrounded by nothing but glorious views.

The home he's likely constructed using the missing funds from DMBS, she reasoned. Was that where it had gone? Would a lien have to be attached to his dream house? It would, if she discovered that the money had been spent on the property.

The truck slowed; the downshifting of gears resounded through the cab, interrupting Amanda's thoughts. They were in a traffic jam. The broad hips of the truck caused her to mentally sweat as they nearly glanced off power poles and city buses. She was thankful to see DMBS's parking lot looming ahead.

Vernella seemed beside herself when they arrived back at the shop. She appeared—one of many—wanting Reece's undivided attention. They all started talking at once, ignoring Amanda altogether.

Amanda's desk had failed to arrive, there was a breakdown on one of the millwork machines halting progress of the guaranteed order he had so much trouble with the day before, and his cell phone had been turned off. He insisted he didn't know how that had happened.

Faces and voices seem to come at them from all directions. One very perky one Amanda hadn't seen before peered from around the corner, sunglasses-covered eyes followed by a giant swath of long blond hair and too-pink lipstick on super glossy lips.

"Shoot me now," Reece whispered.

"What?" Amanda felt the stares of everyone

around penetrating her.

"Nothing," he commented. "Listen, I've obviously got a few fires to extinguish, so if you want to go upstairs with Richard, maybe he could give you a little background on the company and take you through our marketing concepts."

"Good idea. I'll just get changed." She entered ahead of Reece, giving him a single backward glance. He looked as if he was trying to calm himself before entering a den of snakes waiting to devour him.

Vernella called out to Amanda as she tiptoed through the door. "If you're through playing with Reece, Chicago wishes to speak to you."

Her words shot through Amanda as cleanly as a shredder through a sheet of ordinary paper. "Could you be more specific?" she shot back to the redhead.

"Judson Matheney, on his fourth call, for the agent he sent down here to work. Is that specific enough for ya?"

Amanda understood the sudden urge to clench her jaw and grit her teeth. But she only nodded and said, "I'll take it in Reece's office."

"That line's full," Vernella sneered.

"Then upstairs with Richard."

She slowly walked through the reception area before running for the steps, taking them two by two in her boots and jeans.

She practically snatched the receiver from Richard's hand as he reached to pick it up. "Yes. Here," she said between sharp intakes of breath after answering the line. Even in her physical condition, the sprint down the hall and up the stairs stirred heavy breaths.

She could hear the irritation in Judson's voice as he questioned why she hadn't answered his call.

"My cell phone? Yes, no reception at the job site."

"Job site? What are you doing at a job site?"

"It seemed easier to get an understanding of the finished product that way."

"Since when do you need to understand the product *at a job site*? DMBS *is* the product."

"Of course it is." She could think of nothing else to say about that.

"Are you in over your head there? Do I need to send in back-up for you? I'm beginning to fear sending you there alone may have been a mistake."

Her heart pounded, pushing blood through her veins at a force she could literally feel. He was regretting sending her here on her own. Clearly he didn't think she was up to the job at hand. She would have to convince him she knew what she was doing, and that going out to the job site was necessary.

"No sir, you didn't make a mistake by sending me; in fact, just the opposite. Since I do not understand anything about the construction business, I didn't want to be crippled by false apprehensions and impressions of my own making. Seeing it first-hand has allowed me to conduct the inventory here in a better manner."

"Do you still believe it has viability in the market there? Or should I be scheduling an auction?"

"I'm still determining that. Having a millwork shop right on the premises is a definite plus. It could be an asset to the Rock Hill store."

He didn't answer right away. "You are looking at this venture from every angle, aren't you, Amanda? That's good. I hadn't considered using DMBS as a supplement to the Rock Hill store."

A compliment! How divine. "Yes, sir," she said. "I don't want to miss anything here."

"Okay. Give me your office extension there in case you are in another situation without service. I know how *those rural areas* can have dead cell reception."

Amanda heard the distaste for the countryside in his voice; could mentally envision him looking down his nose. "Well, we're still in the process of setting up an office for me now."

"What do you mean? Do I need to remind you who is in charge there? Take the CEO's office and let *him* wait for the new one."

"Yes, I understand. I'll be taking Reece's office and the new one is for him. Right."

"And you'll call me at the first sign of trouble?"

"Yes, sir. Absolutely."

"Keep me posted."

Richard pretended to be engrossed in his own project, but she could tell he hadn't resisted eavesdropping. She hoped he wouldn't disclose the dressing down he'd overheard.

She knew the more she explained, the less powerful she would appear. "Thank you, Richard. I'm sorry to keep bothering you," was all she said before disappearing down the stairs in a hurried clumping.

She grabbed her clothes—cell phone still in the jacket pocket, light flashing to indicate the numerous messages. She caught a glimpse of herself in the mirror. She looked like Reece had this morning—a disheveled mess.

Well, she just couldn't continue to let him get beneath her skin. She stripped the clothing from her body, and slowly redressed herself in the business attire that supported her importance in this endeavor. She wasn't as prone to slip ups in her black and white professional uniform.

The only problem was the shirt. Now wrinkled and stained from the tying above her jeans and the greasy-spoon lunch, it looked worse than Reece's had this morning. Oh well, there was nothing she could do about that now.

Amanda recalled Susan's trick for getting out a stain and had she had more time, would have attempted it herself. She simply buttoned her jacket at the waist and hid the wrinkles behind her expensive suit coat. She finger-combed the long strands of hair and caught them once again, twining and twisting to form the chignon which represented her sternness.

She couldn't get caught up in such things again. She had to exert her authority and move a little faster, or risk upsetting her employer. And that wasn't something she intended to do, no matter how attractive Reece Jordan was.

When Amanda slipped her feet back into her designer heels, the transformation became complete. She pulled her shoulders back and exited as *the woman in charge* she knew she could be.

After making a beeline for Reece's office, she was appalled to see him leaning back in his chair, feet propped up on the desk, talking casually on the phone.

"Up, up, up," she demanded.

He did so, but with a pronounced scowl. Obviously, he was unused to anyone speaking to him thusly unless the place was on fire. "Gotta go, I'll call you right back." He set the receiver back against the phone rest. "What is it?"

"I have orders to take this whole office over. Somehow I've let you make me forget what it is I've come down here to do. From now on this is my office, and if there is waiting to be done for a desk, for an office space, for a phone call, or for a company mascot to learn how to pick its own nose, well then *you* will be attending to that and I'll be in here."

He tried to protest.

"No, no, I will hear no excuses. You get yourself set up the best way you can. I've got work to do."

"And if I refuse." He stood bolted to the floor, looking determined not to give an inch.

"Then I'll make one phone call to legal, and you'll be physically removed from the premises with a cease and desist order preventing reentrance. Understand?" She stood equally as regal, confidant in her attire and quite a bit taller in her heels.

"Well, I wouldn't want to put you to all that extra trouble."

"I assure you, it will be no trouble at all." She said it in her finest high-brow voice, the one that made cold shivers run along the spines of weaker people.

He walked around to the front of the desk leaving her room to move around him and take the seat behind his father's desk. He pulled up a chair opposite her, and flipped the phone around, mashing the intercom button and calling out for three of the burliest men in the shop to come to his office.

They arrived quickly. "Yes sir, what do ya need?"

Each of the quiet warriors in his office looked from one to another. "I need those filing cabinets moved into Richard's old office. Ms. Lassiter and I will be sharing this room."

"What?" she asked.

"You're right. We need to be together so we can get all of the kinks out...for the betterment of the staff and the company."

"We'll try it," she agreed. "But if you don't cooperate, you're gone."

He nodded. "I understand."

Chapter 6

There was so much chaos that another day passed without Amanda finding the answer she was looking for. She hated to ask Reece, but soon she would have to. With all of the moving around and about, the day was shot. The phone company was scheduled for the following morning to set some extra lines for Reece and his computer, and after that—hopefully—they could get down to serious business.

"Let's go for a drink," he suggested as she prepared to leave.

"That's completely out of the question. I've been side-tracked enough for one day."

"There are things which are just difficult to discuss around here that might be easier in a more relaxed atmosphere."

She had known Judson to practice this philosophy as a religion and thought he would approve. "Only if we can agree to keep it focused on business and to limit the time to about one hour."

"Deal."

He extended his hand as though to shake on it, but she walked past him and out to the parking lot throwing the words over her shoulder, "I'll follow you."

They didn't go far, just a few blocks down and into a quaint and quiet corner of a restaurant and bar combination. Amanda ordered a glass of pinot noir.

Reece requested the whole bottle be delivered along with a glass for him. He sat opposite her though his long legs didn't seem to completely fit beneath the table and they kept bumping hers, sending waves of longing throughout her body each time.

"Maybe if we sat on the same side," he suggested, sliding into the booth beside her. "Isn't that better?"

His knees no longer competed with hers for the space beneath, but his entire thigh ran the length of hers from hip downward. When he moved he rubbed against her and set off a frenzy of sensations which caused her to lift the glass of wine to her lips more times than she should have.

"Tell me about yourself," he suggested, tipping the wine bottle into her glass as it emptied.

The wine dulled her senses just enough to let her guard down. "There isn't much to tell really. I work. That's what I do. It's who I am." She ran a finger along the rim of the wine glass.

"Surely you have a significant other, someone waiting at home." He rocked his foot up and down, causing his thigh to brush hers over and over in a series of caresses.

She gave a sarcastic little laugh. "Not even a cat. How about you?"

"Have had, but they didn't work out. The women in my life all wanted more than I could give. I am '*complex, and never around*,' they say."

"And yet I have barely spent ten minutes without having you near me." She said this without thinking. It was her vulnerability to alcohol.

"I enjoy being near you for some reason." He didn't look at her when he said it.

"Yeah, I know *the reason.* You want to keep an eye on me." She caught his eye then and saw the smoky desire billowing there. The breath left her body as she simmered in the heat of his stare.

"I can't deny that," he whispered as he leaned forward. His face was too close, and the room was too dark. There had been too much innuendo, too many heated glances and electrical touches not to lean in and brush his lips with hers. They were soft brushes, the kind a person could walk away from and label a mistake. She hadn't gone too far yet.

She would have been lying to herself if she had said she didn't wonder how he tasted. When he leaned in to kiss her, she couldn't stop herself from responding. It was natural to crave a man, and she had been without one for so long that even the touch of his thigh against hers drove her crazy. Truth be told, he had been arousing her since he first touched her flesh.

His lips parted, just a little, but enough to indicate he wanted the taste of her. Amanda licked the wine from his lips, his tongue, and suddenly there was nothing and no one else in the bar.

"We'd make a good team, working together instead of apart on this," he whispered.

She had been accepting his long sensual kisses, tasting the wine on his tongue while smelling his faint scent of sawdust and glue, until then. That single comment was enough to make her doubt his connectivity to her on a personal level. *He's worried about his damned company.*

Amanda pushed him away. "We can discuss this at the office. I really need to get to the hotel."

She fumed all the way to the hotel. What on earth

was she doing getting involved with him? She couldn't even claim temporary insanity as she just kept on waltzing with the devil.

****

Reece wasn't feeling much better. He had followed Amanda to the hotel ostensibly to assure himself she got there safely, but mostly due to his hope that she would recover her senses and invite him up. He felt every inch of his body ignite.

Everything was at stake with this woman being at the helm of his destiny. To feel so attracted to her was akin to Dante loving the inferno. A stronger man would have run away, but Reece couldn't run fast enough to avoid the energy that pulled him toward her in its tractor beam. How could he even try to reason with her sensibilities where his company was concerned?

"Let's at least get a bite of dinner together," he insisted as she flew past him in the lobby.

"I'm going to order in tonight." She furiously pushed the button for the elevator. Several others waited patiently for its door to open, and she gave them a weak smile as she entered the back of the line.

"Come on, talk to me. What are you afraid of?" he whispered.

"I'm not afraid of anything or anyone, but this situation can't end well." The elevator arrived and Reece pulled her out of the line for it.

"Give me five minutes, please."

"What do you want from me?" She appeared distraught.

"I want to get to know you. I want to understand what this crazy attraction to you is—the one you keep pretending isn't there—but I can sense you feel the same way. I want to explain the importance of my business and the people whose lives depend on it. And then I'll get warmed up."

"Look…" She held up a hand and backed away from him as he attempted to touch her yet again. "I don't know what this crazy attraction is either. It's probably coming from the heat of our differences. But I can't throw away everything I've worked for just to have some hot sex. I work, I told you; it's who I am."

"No, it is not who you are." He grabbed her and pulled her body into his, caressing her in the warmth of his arms. "It may be what you do," he whispered into her ear, "but it is not who you are."

"Then *who* am I?" She stared into his eyes, pleading for something—strength maybe.

"You are a divinely beautiful and sexy lady who needs a man as much as I need a woman."

The elevator opened again, and she pulled him inside of it with her. Between floors, he kissed her deeply and passionately, his hands roaming around her back and along the sides of her face, reigniting the flames she had tried to extinguish mere moments before.

The gentle rising stopped and the sounds of metal sliding open caused her to move outside of the enclosure. She pressed a hand to his chest, stopping him from getting off the elevator. "Please...don't."

Surely she could feel his heart thundering beneath his shirt. "But—" He protested to deaf ears.

"I cannot let the possibility of an affair interfere with my job. You should respect that. If, after all this is over and finished, you still have these feelings toward me, and I you, then we'll talk."

"But what about now?" he protested. "I haven't desired anyone like this in...maybe ever."

She ran a fingertip along the side of his stern chin. "If we slept together now, I would never know whether or not it was to interfere with the job I've come to do. And you would never know if you desired me simply because I held your future in my hands. It can't happen this way."

She reached in and pushed the button, disappearing around the corner as the elevator carried him back downstairs.

****

The next morning Amanda acted as if nothing had happened, and Reece followed her lead. She refused to look at him, or touch him in any way, no matter how foolishly he tried to bump into her. It was probably easier that way.

He recalled all too well the scent of her, the way she tasted, the hot flash of desire he knew he aroused in her. But there was no way to marry that with the intense working relationship they now shared.

She was working on the final figures. Reece watched the delicate movement of her red-tipped fingers on the keyboard. Amanda reached up and ran one absentmindedly around the rim of her coffee mug, and he wanted it exactly the same way on his body, the delicate circling along his thigh and...*Stop it*, he chastised himself.

Reece watched her break down the analysis into smaller and smaller categories. He knew they wouldn't look any better the second time than they had the first.

Amanda looked up. "Reece, there is something we need to discuss."

"Okay." He braced for it.

She laid the statements out—and the analysis she had collected—then pointed sharply to a missing amount of money that shocked even him. "So what do you think can account for this shortfall?"

"Why don't you tell me? You're the one with the expertise in this field." It sounded snarky, even to his own ears, as he said it.

"What's going on here?"

Her intimidating stare had lost its effect since kissing his lips raw in the elevator.

Vernella—always popping in at the worst possible time—chose that moment to appear in the doorway. "Someone is here to see you, Reece."

"Who is it?" he asked, a bit sternly.

"Why don't you see for yourself?"

He glanced out of the window to see the red sportster parked outside. "Oh God," he moaned. "That's about the last thing I need right now."

"Shall I try to handle it for you?" Vernella asked.

"No, I'll just go see what she wants." He stormed out of the door and into the parking lot, cutting the visitor off before she could blow through the office in a perfume-scented wind storm.

****

"What is this about, Vernella?" Amanda asked.

"See for yourself." She pulled open the shutters over the front windows, opening the view to the parking lot where Reece was locked in an embrace with a tall blonde.

He kissed her on the cheek, opened the door of her candy-apple red sportster, and helped her back inside, closing the door gently while leaning inside of the open window to whisper something privately to the woman. Her head snapped back with open-toothed laughter.

"And I suppose you just can't wait to tell me who this is?" Amanda quipped.

"It's none of *my* business. We just call her 'Mrs. Jordan.'" Vernella mouthed the last two words in exaggerated syllables and raised an eyebrow at the shock on Amanda's face. "Tried to warn you, but you didn't want to listen."

"What does any of this have to do with me? Why should I care if he is married or not, seeing someone or not? I'm not here for shenanigans, just business."

"Oh honey, save that act for Reece. He'll buy a bushel, but you can't sell me a pint. I see how you look at him. And I don't blame you. If all you want is a good southern spanking, well, go for it."

Vernella walked off with a giggle, leaving Amanda standing at the window, watching Reece wave to his wife as she pulled out into traffic. She watched a moment too long.

Her anger boiled at the thought of being in Reece's arms in the elevator the previous evening and aching to take him to her bed. Now to see a wife—one that he had purposefully left out of the picture—made her feel humiliated and used.

She had fallen victim to his charms. It was more than clear she had been correct in thinking he was using her in order to send her off the trail of his missing funds. Thankfully, she *had managed* to refrain from sleeping with him—the only saving grace in the whole scenario.

So distracted by her thoughts, she didn't hear the footsteps creeping stealthily behind her.

Reece seized the opportunity to throw his arms around her and whisper in her ear. "Hello, gorgeous. Can you spare a few minutes for a man who finds you irresistible?"

Nausea seized her. Moments ago he was kissing his wife on the cheek, and now he was wrapping another woman up into his hot embraces. He was almost vile to her now.

She burst free of his grasp and turned cold eyes on him. "I do not think it is appropriate for you to display your affections in the work place, even if they were mutual. In the future, I expect our relationship to be purely professional. Understand?"

Reece dropped his arms and frowned. He looked shocked and confused, though she couldn't imagine how he pulled it off.

He must take me for a complete idiot.

"I'm sorry. I totally understand." He backed away, hands up, surrendering. "No more public displays of affection."

"No more affection whatsoever. This is business. Nothing more," she snapped.

"You made your point." He sneered. "No need to go on and on about it." He thundered from the room, mumbling something about "Damned moody women" she chose to ignore.

****

Vernella signaled Reece that Chicago was on the line for Amanda. He had made it clear he wanted to know every time she took a call from headquarters. Before Vernie made the transfer to Amanda's phone, Reece slipped quietly into the office previously occupied by the marketing director, now home to the massive file cabinets from his own office.

Amanda was busily tearing his life apart as he settled in to listen to the information she shared with her higher-ups. He missed a bit of the initial conversation but now followed it perfectly.

"There's a lot of knowledge here that I think shouldn't be wasted. In fact, we might want to merge another branch with this one."

He smiled to himself.

"I realize I have just been a numbers representative to you in the past, but the people here at Dixie have been walking me through the entire process over the past few days."

He grinned again, nodding to no one; hoping he wouldn't get caught eavesdropping.

"I don't think they even need me anymore."

He heard the chair turn swiftly.

"What? No, sir."

The tension in her response sent shivers up his spine. What was it that had her alarmed?

"Super Builders Mart will be glad to hear it." She laughed.

What is she laughing at? Reece wondered.

"When should I plan to come back?"

She's leaving. The realization suddenly hit Reece. A tidal wave of physical desire coursed through his body just as a knot of emptiness fisted itself into his gut.

"Not until then?"

A reprieve. He might have a little time with her.

"Oh, all right. Whatever you say. I'll see you then."

He heard the click of the phone being hung up.

Reece wanted to play cool, yet somehow couldn't

stand it any longer. He had played tough, even arrogant, and now he wanted to know the scoop.

He walked into the office and revealed his own snooping. "I'm sorry. I couldn't help but overhear your conversation."

"Well now, aren't we the crafty little spy?" Amanda looked up at him with raised eyebrows.

"You know I am when it comes to this business." He could feel anxiety creeping into his voice and knew it made him appear vulnerable.

"The problem I am having is in reconciling a balance sheet of assets. There is a huge hole, something is missing. Might you know where it may be?" She pushed the balance sheet toward him along with spread sheets printed off his own computer. *You traitor*, he thought, as he glanced at the box of electronic record keeping.

"You need to come up with an answer, or someone is going up on embezzlement charges. Understand?"

"What makes you so sure it isn't accounting errors or an honest mistake? Why do you just jump to embezzlement as a first theory instead of a last one?" He had found a backbone again and yanked it upright as he faced her.

She met his strength with a sudden surge of vitriolic words. "Oh boy, you are a slick one. You think you can get away with defrauding and defaming and cheating and lying and all kinds of games that we *weak* women can never quite figure out because we're not nearly as smart as you. Is that what you're saying?"

"I've had just about enough of you!" Reece didn't know what it was that had her so worked up. He stormed off, preferring the noise of the mill shop over the noise of the woman who kept him at the gates of hell.

****

Amanda had done all she could until the missing equity reappeared. She had filed a very thorough report, disclosing the discrepancy and the large amounts of money going out to J & S Consulting. Unable to find any information about that particular firm, she knew it didn't look good for Reece Jordan. But she would no longer cover his mistakes.

She couldn't determine who was guilty either, and that was the problem with deciding whether to close the business. If it was Reece skimming the profits, there was an easy mend. What if it wasn't though? What if there was someone in accounting jiggling the numbers on purpose?

Unless the culprit was found, Amanda couldn't recommend keeping Dixie Millwork and Building Supply open. It broke her heart to think of all of the faces of the people she had met and talked with over the past week being told their jobs were gone. In a better economy they might consider it a brief blip on the road of their careers. But in this job-scarce environment, they might have trouble bouncing back.

She typed an e-mail to Judson's private account, hoping to bypass Mary. Attaching the files containing her findings, she hit "send." There was no retrieval now. It was all there for him to see. What happened next was up to him. Her job was done.

It seemed almost silly now that so much upheaval had been caused by her need for an office space to work in. What was the point in having the new desk and the recently rewired office? If her recommendations were followed, the entire building—and everything inside of it—would be sold.

Amanda's phone buzzed almost immediately. Judson's name appeared across the screen. "Yes, sir," she answered.

"Good job, Lassiter! Stay put. I'll send in a team Monday morning to help you with the layoffs and inventory. Meet them at the airport. Mary will verify their estimated time of arrival." The line died.

Brief and to the point. It was typical Judson. But the instant response astounded her. He couldn't have had time to look over the reports. Surely he made the decision based solely on her recommendation.

Amanda began to shake, unaccustomed to the ultimate power one person could wield over the lives of so many people. She sat back down, letting the indentations in the leather chair caress her body one last time. Once the others arrived, there would be no time for sitting, except for the person handing out the pink slips. And she definitely had no desire to be that individual.

Amanda swiveled the chair away from the doorway. She didn't wish to see anyone who might appear there, not Richard, not Susan, and definitely not Reece.

Something caught her eye. The door to the back room Reece kept for late nights and early mornings was ajar. She hadn't inspected it, but as part of the building, it now belonged to Builders Tech.

Feeling like a voyeur, she crept toward it.

Chapter 7

Reece checked his online bank account for the umpteenth time. He had lost count of the number of actual log-ins. Relief surged through his body as he saw what he had been looking for. The funds from Builders Tech were finally available for his use.

He called his accountants together and they began a plan for using these proceeds to replace the missing ones. It was under debate whether they should do so in respect to inventory, accounts receivable, or some other capital investment. They had a dummy company already, J & S Consulting, and needed to make some kind of explanation as to its connection to DMBS and the type of service it provided.

As they argued amongst themselves, Reece was feverishly thinking of which of the ideas wouldn't reflect badly on Amanda. The last thing he wanted was for her to take a professional hit when this was her first solo acquisition.

She hadn't told him so, but he could sense it. He had seen the bead of sweat on her upper lip when Chicago called, and he'd overheard one of the conversations she had with the main office. He didn't want to make her look foolish. When he voiced this concern, it fell on deaf ears.

"Why should you care how *she* looks?" one asked.

"We are at fault here. It won't serve us to make her

the scapegoat." It was all he could think of to say.

They looked at one another, nodding.

Reece assumed they would do whatever he asked. He had always been honest with them. Even now, he was using all of the money he had just received to rectify a situation not of his own making.

"So how do we do it?" Reece asked the group. "What kind of investment should it be? Which would be the easiest to cover for?"

They debated. Ideas whipped across the tables. One suggested an off-site storage facility they could suddenly realize had not been listed with the assets. It seemed a pretty good idea.

Another suggested they might purchase stock in a business they used, such as the lumber company, but they would have to be willing to backdate the sale— treacherously close to the border of being illegal.

"Why can't we call it what it is—a loan?" Reece asked.

"You don't get it," another said. "A loan without permission of the person holding the money is theft, even if it is paid back."

Reece clenched his jaw. "What was I supposed to do? Was I supposed to let my seventy-nine-year-old dad go to jail?"

"Why would he go to jail?" Susan asked.

A snicker went round the table.

Reece was edgy and irritable. He rubbed his forehead. "Would someone explain to Susan what we are doing here?"

"That isn't necessary," she said. She gave a little cough, appearing to gather her courage. "I just don't know why Roger Jordan would be in danger of incarceration when Reece is the one who signed the checks withdrawing money from the J & S account."

Reece jerked his head up. "I didn't sign those checks."

Susan looked confused. She fumbled through the copies she had brought with her to the meeting. "Here. Here they are." She produced a few copies of the astronomic checks drawn on J & S.

Reece grabbed them, scanning each one before slamming it down on the table. "Why didn't you tell me this before?" he snapped.

"Why would I tell you something I had reason to believe you had done yourself?"

Reece motioned to the others around the table. He could barely contain his fury through his clenched teeth. "Did none of you check the signatures?"

Shoulders shrugged as the rest of the people he paid to watch his best interests glanced from one to the other. They were looking for someone to take the fall for letting such a travesty slip through their fingers.

"Well?" he asked again. "Is Susan the only one here with enough sense to follow through? *And* she was the only one who didn't know it was my father behind this crap." He paused and looked at her apologetically. "You all didn't trust her...and I didn't have complete confidence in her either. I'm sorry, Susan. It appears I have paid the price for misjudging you."

Harold leaned forward. "Reece, you are jumping to conclusions. Builders Tech may own Dixie Millwork right now, but they have no right to go snooping into a privately owned company. They won't have access to the bank statements of J & S."

Reece noticed the way Harold locked eyes with

Susan as he spoke, narrowing his to indicate a warning to her and he wondered if Harold's attempts at intimidation ended with Susan. She appeared unfazed.

"Yes, they will," she firmly stated, disregarding his hint. Susan took a deep breath and met his gaze.

Reece looked from one to the other. "Susan, tell us why you think that."

"Builders Tech will find the mysterious disbursements to J & S. There's been at least one check issued since the takeover. Builders Tech didn't authorize any such expenditure. They will seek a subpoena to trace the funds. It will be issued and their records will fall squarely into the hands of the very people you are trying to keep this from."

"That's making an assumption," another said.

Susan looked at her colleagues. "You are unbelievable. You act like everyone at Builders Tech is an idiot. You've certainly treated Ms. Lassiter that way."

Susan addressed Reece. "She would have helped. You know that, don't ya?"

Reece knew Susan was right. "If I have trouble trusting my own employees, why do you think I would trust someone sent from the company who took mine out from under me?"

He had made a mistake by antagonizing Amanda. "Does anyone have a suggestion *now*?"

The table fell silent. All eyes turned downward. Nervous fingers sifted through sheaves of paperwork. Reece looked at each accountant directly, failing to get a response.

Susan finally spoke up. "There's still time, isn't there?"

Reece's head snapped around. "What are you suggesting, Susan?"

"You know what I'm suggesting, sir. She hasn't left yet. Find her and tell her everything…after you replace the funds of course."

"Of course," Reece agreed. He threw the documents into his briefcase and then pushed back from the table, starting for the door. With the knob firmly in his hand, he turned. "And Susan?"

She glanced toward him. "Yes, sir?"

"If we survive this, there's a huge raise in your future."

"Thank you. Just doing my job."

Reece ran from the upstairs office, the place where Richard had been exiled to. He skipped down the steps and headed for his office. *Her office,* he mentally corrected. He hoped she would still be there and wouldn't be in the same mood she had been in when he had last seen her.

Chapter 8

Amanda pushed open the door to the small room in the back of Reece's office—*will I ever stop thinking of it as such?*—and slipped inside. She scanned the masculine array of furniture, sparse though it was: a small bed with a comforter thrown haphazardly over it, an old chest, a tiny table with two ladder-backed chairs, and an armoire which could have been an antique. The only modern thing in the whole space was a wall-mounted flat screen television.

A narrow door led to the bathroom, another dreadfully dull area with the basics and nothing more: a toilet, stand-alone sink, and a tiny shower with room for only one. This certainly didn't look like the kind of place one would associate as a *love nest*.

She started to leave when an old-fashioned scrapbook, angled on the chest, caught her attention. Block letters across the front read "The Beginning." Amanda crooked her finger beneath the cardboard cover and flipped it open. Ten men, three in horn-rimmed glasses, stood in front of a building. It was this building, although it looked quite different in the sepia-colored image.

There were pictures of the shop with what were likely state-of-the-art millwork machines for 1959, the date beneath the pictures. She turned the pages, opening a time capsule. One shot of the parking lot made her laugh as she looked across a variety of tank-sized vehicles, some sporting fins. It was one picture she wished she could see in color.

Another page later and the smile left her face. The man in the photograph shaking hands with the one who seemed to be in nearly every shot, looked incredibly similar to her father. Of course, that was impossible. And didn't all of the men resemble one another with their identical buzz cuts, plaid shirts, and high-waisted pants?

She sat down on the edge of the bed and picked the whole book up for a better view. The date beneath this picture was 1962. She studied every detail she could find in the face staring back at her from across the years.

****

Reece's heart pounded. He barely slowed as he swung open the door to the office that had once been solely his. Having gathered his courage on the way down the stairs, he intended to confess everything to the woman holding the future of his company in her hands.

He pushed the door open. Seeing the office empty, he assumed she wasn't inside. But her briefcase was still on the floor and her laptop perched in open position on the desk. *She must have only stepped away for a moment*, he thought. *I'll just wait on her*.

Something rustled in the back room, and the door stood ajar. Reece tiptoed over and pushed the door just far enough to see Amanda sitting on the edge of the bed with the company's original scrapbook in her hands. For a moment he could only watch as she appeared to be entirely engrossed in something in the book.

When she lowered it, a strange paleness washed

over her face. She looked like she had seen a ghost.

"Oh, God!" She jumped up. "You startled me."

"Sorry," Reece said. "I was just looking for you."

He wanted to ask her questions concerning the sudden desire to spend time in his home-away-from-home. But she looked so stricken—vulnerable even—that he decided to keep quiet.

"I...I..." she stammered. She walked over to him and held up the open book. "Do you know who this man is?" She balanced the scrapbook on one forearm while pointing to a man in one of the photographs.

Reece squinted at the picture, taking the book from her. "Let me get my glasses." He carried it across the room and sat down on the edge of the bed, grabbing a leather case from the top of the old chest. "Don't laugh," he warned. "I don't normally need them, but they help with details."

"You don't have to explain. My vision isn't what it used to be either." She was standing next to him, looking over his head as he scanned the picture.

"Oh, that is Bill Simmons. He actually—"

"Are you sure?" she interrupted. She plopped down on the bed's edge beside him. "Are you absolutely certain?"

"Well..." He looked over at her. She was practically salivating, eyes wide and moving back and forth rapidly. "Why does it matter?"

"*How* can you be sure?" she demanded.

He lifted one edge of the picture out of the old-fashioned corner holder, followed by another, and then slipped it out of the other two. "Yeah, 'William Simmons, 1962'." He held it out to her and she took it, bringing it in close to her face.

She flipped it over, reading the hand written lettering. Whispering in an almost sacred tone, she repeated, "William Simmons, 1962."

Reece pointed to the man standing beside William. "That's my dad, Roger Jordan. He started this business in 1959 and it went gangbusters for about two years. Then, as it has always been with my dad, he overspent and got into financial trouble."

"That's nice," Amanda said, clearly not listening to him.

"What's going on?" he asked.

"What was William Simmons' connection to Dixie Millwork?"

"That's what I was trying to tell you." He repeated the part about his dad. "He would have lost the company then, if it hadn't been for Bill Simmons coming through to the rescue. And it continued to thrive as long as he was here."

"So what happened to him?" Her voice sounded thin and far away.

"Well, he died…killed in a car wreck with his wife. Tragic." He went back in his mind to the night his father learned of the tragedy.

A note of desperation clung to her voice. "Do you remember when it was, when the accident happened?"

"Why?" he asked, unable to conceive of her intense interest in this one man.

"Please just tell me if you remember when."

She sounded so distressed he stopped questioning her and continued answering. "Yeah, it was 1972. I was twelve years old and already hanging out with the workmen after school, so I knew everyone by name. Bill was such a godsend to my father that I thought he was the best guy in the world." Reece paused, seeing the man in his mind, hearing his voice in his head.

"And?" she quietly coaxed.

"And I was listening to him seal a deal with the owner of what would become a condominium complex on a Tuesday afternoon. He was so excited. It would mean a sizable commission for him and would keep the millwork shop busy for a year. He left early saying he was taking his wife out to celebrate. Dad was so excited he told him to take the rest of the week off. Bill wanted to get the paperwork for his kid's college fund set up. I never saw him again. I've often wondered what happened to his child."

"Boy or girl?" Her voice was barely audible.

"Girl," he said. "He talked about her all the time—something with an 'm'—Margie, Marty, Mindy? It's right on the tip of my tongue...wait...Mandy! That's it! Her name was Mandy, Mandy Simmons."

Reece looked back at her and she was rocking back and forth. Giant tears fell silently down her cheeks. "Amanda, are you all right? What's wrong?" He reached out and put an arm around her shoulders.

She collapsed in sobs, soul-racking crying that broke his heart.

"Did you know this man? Did he mean something to you?"

The words came out broken and shaky. "Yes...Bill Simmons...was...my fa...ther."

"No way," he said, shocked by the revelation.

"My father...always...called me...Mandy... sh...sh...short for Amanda..." She cried even harder—raw pain in her voice—as though it had happened a few moments ago, not forty years ago.

"Oh, Amanda, I'm sorry. I'm so sorry."

Reece had forgotten why he came looking for her. He forgot about the funds and the business. For that moment, all he could think about was the heartrending sorrow unleashed by the woman who had seemed to be made of steel. Right now she was more a woman of straw, fragile, brittle, falling apart.

****

Amanda couldn't speak. She couldn't stop shaking and crying. She was shocked. Finding her father in the place she least expected had been traumatic. Hearing Reece talk about him had brought him to life in a way she had no memory of experiencing.

He had been *here*. Bill Simmons had walked these halls and breathed this air. He had spoken about her, planned for her future. It was too much to absorb, all of a sudden.

Her head swirled with Reece's words. He had known him. He had respected him. How was it possible she hadn't known where he worked?

Reece whispered, "How old were you?"

"Six." She peeled herself away from his embrace, trying to gather her wits.

"So…how…where did…who raised you?" he stammered.

"Grandparents," she answered, giving another one-word response as it was hard to talk. Amanda swiped at her tear-soaked face with the back of her hands. Reece reached behind him and retrieved a box of tissues.

"Thanks," she sniffed, pulling two from the top and laying them against her flooded eyes. "I'm sorry. It was a shock."

"I can only imagine. I'm pretty shocked myself."

She gave a little half-cough, half-laugh. "I bet you are." Amanda had ceased the violent crying, but her entire head had become a giant pressure cooker. Her nose was stopped up, eyes sore and swollen, and her throat felt thick and blocked. She snatched another tissue and blew her nose, trying to breathe a little easier.

"So, your grandparents didn't talk about your dad?" Reece asked.

"It was my mom's parents. And no, we rarely spoke of either of my parents. They probably thought it would be too upsetting for me."

"Reece! What the hell?" Vernella appeared in the doorway, looking from one to the other of them.

"Not now, Vernie," Reece snapped.

"But I have…"

"I said *not now*!" He motioned for her to leave.

Amanda groaned, imagining the sight the made, sitting on a bed, her face streaked with tears.

Vernie spun around and marched out of the office, slamming the outer door with a pronounced "wham."

The tension was so tight it had no place to go. It had wound and wound and now needed to release. Amanda gave a half-laugh and said, "Shoot me now!"

His head snapped toward her. He looked surprised at her sudden display of humor. Then he laughed.

It was contagious. Amanda broke into a full laugh too, feeling silly and strange simultaneously. She had been on an emotional rollercoaster since arriving in Charlotte. The past few minutes had been especially difficult and draining. The laughter was a tonic.

What were they laughing about? Vernella's expression? Her comment? The odd situation? It didn't matter.

Chapter 9

"I'd better go see what Vernie wanted and put that fire out before the whole office is alerted we were caught alone together on the edge of my bed." Reece patted the comforter.

Amanda pointed at him. "Yes. You should do that right away."

"You'll be all right?"

She nodded. "Sure."

He shut her in behind the closed door to the room he had slept in the previous evening, and the one before that, and for the past couple of weeks. It was getting old. He'd have to deal with Pamela sooner or later, but for now she was cozy and snug in his condominium in the arts district. Reece shuddered. He couldn't deal with Vernella and Pamela at the same time.

Right now it had to be Vernella. Interestingly, she was absent from her reception window perch. And he didn't have to think too hard to figure out where she was and what she was doing.

He went straight to accounting and peeked in through the open doorway. Sure enough, Vernella's head was pushed against Marlene's cheek as they whispered, with Susan scowling as she looked on. Susan glanced up at him and started to speak but he held his index finger to his lips, signaling her to keep quiet.

She grinned and looked away. Reece slipped, quiet as a whisper, directly behind the two gossiping women. He clapped Vernella on the back, and she screamed, jumping backward. Marlene gasped and Susan laughed.

"My ears were burning, Vernie. Did I hear you mentioning my name?" He blocked the doorway, standing feet apart, arms crossed over his chest.

She blushed and stammered. Reece enjoyed her discomfort, and Susan was stifling more laughter. Marlene looked completely horrified.

"So, Vernie, what is the story? Why don't you share it with us all?"

"Damn it, Reece. How could I not need another opinion on that situation? What was I supposed to think?"

He pointed his finger back and forth between Vernella and Marlene. "Here's the deal. I'm not going to say it wasn't what it seemed. But think about it, I was upstairs in a meeting until a few minutes right before you"—he pointed at Vernella solely—"burst in the door."

Marlene and Vernella wore guilty expressions. But they also nodded as Reece attempted an explanation. "Amanda had just received some shocking news and was upset."

"I *thought* she was crying,'" Vernella said sheepishly, looking embarrassed.

"And you didn't think it odd she would be crying if we..." He dropped the sentence and raised his eyebrows.

Vernella's face turned red, and she met Reece's accusatory stare. "I didn't think it was odd really, old sport," she quipped, springing back to her spicy old self. "In fact, I'd be willing to bet she isn't the first woman to sit weeping on that bed."

Reece laughed in spite of himself. "You are a pistol, ol' gal. But I'm warning you both. If I hear the two of you have as much as raised an eyebrow in her direction, you'll have to deal with me. The gossip begins and ends right here. Understood?"

Both women nodded.

"You too, Susan?" Reece winked at her and she grinned.

"Yes, sir."

"Okay." He turned to leave and spun around again. "One more thing, Vernie. Just wondering who is answering the phone?" He heard the clip-clop of her feet pounding the floor behind him as he walked down the hallway.

"Mr. Jordan?"

The voice came from directly behind him. He turned and saw Susan trying to catch up with him. "Yes, Susan. What is it?"

"Was I wrong? Was your request of Ms. Lassiter what pushed her over the edge and made her cry?"

"My request?" Reece didn't know what she was talking about.

"Yeah, you know. We discussed in the meeting that you—"

He interrupted her. "Dear God, Susan. I forgot all about the reason I went to see her in the first place. Thank you. This is twice you have saved me today."

She blushed and walked away.

He ran back to his office, hoping Amanda was still there. Reece couldn't believe he had gotten so involved with Amanda's issues he had forgotten to explain about

J & S and the missing funds. He had to tell her and hoped she would be willing to help him. His heart was pounding when he opened the office door. *She must still be in the back room*, he reasoned.

Slowly, he edged the door open. When he failed to see her sitting where he had left her, he looked back to see if her laptop was still on the desk. It wasn't. Her briefcase wasn't there either. He raced to the side door, running out into the parking lot. Her rental was gone.

Damn! It was Friday, so he doubted she would be back until Monday. He would have to talk to her then.

Reece tried to put Amanda out of his mind, but he couldn't stop thinking of her collapsed in his arms. If she was really little Mandy Simmons, he hoped she would not be as determined to shut them down. She just might be a little more receptive to hearing his explanations.

He went about the rest of his day, taking calls and reassuring customers who had read about the acquisition.

Vernella had managed to keep quiet; at least he thought she had. Surely the rumbling of an affair with the henchwoman from Builders Tech would have managed to get back to him by this late in the day.

Reece was lulled by the winding down of this horrible week. It had been one of the most stressful of his life.

He wondered if Pamela would be over her tantrum yet. Maybe he could go home to his condo and have a good night's sleep in his giant king-sized bed with the feather topper. He was almost ready to drive out to the small, beautifully architectured downtown enclave known as the arts district, so-called for its starving artists and block parties.

Reece heard her clip-clop before he saw the tangle of red hair. Her voice was, of course, the dead give-away. He was poised to greet Vernie by the time she lunged at the desk, tossing a note in front of him. "Reece, this just came in for Amanda. It's from Chicago."

Reece read over the note: "Estimated time of arrival for back-up team, 10:00 am Monday."

"Who called for her?"

"Somebody named Mary. Said she'd been trying to reach Lassiter on her company phone—which I took to mean cell phone—with no luck. So she left the message for me to give her."

"Judson has a secretary named Mary. I remember her from my earliest dealings with the man." He rubbed his chin reading over the note again.

"What do ya think it means?" she asked.

"If it is coming from Judson's office, then he must be the one sending down a team. And the only reason he would do that is to dismantle this operation. Damn it to hell!" He leaned back in the chair, heart pounding.

"Do something, Reece."

It was the first time he had heard panic in her voice. Vernella was like an old southern stove pipe. She might rattle and chatter but was steady and strong. If she was starting to crack, then there was reason to fear their very foundation.

"Okay, Vernie. Get me her phone numbers—hotel, cell phone—and do it quickly."

She pulled another piece of paper from her pocket. "Here. Thought ya might say that."

He chuckled in spite of himself. "This is why I

keep you around, Vernie. You anticipate my needs and have everything ready. You're the best, even if you are a rumormonger."

Reece dialed both numbers, getting no answer at either. He dialed them both back and left messages, ones he deemed *emergency information* from Chicago. She might not return a generic phone call from him, but her little fingers would dial with speed once she heard he had a message from Builders Tech.

Vernie looked at him expectantly. "What now?"

"Listen. Can you stay late?"

"Of course."

"Great! We'll both stay here until she calls in. I want to know the second you see either number up on the call screen."

"On it," she said, racing back to her desk.

Chapter 10

Amanda's head roared. It was too much. She couldn't imagine advising her employer to dismantle the very company it now appeared her father had spent the last ten years of his life trying to save. And how was it she had no memory of him working for Dixie Millwork?

She had to get out of the office. It was stifling her.

Her clothes were suddenly cutting off her circulation. Wanting to strip them off, and thinking a swim would solve her problems, she raced back to the hotel. If she didn't swim, she would eat. And as upset as she was, she would probably eat until she was sick.

Amanda changed into her swimsuit and grabbed a towel and a pashmina which would serve as a cover-up. It was such a lovely June day. Heat radiated through the windows lining the hallway and she could see the sparkling outdoor pool where several people were beginning to congregate.

She didn't want bright sunshine and the sound of tinkling drinks sporting fruit slices or umbrellas. She needed a cocoon, a cavern, a dark space to float in.

Nobody else seemed to share her desire. The indoor pool was empty, the water still as glass. She slipped in as gently as possible, not wanting to disturb the water any more than necessary. With head back, ears dipped beneath the surface, she floated atop the surface on her back. A gentle hum filled her head.

From the depths of her memory, splices of conversations came back to her. Little slides of her youth slid past her inner eye. She saw her parents, dancing and having a cocktail. She was up on her father's shoulders at the beach, waves breaking as they jumped over them, her father lifting her high in the air.

She was in the old tank of a car. No, it only seemed old now. Then it was new. And it had scratchy seat covers and fins on the back. She heard her daddy say they were taking a vacation because he was getting a nice bonus at work. That was all she ever remembered him saying about his job. He called it work. And it was separate, apart from their idyllic family life in their cottage outside of the city.

She had a sudden compulsion to see it again— assuming it was still there. Could she even find it? She remembered the name of the street, Blackberry Lane. And it was in Mooresville, about fifteen minutes north of Charlotte.

She leapt out of the water and hurriedly dried, rushing for the elevator. Amanda pulled her wet hair into a pony tail, threw on the clothes she had just removed, and tossed her phone into the laptop case without looking at it. She didn't see the blinking light on the hotel phone either. She had tunnel vision, a singular purpose, and sped from the parking lot onto Interstate 77.

****

The minutes seemed like hours as Reece waited to hear from Amanda. The earlier conversation around the table flanked with his trusted employees came crashing back to him. His dad had forged his signature on the bank drafts. *Damn it!*

He buzzed Vernie. "Get my dad on the line while I wait for Amanda to call," he ordered.

She buzzed him back a few minutes later. "Can't find him either. Was there a party somewhere we didn't get invited to?"

"With him, always." Reece clenched his jaw and scratched his head. What in the world was he going to do? He had always had an answer before, but now?

****

Amanda found Blackberry Lane, but nothing looked as it had when she was there last. Of course it had been many years since she had been back, more than she cared to acknowledge.

Aha, there's the church. She was excited to see something familiar. *And the graveyard.* Her hands gripped the steering wheel as she passed the outcropping of stones and bronze markers, most topped with sprays of artificial spring flowers, a sign Memorial Day had just passed.

Her grandparents had brought her here twice a year—once at Christmas and again at Easter—in order to place a flower memorial on her parents' graves. It was always sad. The drive down from their little farm in Wilkesboro was somber and depressing.

It's unfair that this is the way I have to visit my parents, she remembered thinking. Although she had dreaded it back then, she now felt compelled to have a florist prepare a large spray to leave at their resting place. *I will do that before I leave*, she decided, continuing to drive along the lane which was now a rather wide street.

The houses became grander as she continued along

and the reason was soon obvious. A golf course and country club had taken over the little community. Former rolling farmland was now littered with golf carts, sand traps, and little ponds.

Her heart sank. Undoubtedly, there would be no little rock cottage remaining. Someone would have torn it down and built another of these mansions over its remains. It seemed desecrated.

She slammed on the brakes. *Did that sign say "Simmons Point"?* She backed up quickly and made a sharp right. Perfectly manicured greens rose and fell as she crept along the narrow lane. A gabled structure loomed ahead with a parking lot crouched in its shadow. Shiny new automobiles lined the front.

She parked and entered as if she belonged to the country club set. Amanda caught a glimpse of her reflection in the sparkling glass windows and went straight to the restroom. She wiped away smeared mascara and covered everything that wouldn't brush off. With fresh lipstick and some eye drops to remove the ugly red veins, caused by her earlier crying, she entered the bar.

"Club soda with a lime twist," she ordered, and sat down to wait for its delivery.

"Haven't seen you around here before," the bartender—a bleached blonde with a bit too much tan—said. In spite of that, she looked professional in her white shirt and black vest. Amanda guessed she could have been in her thirties, but more apt to be late twenties with premature lines around her eyes from too much squinting at the sun she apparently enjoyed exposing herself to.

"I haven't been here in years." Amanda glanced

around the practically empty space despite the wealth of cars lining the front. "Looks a little dead for a Friday evening."

The bartender scooped ice from a slant-lidded chest and squeezed lime over it before pouring in the fizzy soda. "They're mostly still out on the course." She jerked her head toward the golf course. "Don't worry; this place will start hopping in about two hours. That's how much good daylight they've got left."

"I see. Have you worked here long?"

She inspected the drink before presenting it to Amanda. "A few years. Started in college and just kept it up."

"Well, maybe you can help me; or if not, lead me to someone who can."

The bartender's eyebrows lifted, looking suddenly suspicious of her new customer. "Oh?"

"Yes. I saw the sign at the road referring to this as Simmons Point. Do you know how it came to be called that?"

"Oh yeah, it's an interesting story. But the person who can tell you about that is out on the green. He'll be in shortly though. Always is." She rolled her sleeves up and started running a sink full of hot sudsy water.

"How is this person connected to Simmons Point?"

"Roger? He built this place. They say he named it after his best friend. I don't know if that's true, but you can ask him. I don't think he minds talking about it."

Something quivered in Amanda's mind. *He had built the place…and his name was Roger? Was there any chance? No…of course not.* "You wouldn't happen to know his last name, would you?"

"Sure. It's Jordan. Roger Jordan. Sounds like I'm

stuttering when I say it together like that—rah-ja-ja-or-dan." She laughed. "He owns Dixie Millwork and Building Supply down in Charlotte. I believe I heard his son is running it now though. So he has a lot of free time on his hands."

"He must be quite a character," Amanda added casually, assuming by the bartender's laughter and attitude toward Roger that he kept them amused.

"Between him and his wife—another character to be sure—they keep us entertained."

"What's she like?" Amanda sipped her drink.

"Hang around long enough and you'll find out for yourself. Wherever he is, she eventually turns up. I heard they were quarreling right now, but…"

The sound of the door opening mixed with loud, masculine voices. Two middle-aged men with receding hairlines and stomach paunches sat down at the end of the bar.

"Hey, Daisy, how 'bout pouring me a shot of your best bourbon? No, make it two." He clapped the other man on the back. "Ol' Ted here will be puttin' it on his tab."

"Is that a fact?" she asked, while setting a bourbon glass out on the top of the bar.

"'Fraid so," the other man answered. "The eighteenth hole sank me again." He shook his head but appeared to be in good humor.

"And what'll you be havin'," she asked the man identified as Ted.

"I'll have the same as Randall. And how 'bout makin' it some of that fine barrel-aged Kentucky special mash?"

"Here you go, fellas," Daisy said, pushing two

squat glasses of amber liquid toward them.

"Hey, who's that?" one asked, jerking his head toward Amanda. He pretended to be whispering, but his voice carried. Amanda could feel his eyes on her.

"None of your business," Daisy responded.

Amanda glanced away, turning her back toward them. She had no interest in having to swerve away from two men looking for a little weekend tryst.

The other man said something, but the timbre of his voice was all Amanda could hear. The actual words themselves got lost somewhere fuzzy, as if he spoke into a barrel.

"Don't be gettin' ideas," Daisy warned. "She's waitin' on Roger." She spoke loud enough for Amanda to hear, and she cut her eyes at the pair at the end of the bar.

"Always Roger," one said. "How does he do it?"

The door opened again, and a trio of golfers joined the impending drinkfest along with the pair already on their second glasses of bourbon. They ordered drinks and took them to a table near the large glass window facing the course's expanse.

Just as Daisy warned, the place began to get busy. Four skinny women in white resort-wear appeared. They slipped in quietly and ordered silently by raising index fingers and nodding.

Daisy caught Amanda's eyes and rolled hers upward, then grinned. "They are *so special* I know what their drink preferences are," she whispered as the group of women pony-walked to the table across from the golfers.

Amanda watched as Daisy poured a concoction of cassis and champagne, another of peach schnapps and champagne, another of pear nectar and Prosecco, and a fourth of such a complicated blend of various bottles she lost count.

"What is all of that?" she asked the bartender.

"Kir royale, kir pêche, pear Bellini, and Long Island iced tea," she answered, loading them on a tray in the order in which she had blended them.

"Impressive," Amanda said. She looked at the women—impeccably groomed and coiffed, manicured and pressed—thinking they could have been on a television series about country club wives or girlfriends.

She looked down at herself. She wasn't that different, was she? *Of course I am. I'm in business attire, not courtside skirts. And I work every day of my life.* But maybe they did too. And maybe she was just being hypercritical, something she never appreciated in women who judged her.

Daisy delivered the tray of drinks and followed up with little bowls of nibbles—peanuts, olives, pretzels—for each table. She returned to the back of the bar, washed the first set of dirty bourbon glasses, and set a fresh lime and soda in front of her before Amanda had time to finish sizing up the women.

"You are very good at this," Amanda complimented her.

"Oughta be by now," she remarked. The thump of the door opening and closing caused heads to bend in its direction.

"There's your man," Daisy said as the older gentleman staggered in followed by a pair of guys who pulled up chairs at the table with some of the other men. "And I'd be willing to bet he'll order a bottle of bourbon and sidle up to that booth in the corner." She pointed to the one directly across from them.

Amanda's stomach churned at the thought of approaching him cold. If he figured out what she had been sent to his store to do, he'd have her thrown out of the place.

He walked by and raised a hand at Daisy. "How ya doin', Roger?" she asked.

"I'd be better with a bottle of bourbon and a cold glass." He pointed to the back booth and collapsed into it.

Daisy gathered the tray, the bottle and started to add one glass when Amanda interrupted.

"Make it two and let me take it to him."

"Suit yourself, but I'm not sharin' the tip." She plopped another glass on the tray along with a bowl of nuts and another of olives. "He doesn't care for the pretzels."

"Thanks." Amanda could hear her heart thundering in her chest. It could explode any minute. She had to force herself off the barstool. Every ounce of her dreaded the first moment of introduction.

With tray in hand, she crossed the room, aware that several pairs of eyes followed her. Most likely it was just natural curiosity that had the clubbers wondering who she was and what she was doing there.

Roger Jordan looked up at the sound of the tray being deposited on the table. He caught Amanda's eye and for an instant she had foresight into the way Reece would surely look at his father's age. They had the same sky-blue eyes and light hair though Roger's was more white than blond now. Even the chiseled jaw could have been Reece's.

"Well hello," he grinned. "Don't recall seeing you

'round here before."

"I haven't been here before. Do you mind if I join you for just a moment?" Her resolve kept pushing her forward even when she felt in danger of collapsing.

"No, not at all. Please, sit." He motioned for the bench opposite him. "Looks like Daisy expected you might wish to join me in a drink." He lifted the two glasses from the tray and righted them, setting them bottoms down onto the table. Then he twisted off the bourbon's cap and poured them each a shot.

Amanda speared an olive with one of the fancy toothpicks standing upright in a short vase. The multi-colored cellophane curlicues on their ends looked a bit like something that should be dangling a variety of fruits over a too-sweet summer cocktail. With the saltiness from the olive still blasting her taste buds, she took a sip of the whiskey. It burned, and she winced.

Roger grinned before tossing his back effortlessly. "I take it you don't drink regularly."

"No, sir. I don't. In fact, with the exception of the occasional glass of wine, I rarely drink at all." She took another olive from the bowl.

"Hey, Daisy," he yelled across the room, causing everyone to look in their direction to Amanda's embarrassment. "Bring this young woman a bottle of wine."

Unaffected by his outburst, Daisy hollered back, "What kind?"

"Uh, Chardonnay," she replied. "Please."

"I got a great one from New Zealand." Daisy offered.

"That sounds perfect. Thank you, Daisy," Amanda answered.

Whispers brought heads together around the tables of both the women and the men.

Amanda watched as Daisy snatched a chilled bottle, scooped ice into a round cylinder to keep it cool at the table, and pulled a wine glass from the overhead stem holder. In a flash she was at the table, corkscrew in hand.

"You'll like this one."

"How can you be sure?" Roger asked.

"She enjoys club soda with a twist of lime, so I'm confident this fruity light wine will make her happy." She turned her back to him and winked at Amanda who was busy stifling a laugh. "Men!" she said, exasperated.

Roger laughed. "She slays me," he said, shaking his head. "Won't take anything off of anybody, but still gets the biggest tips in the place."

"Yes, I think she has a gift for handling people." Amanda sipped her wine. She lifted her glass toward Daisy who was already behind the counter washing up empty glasses and pouring fresh rounds.

"Like it?" she hollered.

"Very much," she answered as loudly as she dared.

"Told ya, cranky pants," Daisy teased Roger.

"So, why don't you tell me how we know each other?" Roger asked Amanda.

She twirled the wine glass with both sets of fingertips, looked down into the creamy yellow wine, and wished a vortex would suddenly open up and give her the right way to bring up the subject.

Chapter 11

"Reece, I got someone for you on line two." He jumped at the sound of Vernie's shrill voice coming in through the intercom. On a normal day—one hopping with noise and activity and people flying in and out of his office—he didn't even flinch when her voice boomed out of the telephone speaker. But in the eerie silence now surrounding him, he was a ball of nerves.

"Which one?" he asked her.

"It's the one between lines one and three. Geez, Reece."

"Oh God, Vernie, not which line. Which person?" He scratched his head and took a deep breath.

"Oh, funny. I've got Pamela."

He rolled his eyes and leaned as far back as he could in the chair, asking himself who in heaven he had offended to make his day go so very badly. He snatched the receiver and pushed the blinking button in.

"Reece? What's up, darling? Vernie said you wanted to talk to me."

"Yeah. Better come on over here."

"Do I have to? Can't we just discuss whatever is on your mind over the telephone?"

She sounds tired, Reece thought. "No. I'm sorry, but I need you to come to the office. We need to find Dad."

"Oh, no, Reece. Is something wrong?" The

weariness was immediately replaced by concern. He took this as a good sign.

"Yes, there is. I'll be waiting for you." He clicked the telephone off. He didn't want to hear the string of questions she might start asking. Those would give them something to talk about in person.

Having opened the window to ensure that he would, he heard the car pull up and the door slam. He buzzed Vernie. "Thanks for staying late, Vernie, especially on Friday evening. I'll make it up to you, promise."

"I'm in no hurry, Reece. I'll stay here and keep trying to get the other two on the line if you'd like."

"You're a peach, and I appreciate it. But there's no need. I've left messages for both of them, and they have my cell phone number."

"Call me if you need me to come in tomorrow."

"Sure." He ran for the door, intent on cutting Pamela off before she settled into one of his office chairs.

"Reece," she greeted him in a perfumed flurry. "What's wrong?"

"Everything. We've got to find Dad." He took her by the arm and led her back out the same door she had just entered.

"You mean…you think something's…"

He opened the passenger door of his sports car and helped her inside. Then he pushed the seat back and crawled in behind the wheel.

"Where are we going, Reece? Where do you think he is?"

"Friday night? If he isn't passed out at home, he's probably at the country club. How is it you've been in the family this long and not noticed such routines?"

She frowned at him and looked out of the window. "I guess I've never fit in very well."

Guilt settled over Reece. "Sorry, I'm just jittery. I've got a lot on my plate, and sleeping at the office on that lumpy old bed hasn't helped."

"You're right. You should come back, and I should leave."

"That's not what I meant. You know that."

Reece edged the car in and out of traffic. He missed driving it. Although he loved the giant company truck, it was a different experience to drive this little specialty vehicle. It hugged the road's curves like an extension of his body. Had he not been so upset with the recent turn of events, he would have enjoyed the trip to Mooresville.

"So what's the problem with Roger?" Pamela asked.

"He went too far this time. I spent all of the proceeds from Builders Tech covering his last raid on the company's funds. We should be safe, but if not, he's thrown me under the bus, Pamela."

"You? What do you mean?" Something in her voice had changed. It was small, nearly imperceptible, but Reece picked it up. *She knows. She's known all about it and hasn't said a word.* The accusation he had just made against his own father should have triggered at least a little outrage if she hadn't known.

He hit the gas and accelerated the car.

****

"I believe you knew my father," Amanda said quietly, looking Roger Jordan in the eyes.

"Oh?" He furrowed his eyebrows, making them

appear bushier than they normally would have. "What's his name?"

"Bill Simmons." She watched his face. It went flaccid, every tense muscle relaxing in the shock of her answer.

"Dear God," he whispered. "You're Mandy Simmons?" He pushed the glass away.

"I was. I go by Amanda Lassiter now."

His hands shook, and he pulled them off of the table. "I can't believe it." He did indeed look shocked. His face grew even paler.

"So you married a Lassiter? Is he around here, too?" Roger craned his neck, looking over his shoulder.

"We're divorced. It was rather short-lived. In fact, it lasted only long enough for my name to get established professionally and then it seemed prudent to just keep it." She shrugged, wondering why she had just told him all of that.

"I guess your daddy was a hard act to follow. Most men couldn't measure up."

"So you *did* know my dad?" Her hands were shaking, though she tried not to let him see.

"He was my best friend for at least a decade. Bill taught me how to handle people and how to bid for contracts. We were never more successful than when he was over our sales team."

He shook his head and looked down into the glass as though it was a window into the past and he could see through it into the years in which Bill Simmons was a part of the company.

"Do you know if Simmons Point was named after him?" She held her breath. He may not know.

He looked up and smiled. "Yes. Yes, it was.

There's a plaque with his name on it near the door you most likely walked in here through."

Her father had a plaque on a building and a community named after him, and she had never known. Her head spun with the news. Or was it spinning because he was coming to life with Roger's words, living again after so many years of not hearing his name spoken?

"I'll look for it on the way out," she said.

"But don't go soon. I have a few questions I've wanted to ask you for years."

"Anything." She opened her palms, matching her body language to her words.

He leaned across the table toward her. She leaned in a little as well, meeting his steely eyes. "Have you had a good life? Did you go to college and get a good job?"

Her heart sank at the mention of her job. As soon as he knew what she had done he would throw her out. But she didn't have to start there, did she?

"I lived with my grandparents, and yes, I went to college. I've had a couple of good jobs, and I suppose things have turned out well for me. Most people consider me successful." She shrugged her shoulders.

"Good. Good. I was worried the money might not get into your hands, but I didn't know how else to do it."

"The money?" She shook her head. "What money?"

"Greedy bastards. I was afraid they would…" He reached for the bourbon bottle, the color coming back into his face. He tipped the bottle and half-filled the glass, tossing back a good swig.

"Wait. Maybe I just don't know what you are referring to. Help me out a little here."

"Your dad had a sizable commission coming to him right before he died. And he had some property I bought at a rather large mark-up. I wanted you to have enough money to get started in life."

"There was a trust fund for my education and it paid for most of it. I just thought it was from the sale of the house and possibly some life insurance." She was relieved. Surely that was what he meant.

"Oh, there should have been close to a million dollars in that account by the time you were college age. Unless you went to some college that housed you on private islands, it should have been more than enough."

"No, no, there was nothing like that. I can assure you." She had settled her grandparents' estates. If there had been something left over, surely she would have found it.

"Then they kept it from you, or spent it on themselves." He finished the shot, throwing back his head as he drained the glass.

"Are you certain it was that much?" She could feel her brows inching toward each other.

"Positive. I have the paperwork at home." He jerked his head toward the left. "Come with me now. I'll get it for you."

"No. I couldn't possibly. We've only just met and…" She took another sip of the wine, trying to prevent herself from appearing too eager.

"That's where you're wrong. You may not remember me, but I do you. And your daddy was the proudest man on the planet where you were concerned." He looked down into the glass as if he could see something she wasn't privy to.

"You two were pretty close, weren't you?"

Roger nodded, his white hair bouncing. "Yep. He was a real smart fellow. Although he *worked* for me, I *learned* a lot from him."

Daisy walked past with a tray of empty glasses, then doubled back. "How y'all doing? Need some more snacks?"

Amanda shook her head and Roger declined the offer, too.

"Okay, but if you change your minds, just give me a shout. You know where to find me."

She started to walk off, taking about three steps before Roger called out to her. "Hey, Daisy, would you trust me if I asked you to come out to my house and look at some documents from about forty years ago?"

She turned around. Her eyebrows furrowed toward one another. "Is this a trick question?"

"No. I'm totally serious. Turns out this lady's dad was *the* Simmons of Simmons Point, and I have a few old papers I think she might find interesting." He gestured toward Amanda with his glass.

Daisy's eyes grew rounder, her brows ceasing their inward march. "No kidding! Is that why you were asking about the name Simmons?"

"Guilty," Amanda admitted.

"All bullshit aside, I'd trust this old goat."

"See?"

"Oh, all right." She figured she had this one chance only. When he found out who she was working for and what she had arrived to do, he wasn't likely to extend another invitation.

Roger wasted no time. "I'll get the golf cart and you can follow me." He scooted out of the bench, grabbing both the wine and the bourbon bottles.

Amanda followed him, stuffing the cork partially into the wine bottle so it wouldn't spill. Roger paused at the door, holding it open for her with his one free hand. He shoved the two bottles into the cup holders on the golf cart before pulling it onto the edge of the road.

They didn't go far. He made a sharp right and suddenly they were meandering along a driveway near the backside of the golf course. He zipped his cart up to the porch and motioned for her to circle around the front drive.

Her heart thundered in her chest. There was something familiar about the very air around her. The hair on her arms raised and goose bumps started to prickle her skin.

Amanda couldn't take her eyes from the center of the house. If she could remove the two gabled ends of the building, its breezeway, and garage, she would be left with the cottage she remembered from her childhood. *It can't be. This is just a coincidence.*

She saw it then, and knew it wasn't her imagination. The eyebrow window she had spent so much time in front of, peered down at her as though it were caught mid-wink. She turned around to see what might be visible from it and caught the small grove of magnolias, now so large they made a border.

"You remember, don't you?" Roger called to her.

"Was this *our* house?" She forced her feet to move toward the porch.

"Yes. I added on to it over the years. I bought it and the surrounding land and eventually built all of

128

this"—he made a sweeping motion with his hand—"so his name would not be forgotten."

Amanda couldn't speak. Emotions tugged at her heart. She crossed the porch and touched the original stone. It felt warm beneath her palm. She supposed it was from the June sunshine.

Roger opened the door and held it for her to walk through. She glanced around the interior of the house. Nothing else looked familiar. Of course it wouldn't.

"Sit," Roger commanded. "I'll get the file box."

She nodded and started for the sofa.

"No. Come into the dining room where we can finish our drinks and spread out the papers."

She followed him, sitting in a beautiful padded chair. Its curved back was surprisingly comfortable.

Roger returned with a small portable safe. He punched in a random set of numbers she couldn't—and didn't try to—detect. It sprang open, and he began to pull sheaves of documents out. He whispered and mumbled to himself.

"Aha," he called out, holding up a check register and its accompanying bank statements. "Perfect." He laid them face down on the table. "We should begin in reverse order, start from the beginning." As though turning over cards from a deck for a game of Blackjack, he dealt the statements, until reaching the first one from the year her parents had died.

Amanda wasn't looking at the figures. She was looking at the name on the account. "Dear God," she exclaimed.

****

Reece swung into the parking lot outside of the country club. He took the keys from the ignition and ordered Pamela to "stay put" until he verified his father was inside. He jerked open the door and made swift strides across the floor.

"It's a family reunion," Daisy chirped. "What can I get for ya?"

"Nothing to drink, Daisy. I'm looking for my dad. Have you seen him?"

"Yeah. He was here until a little while ago. Left with some woman."

"Oh God," he moaned, throwing his hands up. "Do you know where he went?"

"Probably up to the house. He left on the cart with a partially consumed bottle of bourbon and another of chardonnay. What's up?"

"I've got to find him. We've got a bit of an emergency at the office."

"Friday evening emergency, huh?" She squinted at him.

"You don't want to know, trust me. Can you tell me what the woman looked like?"

"Middle-aged, yet preserved—nicely—not like those women." She jerked her head to the left and Reece followed her directive to the table where the resort goddesses sipped cocktails.

"Go on," he encouraged.

"Thin, with auburn hair, hazel eyes, and dressed in a business suit. Her name was Amanda, I believe."

"Thanks a million, Daisy." He reached for his wallet to throw down a tip.

"Get on outta here. You can catch me next time."

He ran for the car and raced for the house. He had a strong hunch who had gone home with his dad, and he had better interfere before his father made a stupid pass at her, or worse.

"What is it, Reece?" Pamela asked.

"The woman from Builders Tech has found Dad out here. I've got to stop him before he does something foolish." He wheeled into the driveway.

"What do you think he will do?" she asked.

"I don't know. But I want you to promise to stay in the car. Can you do that?"

"If I must."

He pulled in behind the rental. There was no doubt left. Amanda, the person he had been looking for since earlier in the day, was here. He raced for the door, entering without knocking.

Reece glanced around, devastated that they weren't in the living room. Had his dad done what he feared? Had he gotten her drunk and taken advantage? He sighed with relief when he heard voices in the direction of the kitchen.

He walked quietly through the house, popping his head into the dining room. There they were. Both of their heads bent over some documents. Reece was both relieved and stunned.

"Hello!"

They jumped at the sound of his voice.

"I've left several messages...for both of you. Don't you ever answer your phones?"

"Oh, Reece." Amanda's voice was wobbly.

"You two know each other?" Roger looked from one to the other of them.

"We've met." Amanda's face appeared stricken.

Reece flinched. His dad motioned for him, indicating a chair.

"Come on in, son. Have a seat."

Reece quickly scanned the scene in front of him. The bottles of bourbon and wine were on the table surrounded with documents. *The alcohol explains Dad's lack of inquisitiveness.*

"I believe I will." He pulled out a chair beside Amanda and sat down.

"You won't believe who this is…I mean…who her father is," Roger said, smiling.

"Oh, I don't know. Try me." He knew he sounded sarcastic though that was not his intention.

Amanda's expression seemed to beg him not to expose her. He clenched his jaw and weighed his options. If he wanted a favor from her, he would certainly have to give one.

"This is Bill Simmons' daughter. You remember Bill, don't ya, son?" His father's voice was shaky but Reece thought it was not from too much alcohol. He actually sounded a bit excited.

"I remember Bill very well. He was always good to me. His death was a great blow personally and professionally to our entire community." Reece tried to communicate to Amanda how much her father had meant to them. Perhaps she would be more sympathetic if she knew that.

"It was indeed," Roger agreed.

"Your father was just showing me a few things I never knew. Apparently, I was a recipient of his kindness and didn't even know it."

"There's probably a lot we don't know about each other," Reece said.

"You're right," Amanda agreed. "Take for instance the trust fund I've never seen, and the company which was set up to distribute it, *J & S Consulting*." She cut her eyes at Reece.

"Jordan and Simmons," Roger said proudly.

"Would you excuse my father and me for a moment?" Reece asked Amanda.

"Yes, of course," she answered. "But in my defense, may I just tell you both I have never seen one penny from this, and I had no idea about my father's connection to you in any way."

"What's she talkin' 'bout, son?" Roger asked.

"That's not what I came here to discuss with you." He was having a conversation with Amanda that Roger couldn't follow, and apparently she wasn't getting his hints or expressions either.

"Somebody better start telling me something here." Roger looked from one to the other of the two people sitting across from him.

"And somebody better tell *me* what is going on, too," a feminine voice interrupted.

"Pamela?" Roger asked. "What are you doing here?"

"Reece dragged me out here and then left me in the car. Who is this woman? And what is she doing here?"

"Look it's not what you think. Reece and I aren't involved…"

"I don't give a damn about who Reece is involved with," she snapped. "What are you doing in my house *with my husband*?" She had her hands on her hips and her face glowed red with anger.

"Husband? Roger?" Amanda looked from one to the other of them. "I thought you were Reece's wife."

Reece's eyes flew wide open. "Why on earth would you think that?"

"Vernella said…" She dropped the sentence.

Reece glared at her, his eyes narrowing to slits where they had just been saucers. "What *did* that woman say?" Fury built in his chest even as his face twisted with the strain of the situation.

Amanda laughed. "Of course. I get it now. She only said that she 'called her Mrs. Jordan.' I saw you giving her a hug, knew you were sleeping in the office, and just made the assumption you two were having a spat."

"Why are you sleeping at the office, son?"

Reece threw his hands up in the air. "Because your wife needed a place to stay while the two of you had another of your infamous quarrels. I couldn't very well allow her to sleep at the office now, could I?"

Roger looked at her. "That's where you've been? You've been staying at *his* place?"

Pamela nodded.

"Come, sit," he offered.

She crossed the room and sat down beside him.

"Hey, I've seen you before," Pamela said, as she got a good look at the woman seated next to Reece. "You were at the office."

"I think you're mistaken, Pamela," Reece said. He raised an eyebrow.

"No, I distinctly remember it. And Vernie told me something about you, too." She pointed an accusing finger at Amanda.

"I'm sure you are mistaken." Reece stated it so firmly he thought she would have to be daft not to understand he wanted her silence. He needed it. *Don't say another word,* he silently ordered her with his posture and his eyes.

She didn't heed his code for silence. "No, no, I'm

certain of it."

"I'm sure you are confused, honey," Roger coddled his wife.

"No, this is the woman Builders Tech sent to decide our fate."

"There's been some kind of error. You misunderstood." Roger looked at Amanda. "Tell her. You've just gotten into town. You came lookin' for your roots, to see me. You found me at the club."

Amanda took a deep breath. "No, there *is* no mistake. Your wife is correct."

Chapter 12

For a moment, all within the walls of the Jordans' home was pure pandemonium. Everyone, except Amanda, seemed angry. There was yelling and cursing. Finally, she'd had enough. "Stop!" she screamed at the top of her voice. She scooted her chair back and stood over the table the way she might have if she were Judson Matheney and this was his work force.

They all stilled, likely stunned by her outburst.

"Thank you. I just want to say that I have not led any of you to believe anything of me which wasn't true."

She smoothed her skirt and ran a hand over her forehead to clear it of any wayward strands that had come away from the rest of her carefully smoothed style. "As Reece will attest, until this afternoon I had no idea my father had ever worked for your company. I was only six when he died, and we didn't exactly discuss what he did. I knew he was a salesman and that's all I have ever known."

Amanda went on. "I lived with my grandparents, but they were my mother's parents. I have no memory of my father's family. I think they may have died before I was born."

She stopped and poured a glass of wine, offering some to the others who turned it down.

Reece poured a shot of the bourbon, as did his dad.

After taking a few sips, she continued. "This is the biggest shock I have had in my entire life. I didn't come out here looking for you, Roger." She turned toward him. "I came looking for *this*, my old home. That I happened to run across you was luck. It was serendipitous that I saw the sign for Simmons Point. I drove out to the club where I asked the bartender if she knew who the area was named after. She directed me to you. And here we all are."

She took another sip.

Pamela glared at her, arms across her chest. "And you conveniently managed to convince my husband to bring you home with him?"

"I brought her to show her *this*," Roger declared, holding out the statements for J & S. Pamela tried to take them from him, but Reece beat her to it.

"Funny thing about this," he announced, his face screwing into a sneer. He flapped them at his dad. "You seem to be missing one." He flipped through them. "Where's the most recent one?"

"What are you talking about?" Roger asked, looking confused.

"The one where you wiped out the account and hung me out to dry." Reece glared at him. "How could you do that? What kind of low-life does that to his son?"

"I've done no such thing. Watch your mouth. I'm still your father."

"You're confused now," Pamela said with a nervous laugh. She pointed at Amanda. "This woman is tearing our family apart."

"Seriously doubtful. You left Dad before she arrived. But you know, you've been giving me strange

Renee Canter Johnson

vibes every time the subject of this account comes up. You know something about this, don't you, Pamela?"

"Are you going to let him talk to me like this?" she purred to Roger.

"Yes, I believe I am." He glanced between the two of them. "Answer him."

"I don't know what you are talking about," Pamela insisted.

The truth began to dawn on Amanda. "I think I'm following what is going on here. Pamela has somehow gotten into the J & S account, making *you* culpable for the missing funds." She pointed to Reece.

"What missing funds? What are the three of you talking about?" Roger looked perplexed.

"Dad, the reason we're in the middle of a shit storm is because of your lovely young wife. She must have found the check book which accompanies this account and forged my signature so she wouldn't be responsible, as a spouse, if and when it was discovered. And the whole time I just thought it was you being you. I'm sorry. I should have known better."

"Son, surely you didn't think I'd forge your name on a check?"

Amanda looked from father to son. They both looked hurt and tired. She wanted to drag Pamela outside and pelt her with rocks.

"It wasn't even me who discovered the forgeries."

"Who did?" Amanda asked, wondering how that came into the picture.

"It was Susan in accounting. She told me this morning. That was what I was coming to see you about when I discovered you in the back room holding the company photo album."

138

"And I was falling apart because I found out about my dad. But why did you want to talk to *me* about it?"

"I hoped you might know the best place to put the money back into the company. I didn't want to get you into any trouble. I also wanted to beg you to give us a few more days before you shut us down."

Amanda buried her head in her hands. "I've already sent the report. Judson knows. He's sending a team in Monday." She couldn't bear to look at them. She felt like a traitor.

"I know." Reece touched her arm. "I don't blame you. You are just doing your job."

Roger poured another shot of bourbon. "I feel like I'm on a roller coaster."

"What did you do with the money?" Amanda glared at Pamela, blaming her for the whole mess.

"Don't you dare talk to me that way." She sneered at Roger. "You have no idea what it's like being married to this man. I wanted out. Stupidly I had signed a prenuptial agreement preventing me from getting what I deserve, so I helped myself. Good luck proving it was me."

She got up to leave and Reece blocked the door. "Sorry. I just can't let you leave...until the police get here. And they will be on their way shortly."

"It's just your word against mine."

"And mine." Amanda stood.

Roger joined her. "And mine." He took his wife by the arm and led her back to the table while Reece phoned the local sheriff's office. Roger nudged her into the chair beside him. "I just don't want to let you out of my sight, if you know what I mean."

"You sorry son-of-a-bitch! Let me up!"

Roger looked like he might have an aneurism. His face had gone from pale to red to purple. A giant vein popped out on his forehead, and he tossed back a couple more shots of the bourbon.

Every time she tried to rise, he pushed her back down. She moaned and wailed and cursed.

Finally a car pulled up.

"I'll just go out and play this recording for him. It's the one I made of your confession."

Reece left the room, and Pamela struggled even harder.

Amanda watched them, still a bit in shock herself.

A few hours ago she hadn't known either of the people sitting at the table with her now. She hadn't known about her father or the money Roger insisted he had given her grandparents to put into a trust fund for her—an account he thought should be worth over a million dollars.

She had thought Roger's wife was Reece's, and that Reece was coming on to her because he thought he could use her to keep the store open. She'd even speculated that Reece had taken the money, possibly to spend it on the house at Jordan's Valley.

Worst of all, she had recommended closing Dixie. And in two days, a team was coming in to help her do just that. *What have I done?*

****

The lights flashed on the police car as the deputy drove away with Pamela Jordan. Both Reece and Roger had signed complaints against her.

A private investigator Reece knew was called and agreed to come to see him the next day. He would begin a full search into her background and every possible place she could have stashed the money. Although the evidence was so damning that all agreed she would eventually disclose its whereabouts, they weren't willing to chance having it fall into the wrong hands.

"I suppose I should get back to Charlotte," Amanda said, "It's getting late."

"Too late for you to drive back into the city. Stay the night. I have lots of room here." Roger put his arm around her. "And you might have some questions about your dad I could answer."

"I'd love for you to stay out here in your old house. It has a bit of synchronicity to it." Reece grinned at her and kicked off his shoes.

"I take it you will be staying over."

"The P. I. is meeting me here tomorrow. Besides, I haven't had a decent night's sleep in days."

"That reminds me," Roger said. "If Pamela was staying in your place, could she have left behind some identifying clue such as a key, an address, or a letter?"

"I knew it was too good to be true," Reece said, shoving his feet back into his loafers.

"Yes, if she makes bail, she'll be making a direct run for your apartment," Amanda said.

"If nothing else, to trash the place," Roger agreed. "I'll call a friend down at the police department and see if they can delay her. You two better get going."

"Come on," Reece said, taking Amanda by the arm. "You can ride with me, and I'll bring you back out here tomorrow to talk to Dad. I think he really wants a chance to get to know you."

****

When they pulled away from the house Amanda said, "I'm sorry, Reece. Truly I am. If I had known any of this—"

"You would have done the same thing. You did your job, and I actually admire that about you. I was trying to do mine and make yours impossible. So I would apologize, but given the same set of circumstances, I'd probably do it again." He winked at her as he shifted and put the sports car through its gears.

"You enjoy driving, don't you?" She noticed every detail about the way he drove. He handled the small foreign car as expertly as he had the giant truck with the set of double tires in the rear.

"Yeah, I guess I do. I especially love to drive this little baby."

"So why on earth did you loan it to that awful woman?" She laughed at the mention of Pamela. From the first impression she had sensed Pamela irritated Reece. Yet he had loaned her his apartment *and* his car.

He laughed too, and soon they were guffawing. It was contagious. The more she laughed, the more he did, and then the more she did.

"It's late and we're being silly," she said.

"And even though I hate the way our business has ended, I'm relieved the fighting is over. Do you have any idea how stressful it has been for me?"

"I can imagine."

"But on the bright side, now that I don't need anything from you and your report is finished, there isn't any reason we can't explore our crazy attraction, is there?"

They were traveling along at a decent speed on the interstate highway. No shifting was necessary. He took her hand and brought it to his lips.

It was dark in the car. There was nothing except the

glow of the dashboard lights to illuminate Reece's face as she felt the tender brush of his lips.

He had a firm but gentle grip on her hand. She thought of the way he had caressed the gear shifter, rolling his palm around it and stroking it as he made the gearbox sing. Amanda imagined he would handle a woman as expertly, and she wanted to find out.

She threaded her fingers between each of his, the way teenagers held hands, palm against palm. "It's been a strange day."

"And it may get stranger still," he said. "Lord only knows what we'll find at my place."

His thumb caressed her hand until he had to shift down to enter the slower city speed zones. After a series of exits and turns Amanda knew she wouldn't remember, he entered the brightly lit parking garage beneath the complex.

She started to shut the door behind her after jumping out.

Reece hit the electronic lock button on his key fob.

"Wait. I almost forgot my purse." She looked at Reece blankly.

He smiled. "I'll wait." He hit the fob again, unlocking the door.

She continued to look at him as another thought occurred to her. "Reece, where is Pamela's handbag?"

"I guess it's with her," he said offhandedly.

"No, she left with the deputy, and there was no handbag on her."

"You're right." He ran for the car. "If it isn't in here, it's back at Dad's."

"Maybe you should call him before he heads off to bed. I'll check the car."

"There's no cell reception in here. I'll have to step outside of the garage." He tossed her the fob before disappearing from view.

She looked in the back seat, if one could call the tiny space an actual seat. She looked on the floor and reached beneath the seats. She popped the trunk and looked there. *What am I overlooking?*

In order to assure herself she had looked everywhere, she lifted the lid on the console compartment between the seats. She had never had a vehicle with a space large enough for her purse in that compartment, but didn't wish to leave the slightest stone unturned.

And there it was, glaring at her. She snatched it up and backed out of the car, fob in hand to lock the door back.

"I'll take that," a male voice said.

But the voice didn't belong to Reece. She looked past the man blocking her escape, but could not see Reece.

"Don't bother looking for Jordan. He'll be out for a little while."

There was something familiar about the man, although much of his face was shaded by a baseball cap.

She instinctively stashed the purse behind her back. The brute grabbed her by the arm, taking her wrist and pulling her hand toward his crotch. Amanda balled her fingers into a fist, determined not to feel him.

The man laughed as he rubbed her fist along the front of his pants.

It was worse than she had thought. The hard ridge he wanted her to feel was that of a rather large pistol stuffed into the waistband.

"Now hand over the purse before you force me to do something I would rather not." He grinned at her and nodded, as if he would enjoy the thing he'd proposed.

"Where is Reece? What have you done with him?" She backed up against the car, feeling for the panic button on the key fob.

"He'll be all right if you just hand me what you're trying to hide behind your back."

He lunged at her, and she dropped the purse, kicking it under the car with her foot. She stabbed at the fob. He ignored her as he hit the ground, reaching for the bag. The car's lights began to flash and the horn started to blow.

"Help!" Amanda screamed, looking for something to clobber her attacker with.

He had snatched the bag and was scooting back from beneath the small car.

She had seconds, if that. *Think,* she commanded herself. *What can I use?* There had been something in the trunk. She hit the trunk release and grabbed the tire changing tool from the netting that prevented it from rolling around while the car was in motion.

The man was on his feet and swiftly coming toward the rear of the car. She crouched, braced, and swung with all of the strength in her body, making contact with his knees.

He screamed and went down, face first, onto the cement floor of the garage. As he fell the gun went off, sending a thunderous roar throughout the garage.

Amanda felt numb, although her heart was racing. Security guards were running toward her and the still-blinking car screaming for attention.

Chapter 13

Amanda looked down. A red stain originating from the face-down man on the garage floor grew at her feet. It spread quickly, appearing to be coming for her. She backed away.

"Ma'am, are you all right," one of the guards asked her.

She pointed at the man on the ground whose blood kept pouring across the floor. "That man tried to attack me. He said the man I was with—Reece Jordan—'would be out for a while.'"

"We've already called police and emergency medical services. They're on the way," the other guard said.

"Quick, you've got to find Reece. Maybe that son of a bitch struck him over the head or something." She pointed to where Reece had walked while attempting to get cell service.

One of the guards ran off in that direction. "Yeah, I see him," he said. "Appears to be unconscious."

Sirens in the distance grew louder as they approached the parking garage. One medical technician attended Reece while two others worked on the profusely bleeding man, with the purse still gripped in his fist.

"Whose purse is this?" one of the medical technicians asked.

"It's hers. He attacked her for it," one of the guards explained, pointing to Amanda.

The EMT didn't question it. He just laid the bag at her feet as she answered questions being asked by the police.

"Amanda!" Her named being screamed out echoed inside of the garage. The voice belonged to Reece.

"Over here. I'm okay," she yelled back.

He stumbled over to her. A large knot poked out of his forehead. "Are you all right?" He looked panicked and more worried for her than for himself.

To her horror, she started to cry.

Reece embraced her, stroking her back and whispering, "It will be okay."

"Do either of you know this man?" one of the officers asked.

Amanda shook her head and Reece looked down at the man. "I didn't see him or he would never have gotten the jump on me. And now, well…" he shrugged.

Even after they flipped the attacker over, he was unrecognizable. Landing on his face had caused damage to his mouth and nose, and he was covered in blood from tip to toe.

"We'll get more information on him at the hospital," another officer said.

"Are you two going to be around?" the first policeman asked Reece.

"Yeah," he said, fishing a card from his wallet. "You can find us at Dixie Millwork most of the time."

"Okay, we're going to follow this guy to the hospital and see what information we can get on him. We'll get his statement when he wakes up. I don't know if his leg can be saved. He blew a nasty chunk out of it. So he may be out for a while."

Reece shook the officer's hand, but kept one arm around Amanda.

After getting the attacker on a stretcher and into a waiting ambulance, one of the attendants approached Reece and handed him an ice pack. "That's a vulnerable area. I think you should get an x-ray."

Touching the spot where he had been hit, Reece said, "It's all right. I'm fine. I don't even know what he hit me with."

"Concussions are serious. I understand you were out for a few minutes."

"I played sports in college, so I know what to look for. I promise to get to the hospital at the first sign of trouble."

"Can't make you go, but I do strongly advise it." He walked off and got into one of the waiting vehicles.

"Come on," Reece said. "I could really use a drink now."

They were at the entrance to his apartment before Amanda even realized she still grasped Pamela's purse firmly in her hand.

Reece opened the door to a mess. Pamela had obviously been intending to leave while she still could. Luggage and boxes were everywhere.

"That bitch!" Reece immediately followed with an apology. "I'm sorry, but some of this isn't even hers to pack. It's mine! How dare she?" He pilfered through one of the boxes and fingered through a few items in one of the suitcases.

At first Amanda just watched. Then she took Reece by the arm and led him away from the chaos. "I suggest we deadbolt the door, get you that drink you wanted, and then photograph this carnage before you disturb any more evidence."

"It won't matter. I'm not calling the police over here tonight, and we don't have time to wait for them to file reports and get an investigator on the case. We've got to find where she hid the money before Monday morning."

Amanda winced. "That doesn't leave us much time, does it?"

"No. And if Dad's connection at the precinct isn't able to keep her locked up for long, Pamela may be back here sooner than we would like. " He led her to the kitchen, another absolute wreck.

"I thought you said she had stayed here before," Amanda said.

"Yeah. And I sometimes had to come over to get clothes or documents or whatever and it always appeared immaculate. This is totally out of character."

Dirty dishes were everywhere and empty whiskey bottles filled the sink. They walked through the rest of the apartment. All of it looked equally as ramshackle.

"Well, there is one thing we know for sure," Amanda said. "She didn't expect to be coming back here ever again."

Reece nodded and then grabbed his head.

Amanda pulled a chair over to him and insisted he sit for a minute. "I think the EMT was right. You should get that seen. I've heard about people bumping their heads and thinking it was no big deal, just to have a stroke or worse."

"If it doesn't swell on the outside, you should be worried. Mine is doing that nicely, so I'm not. But thanks for worrying about me. It feels nice." He looked up at her and then pulled her down onto his lap. "I kind of like you; and I believe you like me too."

She traced his forehead with a gentle stroke of her fingertip. "Yes, Reece Jordan. Surprisingly enough, I *have* grown to like you."

Even sitting amongst the mess of the trashed apartment, he appealed to her. Maybe it was adrenaline rushing through her veins from the close call, but she wanted him more than she could have ever imagined.

It frightened Amanda to desire him so fiercely. She was at her best when she had all of her emotions reigned in and her impulses under control. Even at her age, perhaps because of it, she feared letting herself act on instinct.

Her whole body tingled. Every vein rushed with excitement, pulsing against her skin as if it wanted to break out of the flesh holding it back. His hands ran up and down her arms, fanning the flames—growing, threatening to overtake her.

She tried to look away, but his gaze snapped onto her eyes. They were simultaneously searing and cooling. Amanda was too transfixed by them to pull her face away.

As if he sensed her restraint, he reached around her, one palm against her spine as he pulled her close. They were breathing in unison, eyes locked, as if one body already.

Amanda couldn't speak. It was all she could do to remain seated on his lap, her head level with his. She leaned forward just to feel the brush of his cheek against hers.

His face had sprouted a bit of stubble as the long night had turned into early morning. It softly scratched her face, textured like a cat's tongue.

Her hair fell across his face and she tried to secure it behind her ears, but he beat her to it, running his strong fingers through her thick locks, one thumb landing on either side of her head.

His strong hands gripped her head, tilting it for the perfect angle as their lips met—tasting, searching and finding no resistance.

Someone was moaning. *Is it him?* No, the sound was coming from her. She was nearly outside of her body, her hands tracing the tendons of his neck and muscles of his shoulders. She could feel him as his desire became a physical trait growing beneath her hip and all she could think about was how he would feel moving inside of her.

Stop it, she demanded of herself. *Walk away while you can.*

Reece ran both hands along the outside of her thighs, pushing her skirt up. His hands made her tremble with anxious longing and her inner voice faded. She kissed him deeper and harder as his fingers, so strong and masculine in the millwork shop, made soft contact.

"Oh Reece," she moaned, as the tiny strip of silk— the only barrier to the places begging to be touched— was moved aside, making way for his gentle touch. She couldn't wait. Not another minute; not even one second longer. All resolve was gone.

Amanda reached for him, sliding her fingers beneath the waistband of his pants, unbuttoning and unzipping, freeing him. She stood and let him slide her thong from her hips and legs, followed by the skirt he unzipped with shaking hands. She wondered if her hands appeared to be as unsteady on his body.

"I would carry you to a bed if I knew which one wasn't spoiled by her rampage," he whispered, his voice husky.

"Shh," she whispered. Her voice seemed to be coming from a place far away and in a great canister. She had intended to tell him to stop talking about Pamela and the mess, but then he rose up from the chair and tugged at her blouse.

She was going to say something, but he nuzzled the hollow of her neck. Amanda's chin lifted, giving Reece's hungry kisses more space, and then all thoughts were gone. Had there been even an echo of one hanging on for an opportunity to present itself, it slipped away with his lips and teeth and tiny tugs at all the newly exposed flesh.

Reece's nibbles were maddeningly erotic. Amanda tore at his clothing, happy finally when there was no fabric left between them.

He sat back down and scooted his hips to the edge of the chair, taking her by the waist and leading her downward over him. Reece guided her onto him, his blue eyes locked on hers, tugging on her emotions, forcing them to meet his. He was intensely sensual.

Her whole body responded, joining with him. Every response—shiver, graze, touch of longing—she had felt for him, and brushed aside, rushed back to her.

He was liquid light after a long, dark winter. She pressed against him, feeling the heat from his body. Reece was everywhere at once, lips on her lips, hands tweaking every spot they landed, while filling an empty space both physically and emotionally. The angle was magical. The pace was hers to set, and she rolled her hips, building an anxious drumming. It wanted a crescendo, and it received it, sending her into a spasm as she ceased moving and let the contractions spread throughout her body.

Reece pulled her hips back and then pushed them against him twice more before sending out his own moans and pressing her so tightly against him that she could feel his shudder as he released. They sat still for a long moment, still connected.

"You are so beautiful," Reece said, hugging her to his chest. His hands wound around her hair as her legs dangled off the sides of the chair.

"And you were wonderful," she mused, hearing the throatiness in her words. Amanda wanted to curl up and nap. "What a fantastic surprise after such a long day."

"You're surprised that I am wonderful?" he teased, tugging on a strand of her hair.

"Well, it wasn't what I meant, but, actually… yeah…I am surprised." She laughed.

"Do tell."

"I have found you to be rude at times, and at others, arrogant. I even thought you were a bit of a cad who was sleeping at the office because he had been cheating on his wife."

"Pamela!" Reece exclaimed. "I completely forgot."

They scrambled to wash and dress, and then wiped off the dining room table to dissect the contents of Pamela's purse.

After eliminating all of the things that weren't apt to hold hints—the pink lipstick, a pack of tissues, hand sanitizer, and a telephone charger—they began to look carefully at everything else. She apparently had her telephone on her, so they didn't have it to search through.

"Maybe there's nothing in here," Reece said. "She probably has the damning information with her."

"Then who was the attacker in the garage?"

"That could have been coincidence. People get mugged here every day."

"Then how did he know to take you out before coming for the purse? And how did he know that was what I was looking for?"

"What do you mean?"

"He knew you. He said, 'Don't bother looking for Jordan. He'll be out for a while.' And there was something vaguely familiar about him although I can't quite put my finger on it."

"He called me by name? He knew who we were and what we had?" Reece looked at her expectantly, as though a connection was suddenly forming.

"Yes. And when I asked him where you were and what he had done with you, he said you would be all right if I just handed over the purse. So he knew you were going to be there, and he knew to get the purse."

"Son of a bitch!" Reece declared. "She must have called him and warned him we had it."

"Then keep digging. There's got to be something important here."

"How did you manage to keep him from taking it from you?" He was looking through Pamela's wallet, but eyeing Amanda with curiosity.

"Are you going to talk or work?" She gave him her best serious expression and then burst into laughter. The experience she had just shared with Reece made her giddy. "I'll tell you later. Focus right now."

"You are a regular drill sergeant—a version of

myself—in heels."

"Don't bet on that…" She ceased talking, looking off into the distance. A memory was forming. "Bet!" she exclaimed. "I *know* who that man is!"

Chapter 14

"Who? How?" Reece looked and sounded completely perplexed.

Amanda turned toward him, excitement causing her eyes to glance back and forth as she recalled the earlier scene at the club. "I was sitting at the bar talking to Daisy while she worked. Two men came in from the course and one said he was 'having drinks on Ted because he had lost the bet.' Ted then said something along the lines of 'the eighteenth hole had sunk him again,' but he was in good spirits as if the money was nothing. Then he asked Daisy who I was. But *that* was him. The man who attacked us tonight is the one that played golf this afternoon at your dad's club and had a bottle of bourbon put on his tab."

"Ted Logan?" He shook his head back and forth as though he couldn't believe what he was hearing.

"Pamela must have called him or sent him a text, and he must have followed us back here."

"I was so distracted by you I didn't notice," Reece admitted. "Okay, let's keep looking."

After going through everything they thought it might be in, they decided to look through the things they had set aside. Amanda opened the lipstick tube and rolled up the ghastly pink lip color, ruling it out once again.

Reece set aside the charger and the hand sanitizer,

leaving the package of tissues. He started to set them aside as well, when Amanda pulled one out, then another and another. She was about to give up when a slip of paper popped out.

"Aha," she said, holding it up. A series of two digit numbers was written on the slip.

"Is it a combination?" Reece asked.

"Most likely. But to what?" She sat down again.

"Don't give up on me now. We're too close for that."

"Okay, but without knowing what these unlock, they are pretty useless." She grabbed her phone and snapped a picture of the combination.

"Good idea," Reece said. "I'd hate to lose that. Do you think whatever it unlocks is here in this apartment?"

She shook her head. "No. She might think that's too risky."

"Suggestions?"

"Have you got a computer here?"

"Yeah, a full office in the spare room."

"Come on. She probably hasn't had the time or the foresight to erase the browsing history."

Reece led Amanda to the room where a full office occupied the space, flipped on the computer, and stood over her shoulder as she hit a few strokes on the keyboard. A list of websites scrolled down the monitor face.

"Damn. You're good," Reece said.

She chuckled. "I've heard that before. But we're here to work." She winked and he smiled.

"How is it possible that you even make sleuthing fun?" He ran a hand along the back of her head in an affectionate gesture.

She warmed at his touch, but it was her heart feeling the heat instead of her body this time. "Look," she exclaimed, pointing to the screen. She clicked on the link. "Our dear Pamela has been making travel arrangements, train and airport."

"And some airports and train stations have lockers." Reece hit the slip of paper with a finger to punctuate his words. "This might be the combination to one of those."

"But we need the locker number."

"Put the paper back in the tissue pack." Amanda got up from the desk chair and led him back to the dining room.

"Are you kidding?"

"No. Listen. She'll make bail. And if she's as despicable as I believe she is, she won't give a damn that her accomplice is in the hospital. She'll make a run for the locker and her ticket to paradise..."

"And we'll nab her before she reaches the finish line," Reece ended for her.

"Exactly!"

"Okay. Let me make a few calls."

"Better wait a couple of hours. Most people aren't up at this time on a Saturday."

"And they won't release Pamela until at least mid-morning. I think we had better get a little sleep."

Reece pulled Amanda behind him to the room Pamela had been sleeping in. With both hands firmly gripping the top of the bed linens, he pulled everything from the mattress pad to the comforter up in one tug, dumping them in the floor. He grabbed a pair of quilts and two spare pillows and made a rather comfortable-looking space for them to curl into.

"I'm not really used to sleeping with people I barely know," Amanda said. Although she said it with the hint of a joke, she actually meant it.

Reece stroked her cheek with his hand and then leaned forward, his lips close to her ear. "We've made love. I think it's acceptable for us to grab a quick nap." He dropped a few tender kisses along her forehead and nose.

"But I'll never be able to fall asleep in these clothes."

"By all means, let me help you remove them."

She tried to protest, but his lips were so busy leaving a trail of divine joy along her neck—while his hands unbuttoned and unzipped and pulled and lifted—that nothing came out except soft moans. "It's been a long time since I've made love twice in one night," she said, her voice shaking.

"Technically, it's morning." He pulled his shirt over his head while she eased his pants off his hips once more.

Totally nude, they slipped between the two quilts. This was much different than it had been in the kitchen. In the chair she was on his level and completely in charge. Now, with him towering over her, she felt small and vulnerable. His legs felt like tree trunks next to hers, and she couldn't prevent them from falling open at his touch. The back of one finger shivered down her abdomen—and below—promising more, making her long for it.

"Oh my, Reece," she gasped, as he let his finger dip beneath, dragging it toward her center. In its wake it left a trail of heat and vibration. She wanted him more than she had wanted anybody. She lifted her hips, curling them toward his fingertips.

He chuckled. "Don't rush this. I'm enjoying myself."

"And tormenting me," she moaned. She slipped her hand downward and found him.

Amanda had been keeping all of her hungers under strict lock and key, refusing to give in to any of them. Succumbing to this physical craving was a powerful release—pure decadence.

Reece's hand moved to the outside of her hips as she wrapped her legs around his back and let go of all control. He was gentle, much more so than she would have imagined. And he kept making eye contact, making it clear this act of lovemaking was more than just sex.

Amanda got so lost in his eyes that she was taken by surprise when the building storm broke over her body, raining contractions. They caused her to make some noises unfamiliar to her. Her sounds and internal quivers seemed to fuel Reece as well, and he burrowed into her—head into the crook of her neck and shoulder, hips as firm against hers as possible—arms wrapped around her.

He lay that way for a few moments before rolling onto his side. "You're amazing," he said, running his hand along her cheek. Reece kissed her on the forehead and then pulled her into his side.

A breath left Amanda's body, one she had been holding since realizing she was out of control and reacting at will. It felt marvelous. Maybe she didn't have to keep such tight restraints on herself all of the time.

She curled against Reece, feeling strength from his powerful limbs. *He must have been a force to be reckoned with when he was younger,* she thought right before falling asleep.

Chapter 15

Buzz…Buzz…Buzz…

"What the…?" Reece heard the sound, though his head felt fuzzy. He had a terrible headache, and he wasn't alone in the bed. He ran a hand along the curved spine of the beautiful woman lying nude beside of him. Surely he was dreaming.

Buzz…Buzz...

He reached over and hit the alarm, and collapsed back against the quilt. His forehead throbbed and he traced a finger over the swollen, sore knot. The memories of the previous evening flooded back to him.

Reece leaned back and looked up at the ceiling wishing he could see a repeat of the day before playing as a cinematic tape on the white-sprayed space over his head. Had Amanda not been lying beside him he would have thought he had dreamed the entire scenario.

Fury hit him in the gut as he recalled the attack in the garage and the reason he had the souvenir contusion. If Amanda hadn't been so gutsy, she might have suffered something far worse. He shuddered at the thought.

Amanda stirred. She reached for his hand and pulled his arm back around her. He kissed her on the ear and stroked her hand with his thumb. Reece knew he should wake her, but she slept so peacefully he hated to.

She rolled over and opened her eyes, squinting up at him. "So I didn't dream it?"

"No. It only feels like a wonderful dream. But I assure you, it was all very real."

"I don't suppose we took any precautions?" she asked.

He laughed. "None. Should I be concerned?"

"Should I? Are there any diseases or—?"

"Absolutely not. I don't sleep around," he chuckled. "Yourself?"

"No reason to even *be* on birth control." She lifted an eyebrow.

"Well, if you get pregnant, I'll just have to make an honest woman out of you. And if you stay here looking so ravishing, I'm going to add to that possibility."

"Oh yeah? You mean even my horrible morning breath won't kill that desire?" She ran a fingertip along his chest, dropping it to his abdomen and swirling it around his thigh.

Reece hardened. Early mornings found him eager for sex as it was. But with her dragging her hand over his body, it was impossible not to feel the rush of longing. He pulled her on top of him, tracing the outline of her hips with trembling fingers. A confident man, he wasn't used to feeling shaky with a woman. *It must be the blow to my head*, he reasoned.

"I should warn you," she whispered. "I'm not a morning sex person."

"I'll take that into consideration," he said, running his lips over one breast, his thumb over the other.

They fit so well. He seemed to slide into her with no effort as though they were made for one another. Every move she made, every undulation stoked his raging fire. Reece heard her intake of breath, a little gasp, and then he was gone. Amanda was so warm and delicious. And she matched his craving with her own wild abandonment.

He had meant to offer protection, and he would do that next time. He was too close, and so was she. Her face glowed with anticipation and fierce longing. She met every thrust hungrily, and he was compelled to have her.

"Slow down, or I'm going to erupt," he warned as she rubbed circular motions around him.

"Me, too." She laughed as her body quaked, and he lost all control.

For a moment they said nothing. She collapsed against his chest, and he just held her, stroking her head and back. "Tell me again how you are not a morning person," he teased.

"With you, it would seem anything's possible," she said, humor in her voice. "But I suppose we need to get busy."

"As bad as I hate to admit it, you are correct."

They quickly showered and dressed, Amanda still in the previous day's clothes.

The private investigator Reece had spoken with the prior evening phoned him and asked for a photo of Pamela, which was quickly faxed from her driver's license. His plan was to have a contact at the train station and another at the airport. The problem was that they had no certainty it was a locker combination, and even if it was, which one?

Lewis, the private investigator, gave them a list of other possibilities, gyms, spas, bank vaults, even country clubs. Reece heard nothing after he said "country club."

"Of course," he whispered. "It's at the country club. Don't move," he instructed. "I'll have my dad check."

Reece hung up from the PI and telephoned his father. "Get to the club and see if you can find out if Pamela, Randall, or Ted recently rented a locker, and if so, which one." He ripped the piece of paper back out of the tissue pack and restored the loose papery cloths as best he could.

"In the event I am wrong about this, I don't want her to have the combination." He stashed it in his wallet. "In the meantime, let's go out for some breakfast."

"And what if Pamela returns while we are away?"

"I'll take care of that." He picked up the phone and called security, advising them to detain her by any means necessary and to call him immediately. They were to especially avoid giving her a key. He had the one she'd been using in her purse.

Amanda grinned. Reece's phone rang just as he was slipping his shoes on. He glanced down at the screen.

"It's Dad," he called out to Amanda. "Yeah, go ahead," he said into the phone.

"Um-huh...really...you don't say?" He lifted his eyebrows, animating his face for Amanda. "It's possible. Want to try?"

Amanda slid next to Reece and laid her ear to the other side of the telephone. Reece angled it so she could hear what his father had to say.

"What if it is his private locker? Should we open it?" His dad sounded concerned.

"Well, Dad, if it isn't connected to Pamela and the stolen funds, the code I have shouldn't unlock it."

Amanda nodded and opened her phone's picture album, displaying the code in an enlarged feature.

"Okay, Dad, here it is…"

"Wait a minute. Let me get my glasses on. Okay…"

Reece called out the sequence. His heart beat wildly, almost as wildly as it had when he was making love to Amanda. The memory caused him to reach out to her, stroke her face. She wasn't wearing makeup, but still looked fresh and dewy. He called out the last number and waited.

The silence was deafening. Would it open? If it did, what would be there?

"It's opening, son. Oh my God."

"We're on the way out there. Stop, lock it, and call the sheriff and see if you can get a search warrant. Now that we know this is the most likely place for the proof we're seeking, we'll need to make sure it's all handled appropriately."

"What if someone tries to get into the locker?"

"Why don't you call your friends down at the police department and see if they can send someone over to secure the thing. I doubt he'll risk being connected with the stolen money, assuming he has the combination."

"Okay. Hurry." Anxiety resounded in Roger's voice.

Reece and Amanda stepped over Pamela's mess, raced to the elevator, and down to the garage. For a moment Amanda stopped and stood glaring at the spot behind the car. The blood had been cleaned, but the cement had absorbed some of the liquid. They could still see the dark shape of the profuse blood stain.

"Come on," Reece encouraged. "It's just a bad memory. He got exactly what he deserved."

"Do you think he'll lose his leg?" she asked.

"If he tries to hurt you ever again, he'll lose more than that. Jump in the car. We've got to hurry."

She snapped out of her fog of recollection and made her way to the car.

Reece barely nudged the accelerator until they were clear of the garage and the inner city speed limits. Once they hit the interstate, he floored it, leaving Charlotte behind as they raced for Mooresville.

"What will your dad think when he sees me in the same clothing as last night?" Amanda asked.

"I've never known my dad to take notice of anything a woman was wearing. It's the absence of clothing he appreciates."

She laughed, and he realized he rather enjoyed the sound of her laughter. It wasn't cloying or annoying or silly. It was real and seemed to generate from her diaphragm.

****

Amanda braced as Reece careened the sports car into the parking lot outside the Simmons Point Country Club. She leapt out of the car, racing into the building on Reece's heels. Although the sign said *Gentlemen* above the door leading into the locker room, she didn't pause.

Roger was leaning up against a set of steel storage units talking to a deputy. "Okay, here they are now," he said, pointing at Reece and her as they approached.

Reece greeted the deputy, introduced Amanda, and

pulled his wallet out in order to retrieve the slip of paper with the codes.

Roger sidled up to Amanda. "Long night?" he asked, with a hint of mischief in his voice.

"Excuse me?" She looked at him strangely.

He motioned with his hand pointing up and down her body. "You're wearing the same clothes. I was just wondering if you and Reece had a long night." He raised one eyebrow in exactly the same gesture as Reece often did.

"'I've never known him to notice what a woman was wearing.' Really Reece?"

He laughed. "Dad!"

The deputy interrupted them. "Does this locker belong to one of you present?"

"No," Roger said, growing serious again.

"Then we'd better wait for the search warrant."

Roger excused himself and stepped outside of the locker room. When he returned, he had a different expression on his face. "Don't leave," he said to the deputy. "The warrant is being processed as we speak."

"And on the weekend, too. Impressive." The deputy eyed Roger with what was clearly admiration.

"How did you do that, Dad?"

"Do what? This is criminal activity. It needs resolution." He feigned innocence while looking a bit sheepish.

"You have a talent for getting people to act so quickly it amazes me." Reece had spent the last few months thinking poorly of his father. To see him so authoritative was like seeing the man he used to be.

"It's one of the few perks of aging. I know people. I've done little favors for them, donated building materials for their pet projects. I'm not asking for anything illegal, just that all of the paperwork gets pushed through quickly. That's all."

The search warrant arrived, and the locker was emptied of its sparse contents, the most important one being a locked metal box. It was tagged, and the few other items which looked pretty generic—tennis shoes, a bottle of antiperspirant, an old towel—were placed back inside.

"We've got a snap gun at headquarters. It can get this open in a flash." The deputy handed a receipt for the metal box to the club manager and turned back to Reece and Roger. "You can come down to the station if you like. Your help in identifying whatever might be inside could prove beneficial."

They all agreed and set out for the Mooresville Sheriff's Department. Anticipation mounted. What if the box didn't contain anything having to do with the missing money? What if Pamela and Randall were escaping with the cash while they tinkered with some old box?

****

The deputy presented the box to the front clerk for tagging into evidence. "Got the snap gun handy?" She nodded and disappeared, returning with something reminiscent of a staple gun. "This little jewel alleviates us from having to learn lock picking skills or waiting on a locksmith when we need to open something quickly. You just insert the prongs and pull the trigger."

The anticipation was palpable. Amanda's heart thundered. What would it be? What were they hiding? How was this guy involved? Questions formed, rolling over one another.

Amanda watched as the deputy lifted the contents, handing them to the clerk to document. Hurt was obvious on Roger's face. His eyes watered. He suddenly looked his age, his mouth pulled inward like a prune, all color leaving his complexion.

The deputy named each item as he retrieved them. "We have a passport under the name Pamela Porter."

"Her maiden name," Roger interjected.

The deputy continued. "A pair of train tickets to Atlanta, an airline e-ticket to Switzerland…" He pulled out a small manila envelope, pulling it open from one short end. "A cashier's check for seven hundred fifty thousand dollars made out to Pamela Porter from the Bank of Georgia in Atlanta, and…" He stopped talking and flashed a wad of cash which he fanned out like a deck of cards. "Let's count it and add it to the list of evidence."

For a few minutes, nobody spoke. They were all looking at the stash. Most likely, as Amanda was, they were wondering how, why, and exactly what Randall and Ted had to do with all of this.

"If you can't prove she stole these funds from you, I'll have to give them back to her; you do realize that?" The deputy looked from Roger to Reece.

"Don't worry," Reece said. "We'll prove it."

****

"I'll get Detective Stephens for you," the deputy said. He then disappeared behind a wall, taking the box and all of its contents with him.

Reece's cell phone rang. It was Security from his apartment complex. Pamela was there, locked out, and throwing a fit. And she was with a man—a surprisingly healthy one.

A second call came in from Lewis. Reece translated the messages to Amanda. "It would seem that Mr. Ted Logan has recently filed bankruptcy, making him vulnerable. Pamela and *Randall* apparently paid Ted to rent the locker and later to get the purse. Undoubtedly, that explained his exuberant humor about losing at golf. That way Randall could get the money and the tickets without implication.

"And the cash was most likely for Ted."

"I hope it was worth what he is going through now." He rubbed the knot on his head.

"Is it still throbbing?" Amanda asked, seeing his hand stroke his forehead.

His head snapped playfully toward her. He grinned and whispered in her ear. "How did you know?"

She punched him in the arm. "You really are a rascal, Reece Jordan!" Then she glanced around to see if anyone heard his playful jibe.

"And *you* have some power behind that punch." He reached over to feel her bicep just as the deputy rounded the corner accompanied by a short, balding fellow with a serious expression on his face. The deputy pointed toward the three of them, and the man marched forward.

"Hello," he said, offering handshakes. "I'm Detective Stephens."

They all introduced themselves, and he nodded between them. "The good news is Ted Logan has awakened from surgery and admitted he had been hired to obtain that purse under any means necessary. Mrs. Jordan must have used her one phone call to alert her accomplice."

Reece felt his jaw clench as he realized what

Pamela had nearly cost him. Maybe DMBS could be saved now. If only he had talked to his dad earlier about the missing funds. If only he hadn't suspected his father was the one taking the money. If only...

"Is that enough to arrest Randall and Pamela?" Amanda asked.

"Yes. Logan is willing to cooperate to spare his neck. If they manage to save his leg, he's going to have a long and painful journey. And your complaints against them strengthen the case." The detective looked from one to the other of the trio.

"You can find Randall and Pamela at my apartment building. Security is holding them as we speak."

"Same one you two were attacked at in Charlotte?" the detective asked.

Reece nodded.

The detective made a call to the Charlotte-Mecklenburg Police Department. "They should be in custody shortly."

"How long will it be before the stolen property is returned?" Amanda asked.

"Not 'til the case has been tried and the rightful owners determined by the courts. Sorry."

Roger spoke quietly. "I feared as much."

"And when it's determined the money was stolen from J & S, it will be returned to the company, not to either of these two?" Amanda spoke the words all three were likely thinking and didn't want to say.

"Once it is determined where the cash was taken from, it will be returned to that same entity."

"Even if it doesn't exist anymore?" Amanda knew the minute Builders Tech took over Dixie and shut it down, every subsidiary would also be closed and their assets seized. Builders Tech would then be the recipient of the returned monies.

The detective nodded. Reece grabbed Amanda by the arm. "We need to get back to Charlotte."

"I think we already have your contact information. Sign these papers and you can go," the deputy said.

"My information may be lacking a little," Amanda said. "You need to add my Chicago address and phone numbers to your list." She scribbled them down for the deputy and left with a sullen Reece.

****

Reece's head was about to burst. The realization of what he had done and what it was about to cost him made the knot on his forehead pound like a fist into his brow bone. By not trusting his father, he had just lost every dime of what he would have had to start over with. When his dad discovered this, he was going to be furious.

He was acutely aware of the silence that had just settled over him and Amanda. Apparently she had been talking and he had completely tuned her out. There had just been the droning of another human voice he relegated to background noise.

Reece glanced over at her and raised his eyebrows.

She was looking at him expectantly.

He should answer, comment, something. But he couldn't remember one thing she had said, if he had ever known at all.

"Well?" She clearly was waiting for his response.

Reece opened his mouth to speak. It was useless.

"You didn't hear a single word I said, did you?" Amanda asked.

"No, I'm sorry. There are so many emotions and

crazy thoughts circulating inside of my head I simply can't focus."

"I can't say I blame you. This has been a lot to process. And your poor father..." She shook her head, openly empathizing with him.

"Yeah, poor Dad," he said. *He's much poorer than even he knows*, Reece thought.

The drive to his dad's house loomed ahead. Reece pulled in behind Amanda's rental car. "I'll follow you back to Charlotte."

"I'll be fine. You really don't have to." Amanda opened the door and jumped out of the sports car.

It dawned on Reece he should have opened her doors for her. He tried to reach her door first, but she was already scooting in behind the wheel.

"I'd love to see you again tonight or tomorrow. Can we arrange something?" It sounded feeble even to him, but cleverness was absent from his mind at the moment.

"I would like to see you too, Reece, but I have to get prepared for the team coming in on Monday morning. And there's a personal issue I need to look into as well."

The knot on Reece's forehead pulsed wildly as the vein that fed it seemed close to exploding at the mention of the looming Builders Tech team visit. "I don't suppose after all that's happened between us I'll be getting a reprieve?"

"I see." Amanda took a deep breath which she then exhaled loudly.

"No...you...I..."

She held up a hand. "Don't bother explaining. I knew what I was getting myself into." Amanda snatched the shoulder belt and pulled it snugly around her, snapping it into place as she started the engine.

"Amanda, wait!" he called out.

She ignored him, circling the drive and heading out onto the street.

Reece jumped into his car, intending to follow her.

His dad pulled in as he was about to exit. Clearing things up with Amanda would have to wait. His father needed to know what the stakes truly were at this point. He might as well get it over with.

Chapter 16

Amanda's thoughts ran from Reece's stupid comment about being offered a reprieve—which was likely the only reason he had appeared to desire her—to the mugging attempt, and finally settled on the conversation Roger had with her concerning the trust fund he had given her grandparents for her. Was there any truth in that?

It had never been mentioned, not even once that she could remember. Her grandparents had lived a very frugal life. She hoped they had spent it a little frivolously. At least they could have had some fun and a few luxuries.

She glanced onto the floorboard of the passenger seat and saw the gym bag with her job-site clothing was still there. That was all she needed to skip the southbound exit and head for the one leading north.

Amanda knew she would not be comfortable scratching around the old house in her expensive suit and high heels. They had already taken a pretty good beating from the previous evening's attack. She whipped into a rest stop and changed into the boots and jeans and secured her hair into a high pony tail.

The day grew steadily warmer even though she was headed for the foothills of the Blue Ridge Mountains. She made a mental note of the wineries she passed. *I certainly don't recall those being here before,*

176

she thought. One exit alone claimed to offer access to six different wineries. *Wow, when did this happen*?

Amanda took the Little Brushy Mountain exit and drove atop the ridge connecting her community to the interstate. Sweeping views of the valley below lay to her right, large mountain vistas to her left.

This stretch of asphalt marked with yellow center lines and white edges had not been part of her memory. *It's paved*, she mused. *That's something else I don't remember*. She had expected a kick of dust to rise up behind her back tires as she sped along, or muddy puddles to contend with if there had been a lot of spring rain.

Her memory jolted awake. How many times had she traveled this road sandwiched between her grandparents in their old farm truck with the single bench seat? They hadn't worn seatbelts then. In fact, she didn't think the old truck even had any in it. But she had never felt unsafe as her grandmother—usually in sensible shoes and something she called a house-dress—wrapped an arm tightly around her while her grandfather shifted gears on the steering wheel column.

When the ridge road came to a fork, she took a left and continued to the place where the pavement did end. That brought a smile. At least urban development hadn't gotten as far as the old home place.

She took the first right, which was little more than a path through the woods. It had always been shaded, and now the tops of the trees made a canopy she drove through. Amanda had to stop to pull a limb from the driveway. Only then did she stop to think that the whole place was probably dilapidated. It had been years— three, maybe closer to four—since she had been back.

Amanda tried to remember when she had last been home. After the strange day she had yesterday and with such little sleep, she had trouble recalling anything except Reece. He had been so perfectly wonderful and for a moment she had thought there might be something real growing between them. Then he had to go and ask her if she had changed her mind about Dixie Millwork. Now all she could think was that he had used her in order to accomplish that end.

She felt foolish and knew she had behaved recklessly. Falling into his arms had been so easy. After the attack, it had all felt a bit like surviving a war zone and wanting to know the rush of feeling alive again. The events had left her unarmed with her normal wits.

They hadn't even used protection. Fortunately she was entering perimenopause. That would surely make it less likely she could get pregnant.

Amanda couldn't help recalling how Reece had pulled her onto his lap, both hungry and ready for each other. It had felt so right, so wonderful, and they had made love again, both that night and just this morning.

Or was it all a dream? Had it really happened? Would she awaken to find herself in the hotel?

She exited the woods and landed in the midst of the old farm. Weeds and brambles and heavy vines covered everything. What had once been a lovely stretch of pasture dotted with barns and sectioned with fencing, was now unkempt. The fence posts leaned like rotten teeth across the ragged field. The structures used for silage and feed were so vine-covered the very earth itself seemed to be pulling them back into the ground.

The house was a complete disaster. A tree had fallen onto the chimney, knocking bricks out of line.

Some were on the ground; others were dangling with bits of cement the only connection to the next brick and their certain release. The front porch was still viable, though bits of weeds poked through the cracks between the boards. A shutter had fallen and another was hanging against the house by one hinge.

Guilt consumed Amanda at the shoddy appearance of her grandparents' home. They would be devastated to know that not even routine care had been provided. There was no way around it. This would have to be rectified.

After taking a few pictures with her cell phone, she pried a stone up from the path to the rear of the house searching for a key to the front door.

Her grandparents had both grown up near here during a time when there was no necessity for locking doors. Once the threat of violence growing in the surrounding communities began to appeal to their better senses, they had at least attempted to stop a robber or attacker by bolting the main entrances. But after her grandmother had locked herself out with something boiling away on the stove, they had hidden a couple of keys around the old place.

Several spare keys were wrapped in foil and placed beneath stones on the path. They had always been there, for as long as Amanda could remember. Sure enough, after upturning the third stone, she found the item she was looking for.

The lock was "tetchy," a word she hadn't used in years. It didn't want to give. She rattled the knob while twisting the key, fearing it might break off and make matters worse. Amanda gave up on the front door and walked around the house, but every window and the other door was fastened as tightly as the one on the front.

Back on the porch, Amanda contemplated her options. She could go back to Charlotte and forget about the house and everything Roger had said. She could break in by smashing a window, or...she could try to get in through the upstairs window. She remembered it didn't have a lock.

But how on earth would she get up there? She darted off the porch and looked back at the house. The window she had thought perfectly-sized as a child, now seemed incredibly small. Even if she managed to crawl up there, she might not fit through the opening.

Her phone vibrated. She had turned the ringer off, something totally unusual for her. The caller readout said it was Reece. *Should I take it?* Debating too long, it went to voice mail.

She listened to the message. "Amanda, it's Reece. I've been trying to contact you at the hotel. They are growing tired of taking my messages. Wherever you are, please call. I need to speak with you."

He sounded weary. Maybe his head injury was worse than they'd suspected. That had been a pretty hard thump to knock him out and leave such a knot.

She hated calling him back though. *If it's important, he'll call again*, she decided, and went about trying to open the door again. It was as stubborn the second time as it was the first.

About ten minutes later the phone buzzed again. Reece's number scrolled across the display. *Geez, he's just going to keep calling.*

"Hello," she answered. "It's Amanda."

"Thank goodness. I've been worried about you.

Didn't you get my message?" Reece did sound worried.

"What's wrong?" she asked, ignoring his question.

"I need to see you."

"Now?"

"Yes, now. Can we meet up somewhere?"

"Why?" Suspicion edged its way back into her mind as she recalled the way he had expected her to change her mind regarding his business. If that was all he wanted, there was no use in seeing him…ever again.

"I have some papers you need to sign regarding your statement about the attack." He paused and she didn't respond. "That's not true. I just want to see you…because of last night and this morning. I want to—"

"To try to convince me to change my recommendation about Dixie?" Anger crept into her voice.

"No. That's not it at all." His voice morphed from concerned to angry. "Damn it, woman. At least give me time to complete my sentences before you change them around for me."

"Why then?"

"Do you really have to ask? Are you that jaded?"

She rubbed the spot between her eyebrows, trying to smooth them out as they knotted toward each other with her skepticism. "I'm not exactly in town."

"Where are you?"

"I'm in Wilkesboro."

"What in hell are you doing there?"

"I'm at my grandparents' house, the one I grew up in after my parents died."

"Are you coming back soon?"

"Probably not. I'm trying to get in, and the lock is

stuck."

"I can get you in," he said confidently. "Will you wait for me?"

"You're an hour and a half away!"

"So? Go have a burger, and I'll be there before you know it. Just give me the address."

Although she shuddered at the thought of eating a burger, she could use his help. She had her laptop with her, so it wouldn't be difficult to work on a few things while she waited. Thinking better of it, she gave him the address and general directions.

The afternoon was too beautiful to spend working on a computer. It quickly got shoved back into the car as she decided to go for a walk.

Amanda looked down at her boots and congratulated herself for making such a wise purchase. She took off down the hill, across the creek, and along the old path to the Buzzard's Roost. It was no secret as to why it had been nicknamed that. The huge outcropping of rocks absorbed the sun's heat and made the perfect gathering place for buzzards to unite. They reminded her of little old men with their wrinkled bald heads and wobbly necks attached to broad shoulders, all anchored to scrawny feet.

Several of the feathered creatures perched at the rock's edge while off in the distance a half dozen circled something. Undoubtedly when they landed, the others would take off and join in the carnage, feeding until they came back here to roost for the night. The buzzards on the rocks lifted off, and now she could move a little closer in without having to worry about the regurgitation of the foul birds.

A small rustle in the leaves indicated something

moving behind her. She turned in time to see a pair of coyotes had spotted her and apparently decided she was small enough to take down.

Amanda had nothing with her except her phone, which was useless as a weapon *or* rescue device. Buzzards Roost was too far off the beaten path and too surrounded by woodland to allow a cell phone signal through.

The canids snarled, and focused on narrowing their circle. Amanda reached down for a stick and some rocks. When she pelted one, the other would move a little closer. Amanda's heart thundered with fear and she could feel its pulse in her ears.

It was difficult to think or reason. What should she do? *Think*, she commanded herself.

Chapter 17

The coyotes continued to circle, as Amanda thrashed the stick about. One inched forward aiming for her ankles, while the other kept arcing behind her. It was unusual for coyotes to attack large prey, wasn't it? She swatted at the one in front and spun to catch the one behind her on the nose as it leapt forward. The yelp brought out tiny whines from the rocks and a trio of tiny coyote pups toddled up together.

The pair jumped onto the rock and finally, without even a backwards glance, they skipped off across the ridge, babies in tow. Amanda laughed at herself, relief surging through her body. Apparently they had been trying to get up to the rocky cliff to feed on any remains left by the buzzards. They were protecting their young, not trying to kill her.

Amanda had had enough wildlife for one day, and scrambled back to the path and across the creek to the little old house stubbornly refusing her entry.

She righted a rocking chair, most likely left overturned by her grandfather. It had been this way when she came home for his funeral, and she couldn't bear to lift it up then. She had wanted to keep everything just the way he had left it, his hand the last to touch it.

She hadn't wanted to face the pain. She had zoomed in and out, though she followed a detailed prescription of what one should do when a loved one passes away. Once the items on the list had been checked off, she locked the door, boarded a plane, and hadn't been back since.

The thick layer of cobwebs and dust and old bees' nests embedded in the underside of the chairs, reminded her of the negligence. She marched off the porch, broke a lower limb off of the nearest pine tree, and returned to the chair intent on using the bough to spank the offending dirt and sticky webbing from its peeling paint.

When she was satisfied with the cleanliness of its lap and ladder back, she settled into it and began to rock. Amanda had to laugh at herself. She had become her grandfather, whose penchant for cleanliness had nearly driven her to distraction as a teenager.

He had once bought barrels of oil drained from vehicles at the local car maintenance station and then had her drive the old truck while he dribbled the oil onto the dusty drive. It had alleviated most of the dust blowing onto the immaculate white house, but then had caused angst for him as he worried a footprint of oil might end up on his freshly painted porch or—worse—inside of the house on one of the ancient wool rugs covering the hardwood floors.

To solve that problem, he had laid a succession of rugs in different naps and thicknesses from the drive, along the walk, across the porch, and right up to the front door with the brass plaque where his name was engraved as though he were a historic figure. If he failed to see her feet hit each and every rug along the way, she would simply have to go back to the very first one and start over.

And he never let anyone sit down on the porch without inspecting the rocking chairs for dirt, bees, and spider webs.

The worst was the indelicate way she had to eat the delicious sugary, crumbly treats made by her grandmother. If it wasn't mealtime and eaten over a plate at the table, then it simply had to be eaten over the sink so as to assure no crumb found its way onto the floor.

She shook her head, smiling at the memories. Whenever he was away from the house, she and her grandmother ate whatever they pleased wherever they chose. And then they held a finger over their lips as a sign they would never reveal the sin of biting into a cookie in the living room or while climbing the stairs.

Amanda put her feet up onto the porch rail, something else her grandfather would have cringed over. She crossed her arms and sat back, propped comfortably between the rail and the chair rockers. The sun was casting shadows across the porch, the pines seeming to reach out for her. The warmth soaked into her bones, and she closed her eyes in complete contentment.

****

Reece wasted no time in setting out for Wilkesboro. He punched the address Amanda had given him into his global positioning system and compared the directions it gave to the ones from her. They were a perfect match. Excellent!

He zipped along in the little sports car. It was the perfect day for a drive out to the country. Giant cotton ball clouds puffed into a bright blue sky. Everything on the ground was green and blooming. Here and there, dotting the landscape like little visual gifts, were sprays of roses scrambling over fences, giant blue hydrangea heads, and the first of the daylilies.

Reece rarely noticed such things. But today he felt compelled to see things as Amanda might, to pay attention to the things she may wish to talk about.

He took the exits as directed by the annoying voice from his GPS and made the same mental note he always made after taking a trip that required its use: *change the damned voice.* But once he got where he was going, the importance of spending valuable time stuck in the car fiddling with a technological device made no sense to him, and so he was once again listening to the nagging of the dashtop woman.

"Turn now," she said, in the best hen-pecking tone he had ever heard. Surely this couldn't be right. It was little more than a donkey path. On closer inspection of the trail's edges, he saw broken limbs indicating someone had been through recently.

Reece kept going and grinned when he saw Amanda's rental in the drive. He was out of the car before he spied her feet resting on the porch rail. Her head was lying against her shoulder, and she was sound asleep. Tiptoeing up to her, he took hold of the chair to steady it so she wouldn't rock backwards if startled.

She looked peaceful, belonging to the countryside in her boots and jeans. He knelt down beside of her, his head level with hers. As though sensing his presence, she opened her eyes, and jumped.

"It's okay; I've got you," he laughed, glad he had the forethought of steadying her.

"I must have fallen asleep," she said dreamily.

"You probably needed it. We had a bit of a long

night." He reached up and caressed her cheek, immediately desiring her again. Every time he drew near her, all he could think about was making love to her. He couldn't seem to get enough.

She reached in her pocket and pulled out the key. "It's stuck. The lock, I mean."

Reece held up a small tube. "Graphite powder will help." He put the nozzle in the keyhole and gave it a squeeze. Then he took the key and jiggled it in and out before trying to turn it. The tumblers creaked, but gave, and he opened the door slightly for Amanda. "Voila!" He held his arm out toward the opening.

Amanda leapt up and ran toward him. "That was fast!" she declared. "I'm totally impressed."

Reece smiled. Why was it so important to him to please this woman? "Would you rather spend a few moments alone inside, or shall I join you?"

She took him by the hand and tugged. "Come with me. I've faced my ghosts already."

****

Or have I? Amanda wondered. Stale, dusty air billowed as the door opened and closed. She suddenly felt claustrophobic and snatched the front door open once again. "We need to get some air and light in here." She waved her hand in front of her face.

Reece immediately tried to assist in the effort to open curtains and blinds and windows. They both coughed as dust blew into their faces and irritated their throats. "How long has it been since anyone was in here?"

"Three years," she answered calmly, as if that were normal.

"Nobody has checked on this place in three years?

What if the pipes froze or someone broke in?"

She shrugged. "I turned off the water and drained the pipes. Then I set the heat pump to fifty-five to keep the floors from freezing and cut the breakers to everything else. Frankly, I'm surprised I had that much presence of mind." She immediately recalled the last time she had shut the door behind her.

The loss had been crippling and the guilt of how miserably horrible she had been to the people who had raised her weighed as heavy as lead weights on her chest. The urge to eat—her life-long coping mechanism—had been overwhelming. Amanda had known if she didn't escape quickly, she would do the very same thing she had done when her grandmother died. And there was no way she was going to allow that kind of collapse.

Reece was looking at her as though he expected more in the way of explanation. He rubbed his chin and squinted.

"I did forget to take into account the possibility of storm damage," she continued. "The chimney seems to have suffered, and I suppose I need to get that fixed."

"What pulled you out here today? Was it just being this close or is there some other reason?"

"I didn't come for sentimental reasons." She turned from the spray of dust as a breeze kicked up creating a spiral of grit in its wake.

"So?" Reece looked at her with an intense stare.

She wanted to hide from his accusing eyes. How could he care about someone like her? She was obviously a very cold woman. "It was something your dad said yesterday that brought me out here."

"My dad?"

"Come with me to the basement. We'll need to get the breakers back on, and then I'll tell you about the conversation that led me back here."

The basement showed signs of mouse infestation, another surprise to Amanda. In her Chicago high rise she never had to think about things such as chimneys and basement issues.

"We'll pick up a few mouse boxes to fix this problem," Reece assured her. "But you might want to get rid of the draw for them." He pointed to the root cellar and the shelves of canned and dried goods. All of it was beyond recognition. Something which might have been dried beans was scattered around the gnawed-through faded package.

"No kidding! I forgot about this stuff." She would need to take a vacation, something she rarely did, and come back to clean out and sort through. "But we're not going to do anything about this today." Amanda pulled him back upstairs where she gave Reece a quick recounting of the information she had received from his dad.

"Ah yes, I remember now. You two were talking about J & S and the money that went out to Bill's family—your family—when I arrived with Pamela. We got so sidetracked with the theft, the charges, and then the attack that I forgot all about it."

"So, if your dad gifted my grandparents with my dad's commission and other funds, where did it go? What did they do with it?"

Reece shook his head. "I wondered how he dealt with the guilt."

Chapter 18

"Guilt? Why would your father feel guilty?" That wasn't mentioned in Roger's conversation with her.

"He didn't tell you?" Reece asked, frowning.

"No," Amanda replied. "He just said he was worried about Bill's daughter."

He took a deep breath. "Dad thinks your family would be alive today if he hadn't asked Bill to take a dozen or so window grid sets out to a job site on his way to dinner. The customer was complaining they'd arrived broken yet again. They were such fragile things back then that they probably did."

Reece continued, "Your dad said he was going near there to celebrate with your mom at the old country club they enjoyed so much. He was pulling out from the site when a truck jackknifed and…"

Amanda couldn't hold back her tears.

Reece immediately began to apologize. "I'm sorry. I shouldn't have brought it up."

"No, no, it isn't you, or anything you said," she managed through broken sobs.

"Sure it is." He pulled her into his chest, running a hand over her back.

"No. I always *thought* it was my fault. All these years *I* have felt responsible."

"Why? How on earth could it have been your fault?"

"The same way your dad thought it was his." Amanda pulled away from his embrace and tried to stop crying. "I threw a tantrum. I didn't want to stay with the babysitter. I wanted to go with them. They were delayed by my selfishness. If they had left when they wanted to, they would have been way down the road by the time the truck wrecked."

The words tumbled out of her, bringing up old emotions anchored in her psyche at the moment they had happened. Experiencing the pain again wasn't as an adult, but at the age she was when the events took place. It was a time warp, taking her back to that age, especially as she now stood in the house she would come to think of as *home*.

As she turned away from him, Reece reached out to her again—this time from behind. He seemed determined not to let her shut him out. His strong arms wrapped around her, cocooning her into his body, her back to his chest. He rested his head against hers.

"Do you think your parents would want you to suffer like this? Do you think they would want my dad to blame himself? Do you believe the accident was preventable?"

"Of course not," she answered.

"Then let it go." His voice sounded confidant and assured. "Look at me, Amanda."

She turned in his arms, now face to face.

"That's better." He kissed the tears from her cheeks, softly, tenderly.

Amanda's heart swelled with adoration. Reece had managed to touch her in a place she had kept hidden and locked away. As much as it frightened her, it also felt warm and alive, and soothing.

How could a man, so harsh and sharp in so many facets of his life, be so caring and gentle in others?

He lifted her face with a finger beneath her chin. "Now let's find what you came out here to seek and then go have some dinner."

She nodded.

"Where do you think they might have left their important papers?"

****

Reece threw up his hands. "This is getting tedious," he admitted. They had looked in all of the places where people normally kept valuables and came up empty-handed.

"I know. And I had already looked in most of these nooks and crannies," Amanda said. "I just can't think where they might have left information that is so important." She ran a hand through her hair and then let it drop to her side.

"Could there be a secret compartment or a wall safe you failed to see?"

"I suppose..." She threw up her arms again.

Reece placed his hands on her shoulders at the base of her neck and kneaded into the tight muscles. She gave a little moan before saying, "Ooh, that feels good."

"I know you are tired, confused, and frustrated. So much has happened in the past couple of days. I think we are all still reeling. But let's try to focus for a little while longer." He leaned close, his lips brushing her ear. "Or we can say the heck with it and go back to bed."

"Here?" She turned around to face him, shock blossoming across her face.

He laughed in spite of himself. "What are you, sixteen? Of course here! You own this place, don't you?"

She gave a chuckle. "Yeah. Being here does make me feel a bit childish. Go figure! But it is musty and dusty and falling apart."

They were standing in her grandparent's bedroom, and he patted the old spread littered with bits of fly speck. A storm of dust sprang up, and they both turned away from it. "I know this isn't what we came here to do, but maybe you should consider having the place cleaned up and ridding it of the old clothes and comforters which can't be saved."

"You're right. And maybe there is something behind them or underneath them. Old people are infamous for stuffing money in mattresses, aren't they?"

"I've got an idea. Why don't we go find a hotel room and get a bite to eat? Then we can come back here in the morning and get a fresh start."

"Okay. But let's not go just yet. I want to look a while longer."

She had dogged determination, Reece decided. Of course, he already knew that about her. "All right. But let's start cleaning out as we go. Any trash bags around here?"

While Amanda scrounged around for trash bags, Reece made a list on his phone's notepad of all of the likely hiding places: false drawer bottoms, hidden wall panels, underneath mattresses. She returned with a huge roll of black lawn bags.

"I definitely need to clean things out. There's a lot of old food in containers in the pantry."

"Pick a corner and we'll just get started."

He showed her the list, and she smiled. "A bit of a sleuth, aren't you?" She pointed to the chest of drawers in the far corner, and they began to disassemble the chest, sorting through layers of clothes and tapping along the edges where a false bottom might present itself. Nothing of importance showed up.

"This is all Grandpa's," she commented when the bag was full to bursting of old T-shirts, ties, socks, and underwear. "So if he got rid of the rest of Grandma's clothing after she died, why are her dresses still hanging in the closet? Why didn't he get rid of those too?"

"Maybe he couldn't bear to. Some people hang on to things that remind them of the people they lost." Reece shrugged.

"Or maybe they are hiding something." She ran to the closet and peeled back the dresses and old housecoats.

"Just toss them out to me," Reece said, holding open another large bag.

She grabbed a handful of hangers, each covered in braided fabric or crocheted in various colors of yarn, and lifted them off the rod. Reece caught the pile, coughing in the spray of dust.

While Amanda crawled around in the closet looking for a slit in the panels or a slot where a hidden safe might lurk, Reece began searching the pockets of the dresses.

"Anything here you want to keep?" he asked, eager to toss them all into the trash.

"Let me have one last look," she said, taking the one he was holding up by the hem. A crunchy noise escaped as she squeezed. "What in the world?" she exclaimed.

"What is it?"

"Feels like tin foil. That's weird."

Reece dropped the stack and grabbed the dress she was holding. He tugged on the hem and it fell open, revealing a piece of exactly what she had suspected: tin foil. Amanda peeled it open and inside were ten $100 dollar savings bonds, dated 1974.

"Wow! Those are likely worth twice that now!" Reece stared at the weirdly disguised handful of bonds.

"And if there is one of them, there are probably more," Amanda said, tearing into the opposite side of the garment while Reece inspected other pieces of clothing. The stack of bonds grew taller as they disassembled one after another of the garments. Some were hidden in the linings, others in the sleeves, more in the hems.

"This seems like a risky place to store valuables," Reece said, looking at the fortune piling up on the dresser top.

"Not really, if you think about it," Amanda said.

"My name and social security number is on each one." She pointed to the row of numbers beneath the name: Amanda Simmons. "If someone had tried to cash them in, I would have received a notice from the Internal Revenue Service about the tax owed on the interest. And it would be difficult to get a bank to cash them without the proper identification."

"What about a fire? They would have just burned up, a fortune going up in flames."

She grinned. "That's what the tin foil was for. Ever roast a potato in the coals of a fire?"

It dawned on him the plan was genius. "But why

didn't they tell you about them?"

"You know, they probably tried. I kept promising to come home. When Grandma died, Grandpa was too upset to think of anything else. And every time I planned to visit, something came up, even if it was trivial. He died from a heart attack in his sleep before I made it back here."

"What are we going to do with these bonds? You can't deposit them before Monday." Reece rubbed his chin as he thought of the possibilities. "We could go back to Dad's house. He has a vault in the basement. Your bonds would be safe, and he could probably use a little company right now as well."

She squinted at him. "You don't think he would mind? After all, I'm the enemy."

"To be precise, the company you work for is the enemy. You've saved me from being accused of embezzlement by helping to uncover Pamela's plot to ruin my father and me. I'd say that absolves you from any blame in recommending we be shut down. In fact, I think it just underscores your honesty and reliability."

He caressed her face with his palm, letting his thumb linger along her lips. She opened her mouth slightly, and he pulled her into him, holding her tightly against his chest.

"I really am sorry, Reece. If I had just waited…"

"Shh," he whispered. "You were only doing your job."

"My job," she whispered. Amanda pulled back from him and looked quizzically into his eyes. She caught her lip in her teeth and let her hands drop from his waist. She turned away, head slightly bowed, obviously lost in some internal thought. "It's odd, isn't it?"

Reece didn't respond. He knew something was brewing in her mind; an idea bursting from fertile ground, a seedling in warm spring soil.

She turned and pointed a finger at him. "How likely is it this is a coincidence?"

His mouth flew open. Was she going on a tear about them again? "Us?" he asked, pointing first to her and then to himself.

"No, not us; Judson!"

Reece shook his head. "I have no idea what you are talking about."

"Of course you don't. Let's pick up some food along the way to your dad's house. I'll explain as we drive."

"My car or yours?"

"Yours. It will look better sitting in your dad's driveway in the morning," she reasoned.

They loaded the bonds—over two thousand—into the gym bag from Amanda's car and then set off in Reece's for Mooresville.

Chapter 19

Amanda felt hungry, really hungry. She had denied herself the physical recognition of the gnawing pangs in her belly for years, eating as little and as infrequently as possible. But she had faced an attacker, made love with abandon, and worked to exhaustion. A nice meal was in order!

Reece promised a good steak from a little joint he knew about on the way to his father's and ordered three of their special marinated-in-bourbon rib-eyes with creamy spinach and garlic mashed potatoes on the side. The scent of the seared meat, garlic, and yeasty bread made Amanda's mouth water as she held the huge sack of food on the way to Roger Jordan's house.

Though they had called ahead so Roger could attempt to make himself presentable, he had clearly had too much to drink and looked miserable.

Who wouldn't? Amanda thought, *given the information he had received over the past twenty-four hours.* His wife was planning to take off with another—much younger—man, wiping out his company's account and leaving his son out on the limb for the theft of it.

How ironic that the company using this vulnerable moment to seize theirs had sent *her* to finish them off—a woman whose father had once saved that very company. That was what was bothering her most at the moment.

Reece threw the gym bag into his father's vault, while Amanda gathered dishes and silver, and set the table.

Roger busied himself looking for a wine to have with their meal, and then made himself a pot of coffee. "I think I've already drunk enough for one day," he declared.

Reece and his father carried on about baseball and stock car racing as they sat down to dinner. Amanda immediately began to cut her meal in half, plating only a portion of it. She was aware of the eyes of both men on her and the meager portion she had on her plate. She looked from one to the other of them.

"It's right there if I want more of it. Geez. I'm not as large as you two. I can't eat as much."

"Eat whatever you like," Roger said. "We're not used to it, that's all."

Reece winked at her. "I would have thought we had both worked up an appetite."

She blushed, feeling the heat scalding her cheeks at his barely concealed reference to their lovemaking. "This is what having an appetite looks like for me, okay?"

They all laughed, happy for the opportunity to relieve a little tension. She was aware of Roger's eyes glancing back and forth between her and Reece. He pointed his fork toward Reece.

"There is something going on between you two, isn't there? You have a spark; electricity following your path like the trailing wake boats leave on the water."

"Now, Dad…"

"No, it's good," Roger said. "There is symmetry to

it. I like that."

Amanda couldn't speak. She certainly couldn't deny it. And for once, she didn't even want to.

****

"You're awfully quiet," Reece said, tugging on a lock of Amanda's hair. She lay in the crook of his body, spooning her back into the curve of his chest. "I didn't disappoint you, did I?" He caressed her slight body beneath the sheet.

Amanda flipped over, arms extended above her head, forcing her breasts upward. In the afterglow of their intimacy, he ached to touch her. She had strength forged from by a tragic past. She had turned that tragedy into a determination to be successful.

Her silence drummed into the atmosphere as clearly as a thumping gong. She had something on her mind, had since they left Wilkesboro. He had thought she was going to share it with him, but now wondered.

Amanda slowly turned to face him, knocking her bony knees against his. "I have this feeling…" she said in a faraway voice. Her eyes wafted toward the ceiling as though she could see something he could not.

"Tell me about it," he encouraged, stroking her back as he draped an arm around her.

"Something is not right. Something is off. I can't put it into logical sentences. But I just have a feeling…"

Reece waited for her to finish the statement until he thought she might have fallen asleep. "It's all the drama, that's all. You've been shocked and attacked and thrown into your past rather dramatically. You'll feel better tomorrow."

"No, that's not it. It's…" She sat up, pulling her body free of his embrace. "It's Judson and Builders

Tech, and how he suddenly sent me here alone when he had never done that before, and…"

Reece sat up with her. "It's coincidence, that's all. How would Matheney know about any of this? *You* didn't even know about your father's connection to us or J & S."

"That's just it. Judson is thorough, completely thorough. He covers every single base, anticipates every likely outcome. And if he knew, why would he send me here alone?"

"How could he know?"

"I don't know; unless he managed to get the incorporation filing for J & S Consulting and made the connection between my father and yours."

"Then he wouldn't have sent you, would he? And you go by Lassiter now, not Simmons. I really think you are making far too much out of this. It is simply coincidental."

Reece pulled her back into his arms. "I think the real question is why your grandparents never told you about the bonds. You could have thrown away a fortune if you had cleaned out those closets and just dumped everything into boxes and trash bags."

She slid against him. "Yeah, but the fault there is mine. Several times they mentioned having something to tell me when I came home. And they were survivors of the Great Depression and World War II. They didn't trust giving information over the telephone or putting away hoards of money in the bank. I remember being told my great-grandparents had lost a fortune when the banks collapsed."

"And after your grandmother passed away, didn't your grandfather feel the need to disclose this?" Reece was totally perplexed. Why would they keep a fortune in such risky places?

"He was distraught. I was inconsolable. I promised to come home at least once a month and then didn't. I don't blame them. That was my own fault."

"But not to leave instructions should he pass away suddenly seems irresponsible, don't you think?"

"I think he wondered how he would explain it. How would he justify keeping that much money from me? And although I think the reason was to make me be responsible for myself and to give me a strong work ethic, he might have thought I would resent it."

"And he might have seen it as blood money, having come on the heels of losing their only daughter."

"True," she said.

"Well, let's get some sleep. It won't serve anything if we can't function tomorrow."

****

If Judson Matheney had been like other men, Reece would have been correct. Amanda knew him as few people did. Only those who worked closely with the mogul understood his dynamic drive and obsessive personality.

A small detail that would make the average person shrug would cause Judson great turmoil. He kept a team of investigators, and they returned tiny bits of minuscule so-what information that he parlayed into multi-million dollar deals.

There was the time a wife of a well-connected builder-turned-politician in the Chicago area had been clueless to her husband's affair with an intern. Rather than have his professional reputation and advantageous marriage ruined, the husband succumbed to Judson's determination to possess his company. Nobody knew precisely how Judson had received that information. Only the people in his closest circles even knew that was the reason he had been able to acquire it.

If her father's connection to Dixie Millwork had gone undetected, it would be the first time any such detail that could have bearing on the outcome of a deal had slipped past him. But if he knew, and didn't tell her…

No, it isn't possible. He couldn't have known prior to sending me here. Judson would have asked me about it. He trusts me.

She glanced over at the bedside table's clock. It flashed 4:23 a.m. in neon green. At least she had gotten a little sleep.

Reece was knocked out, his chest rising and falling only slightly as he slept. She smiled. He needed the rest. Undoubtedly, all of this had been hard on him as well.

Amanda tried to go back to sleep. It was Sunday. There was no need to jump up and get the day started at a run. She could sleep in, doze until sunrise at least.

She closed her eyes, and Judson's face appeared in her mind's eye. The suspicion that all of this wasn't mere coincidence clanged in her head like clashing cymbals. He hadn't even questioned her recommendation to shut the doors on Dixie Millwork. In fact, she had heard something akin to laughter in his voice as he agreed to her suggestion.

That was wrong. That wasn't the Judson Matheney she knew. He questioned everything. Why hadn't she thought more of his quickness to accept her decision?

Ego. It was my ego. I liked that he placed so much

confidence in my opinion. It was powerful and gave me a sense of importance and belonging.

She rolled over, and Reece took a deep breath, exhaled it in gasps. She was disturbing his much-deserved sleep. Slowly she peeled back the covers, reaching for the bathrobe Reece had found for her the previous evening following their showers.

She crept silently toward the door, slipped from the room through the merest crack, and shut it behind her as noiselessly as possible. A pair of nightlights illuminated the hall and the staircase. Amanda remembered the way to the kitchen and padded off with a sure step.

Feeling the wall for a switch, and finding it, she suffused light into the dark room.

"Whoa," a voice called out.

She jumped and squealed.

"Sorry, didn't mean to startle you," Roger said. He was sitting at the table, in the same spot he had been sitting in the night before.

"Have you been here all night?" Amanda squinted in the sudden brightness as her eyes adjusted.

Roger shielded his with one hand and blinked several quick blinks. "Most of it," he admitted. "What are you doing up at this hour?"

"So much has happened, and there are too many questions rolling around in my head to allow me to sleep. I figured I might as well get up and have some coffee. Do you mind if I make a pot?" She pointed to the coffee maker.

"Help yourself. The coffee's in the cabinet above it and I think there's cream in the fridge."

Amanda found all she needed to get a pot going.

The smell invigorated her, the scent of its perking and brewing signaling her brain it was time to get the day started.

She gathered the cream and sugar and placed it on the table in front of Roger, along with a steaming mug of the hot liquid fresh from the pot. His hand shook a little as he reached for it. She pretended not to notice.

"Ah, that's good," he said.

"What are you still doing up?" she asked him, having answered that same question herself.

"That's another perk of getting older. You need less sleep."

"Liar," she teased. "You have a lot on your mind, and my showing up here after all of these years has likely not helped, especially given the circumstances with which I have been sent."

He pulled his lips inward as if the coffee had turned sour. Reaching up with one hand, he scrubbed at his scalp like the friction would kick his brain into gear.

"We have a history," he said. He suddenly became steady and alert. His sleepy eyes turned eagle-sharp as they fixed on her face.

"Yes. You and I have a history I wasn't aware of until now."

He sat his cup onto the table with a thump that sent a splash of coffee onto the table. "Yes, but I wasn't talking about you and me."

"Who then?" she asked, feeling confused once again.

He spat the two poisonous words from his lips. "Judson Matheney."

Chapter 20

Amanda shuddered. Goosebumps prickled her skin. "You and Judson are acquainted?" Surely she had misunderstood Roger.

"We met a long time ago under similar circumstances." Roger took a long sip from his cup of coffee. "If it hadn't been for your father, Matheney would have made Dixie his first acquisition."

The blood rushed to Amanda's feet with a thud, leaving her head weightless and without the ability to think clearly. She couldn't have stood up even if she had needed to. Her toes tingled, and her heart seemed to cease beating.

Roger set the now-empty cup down on the table. He appeared to grow more alert as Amanda became more confused. He gave a chortle.

"Your father helped us thwart his plans. Judson was considerably less savvy back then, but eager to make a name for himself. He headed up north and, as I now understand it, was quite successful. I believe Dixie was the only company that managed to avoid his talons. And now, even we have fallen victim. I bet he is gloating."

Amanda was speechless. Judson Matheney had failed to mention any prior association with Dixie Millwork to her *on purpose*. Could that have been due to pride? He may not have wished her to know he had tried and failed to acquire it in the past. But if so much was at stake, why wouldn't he have mentioned the pitfalls? He had said nothing to her, not one word.

Roger continued talking, working out his thoughts aloud. "What did he tell you about us?"

Amanda's mouth fell open. She lifted her cup of coffee, sipping it slowly, buying time in which to coax her brain awake. "That's just it, Roger. He has said nothing about ever having met any of you or even being here in the south before."

"And he just happened to send you because it was your turn to handle the first stages?"

She met his eyes with her suspicious ones. "He has never sent me alone on a project before. This is the first time."

Roger's face became animated. His eyebrows shot upward and his mouth pulled to the left, leaving a strange lopsided slash across his lower face. He rubbed his hands together. "Well, well, isn't that a coincidence?"

"Is it?" she asked.

"You can bet your ass that it isn't. This has been one long game of chess for Judson Matheney. I can almost guarantee he hired you for this moment and used you as the pawn to make his track record a complete success."

"But how could he have known when I didn't even know?"

"How does Matheney know anything? How did he know Pamela stole funds from J & S? How did he know the missing funds were making us weak and ripe for his picking? How did he happen to hire the child of the man who had caused his only failure? How was it he just happened to send her on the inaugural venture of the one company her father had saved? How?" He had grown louder as each question left his mouth. "You tell me!"

Amanda hung her head. She could sense the anger and confusion but had no answer for him. "I've been asking myself some of those same questions," she admitted. "Perhaps he thought I did know. Perhaps he was testing me to see if I could be trusted to always have his best interest at heart." She shrugged, remembering the delight in his voice when she had last spoken to him upon recommending Dixie's closure.

"No, he doesn't need proof of your trustworthiness." Roger grabbed her cup and his and got up. He refilled their coffee mugs and returned them to the table. In a sudden gesture, he gave her a hug from behind, resting his chin on her head. "It's a game, my dear, and the fact that you were clueless about your true role in it only serves his ego. This acquisition completes his record of achievements. I don't hold you responsible. If it hadn't been you, it would have been someone else. You were only doing your job."

His understanding melted her heart. Giant tears fell from her eyes as her chest heaved.

"What's going on?"

The sound of Reece's voice luckily caused *both* their heads to jerk upward, or else she would have hit Roger in the mouth with the back of her head.

"Are you crying?" he asked, racing to her side.

She burst into a full scale sob, the sounds of her wails echoing through the kitchen.

"Dad, what did you say to her?" Reece asked harshly.

"It wasn't his fault…He…was being…nice. I just can't…bear…what has hap…pened."

"It's true, son. I told her I didn't blame her. I didn't mean to upset—"

She took Roger's hand with one of hers while wiping her nose with the other on the napkin Reece handed her. "You didn't upset me. I was just touched by your ability to forgive and the fact that you weren't blaming me."

Reece poured a cup of coffee for himself and joined them at the table.

Roger sat back down. "So what are you doing up so early, son?"

"I heard loud voices and when I realized Amanda was missing, figured I'd better come down and see what the commotion was about."

"And then you saw me crying and thought the worst."

"Judson didn't tell her about his previous attempt to take over Dixie," Roger said bluntly.

"Why would he?" Reece asked. "What would that have to do with this acquisition?"

"He doesn't know Judson Matheney as you and I do, does he?" Amanda asked.

Roger and Amanda filled Reece in enough for him to acknowledge he now understood their point of view.

"So what are we going to do about it?" Reece asked.

"You've got to get your money back." Amanda looked from son to father.

"How? Aren't the henchmen coming first thing in the morning?" Reece asked.

Amanda's face revealed a devious expression.

"Well...nobody knows that I know any of this yet."

"Go on," Roger encouraged. "I'm likin' the sound of this."

"Okay, I'm supposed to meet the team at the airport. They'll be flying in on Judson's private plane. If I can stall them until the bank opens, you might be able to retrieve the funds you deposited."

"But we still lose Dixie," Roger pointed out.

"Maybe you will. But maybe you won't. The charges against Pamela are already on the books. The crime happened before Judson's take-over attempts and will supersede his ownership. If he wants to take the company, he'd have to be the one involved in the effort to pursue action against her. He'd be assuming all liabilities as well as assets."

Roger and Reece looked first at each other and then at her. "You mean we could leave him with the burden of proving the theft against Pamela while needing our testimony to do so?"

"Yes, and although he could have a subpoena issued, he would need your cooperation to win the case or it could cost him dearly."

"Giving us a little more time and bargaining room," Reece concurred.

"Absolutely. Then, even if you decide to move on, you will have the time required for starting up something under a different name."

"Do you think I will have any trouble getting the funds back out of J & S that I deposited?" Reece asked her.

"No. I think he was so focused on Dixie that he saw no need to be concerned with the consulting firm. It was at a near-zero balance and of no use to him."

Roger looked completely coherent and alert. "This could work. It could honestly pan out."

"A Simmons has shown up to rescue the Jordans once again." Reece pulled Amanda into the curve of his chest.

"Don't count your chickens and all of that," Amanda said, though she looked up at him with adoration.

"Can we go back to bed now?" Reece asked.

"Absolutely," Roger said. "I think I might actually be able to sleep now."

"Sleep isn't what I have on my mind," Reece whispered to Amanda.

She blushed but fell into step with him as he pulled her toward the stairs and upward to the room they had just shared.

Chapter 21

Reece gave the sash holding Amanda's robe together a gentle tug. It fell away and the oversized, bulky body wrap slipped open and dropped off her shoulders. He couldn't get enough of her. The more they were together, the more he wanted her.

He slid his hands along the sides of her body, savoring the feel of her soft flesh against the palms of his hands. She threw back her head, appearing to enjoy the touch of his fingers. He lowered his head and nibbled her chin before dipping along her neck and placing kisses into the hollows of her collarbone and down toward her still-firm breasts.

The robe dropped to the floor, leaving her naked in front of him. He pulled away long enough to gaze the length of her and take in the visual effect of her perfectly tantalizing figure.

Amanda tugged at his T-shirt and then at the pajama bottoms he had thrown on before descending the stairs. Moans of excitement escaped him as her hands passed over his body.

Reece backed her toward the bed and lifted her onto it. She had ceased resisting, giving in to their desire, spreading her legs as he eased between them. In one gentle movement he slipped inside of her. He took his time, slowly savoring the moment.

She arched against him, moaning softly with each

press, until he could tell she was close. He could have made a couple of swift thrusts and exploded, but forced himself to wait, to hold back. Amanda's satisfaction had come to mean more to him than his own.

She began to quiver, and he held her buttocks in his hands as he crawled forward as deeply as possible. Once he was certain of her pleasure, he made a swift thrust and joined her, holding her long after his body had ceased its shuddering.

Reece rolled away and cocooned her into his body, pulling a sheet over them so that sleep might find them and grant them the rest they so desperately craved.

****

Amanda awakened, naked and still pressed into the curve of Reece's body. It was hard to remember where she was for a minute and why there was a man in the bed with her. She had been dreaming of Chicago and that she was late for work.

Then it all came back to her and she remembered the sweet moments of lovemaking that seemed to always be following some kind of trauma. *Are we using each other's bodies to soothe other wounds?* she wondered.

She overruled the thought, recalling with distinct feeling the way he had inspired desire within her from the very first. Even when she had thought him the worst sort of cad, she'd felt a carnal response to his presence.

Behind her he moved and tightened his hold on her waist. She felt him elongate and harden against her back and instantly craved him. It surprised her to experience such longing for a man she barely knew. And yet, they appeared to have had been crossing paths since childhood.

214

Amanda rolled over, and Reece flipped her on top of him. She couldn't tell if he was asleep or awake. Without thinking about it, she straddled him.

He felt huge this morning and hit a spot which instantly tweaked a cord with her satiety, like strumming a guitar until the crescendo. She circled and pressed, taking him as deeply as possible and winding up toward the explosion. It drummed and throbbed and her whole body fell victim to this one act of pleasure.

With a force that sent a multitude of moans from her, she contracted and expanded and laughed and nearly cried as the most vigorous of all orgasms she had ever experienced left her body.

"You are incredible," Reece whispered, removing any possibility he was still sleeping. "And I am not finished with you."

He flipped her easily off of him and onto her stomach against the cooler side of the bed. Reece could toss her around as easily as a rag doll, and she recalled the first time she had met him and how much he reminded her of a jungle cat, lithe, muscular, and sure-footed.

His hot breath searing the back of her neck brought her back to the present as he dropped kisses and nibbles along her spine. They coursed through her body, stirring up another flame that licked at spots she had just *thought* were sated.

Reece was toying with her, teasing her, and she loved it. It had been so long since she had loved with such abandon. It was as wild and free as if it were happening between two tigers. She felt her hips curling upward of their own accord. Her spine curved and arched bringing her knees up underneath her to give the slight lift she needed.

He let out a sharp breath as he found her again, joined with her, penetrating as deeply as he physically could. The strength of his legs pushing against hers was apparent through the muscle contractions that pushed him forward, rotated his hips against hers, and pulled him back before sinking in deeply once again.

Not being able to see him, only feeling him, added to the momentum.

He reached around her midsection and let one hand caress her stomach and breasts before sliding downward and finding the tiny bundle of nerve endings just to the north of where he was conjoined with her. Gentle as a whisper, he brushed it with a fingertip, and it was all she needed to send her into another spasm. This time she could tell he was joining her.

His legs tensed, pushing him deep and holding him there as his body shook with the eruption. Although he momentarily tried to keep his weight off her by holding himself up with one hand, Amanda felt him collapsing against her, and her knees folded.

"Sorry," he managed, breathless as he rolled to lie beside her.

She turned and raised herself up onto her elbows to look him in the eyes. They were soft in the afterglow, dreamy and full of emotion. "That was fabulous...and so are you." Her voice betrayed her growing affection for the man she had spent most of the last week trying to avoid.

Regret tinged his words. "I don't want to get up, but it *is* after noon already."

Reality hit her hard. She had hoped to get back to Wilkesboro and to digging through her own ghosts.

Instead, she needed to prepare for the next day's schedule and devise a plan to delay the crew from Builder's Tech. "We better shower and get back to Charlotte."

****

Clouds rolled overhead. They were not beautiful fluffy white cumulus clouds that brightened the sky. Gray and ominous, they promised rain and lots of it.

A drop splattered, followed by several more, and then a torrent broke open from the sky onto their windshields before Reece and Amanda reached Charlotte. He slowed to a crawl, visibility low in the sheets of driving rain. She slowed up behind him, driving on unfamiliar streets back to the hotel.

Reece still wanted her to come back to his place. It was tempting, but she needed to clear her head. It was fuzzy, too fuzzy. She needed exercise, physical exhaustion that would come from overloading her body, not her brain.

The past few days had been psychological drains. They had rendered her weak and tired. After the large, delicious steak she had eaten at Roger's house, she craved meat again. After the beautiful lovemaking sessions with Reece, she craved a man again. And she craved belonging—the very worst craving of all.

Belonging to someone, or to a family, brought its own special brand of interdependence. She had lived alone and on her own, with no support except that of her work family, for such a long time. Could she relearn to be part of a familial whole?

Amanda's head spun with conflicting thoughts. What was going to happen tomorrow? What would happen if her peers discovered she was sleeping with

Reece? She had waited such a long time for the opportunity to head a team and to blow it because of a man seemed a pure waste.

Maybe that was the reason. Did Judson have those plans in mind for her when he sent her to Dixie? No, there was no way of predicting a mutual physical attraction. The circle wound itself round and round in her mind.

What about the Jordans? Reece couldn't fake such sentiment toward her, could he? And Roger didn't even know who she was when he first allowed her friendship at the table.

The pictures couldn't lie either. Her father had worked for them. And obviously had been beloved to leave such an impression on the people he had befriended there.

How could she sell them out? How could she help them?

She barely remembered how she had gotten to the hotel. She'd just followed the lights of Reece's car as if part of a convoy. Running for the door, she threw up her hand at Reece as a salutation before dashing inside and up to her room.

Amanda slipped into her bathing suit and headed for the indoor pool. She made quick laps around the pool's circumference. Her arms pulled her body through the water swiftly aided by the scissor-shaped kicks of her legs. The pent-up energy coursed from her core into her appendages until she became pleasantly tired.

She flipped onto her back, floating with her chin pointed upward, ears pinned to the surface of the water until it filled them as a balancing mechanism. The fullness against her ear drums brought a slight roar with it. It drowned out the sounds of her spinning mind.

Weightless, thoughtless, she floated.

A scene flashed through her memory from childhood.

"Hey blimp," the boy had called out, "how about making some room in the pool for the rest of us."

Children were cruel. They wanted to fit in with each other and found that poking fun at her was a great way to have common ground.

Amanda had slipped out of the water on that day refusing to let them see the tears were about to fall. She had made jokes about being allergic to chlorine whenever the opportunity to swim had presented itself again.

Her grandparents had soothed every hurt the only way they knew how, with food. Even now, in the cool water, she experienced the hot sting of remembering how it felt to be the fat kid.

It would be many years, and many diets later, before she would actually pull another swimsuit onto her body.

Staying thin was nearly a religious fervor for her now. She couldn't let the stiff and sore joints from the altercation in the parking garage prevent a work out.

She couldn't let the sudden companionship of Reece and his father cause her to overeat. It was too difficult to smell the mouth-watering aroma of seared steaks from a charcoal grill and not indulge. And the burgers and fries Reece liked were loaded with calories and fat.

Perhaps it was the culture of the south, with its emphasis on food that had aided in her weight issues.

She had to get a grip on that, now, before it got out of hand. Of course, once she was back in Chicago it would be easier.

Back in Chicago…

Amanda plunged beneath the water. The shock of thinking the words broke her cool flotation. What was she doing? Had she suddenly become obsessed? Lost her mind? She bobbed in the pool like a buoy, treading water to keep her head above the surface.

As she assessed the events of the weekend, she struggled once again with the conflicting issues of discovering her father had been associated with Dixie and her obligation to fulfill what Builders Tech had sent her to Charlotte to do.

How can I assist in destroying what my father evidently worked so hard to save? But how can I pretend to represent Builders Tech while aiding its prey?

The two opposing forces batted about in her head, a tennis match between the right and left sides of her brain. Every emotion in her body undulated toward helping the Jordans. Every bit of the thinking and reasoning side of her knew there was no choice.

Her stomach growled. It burned and begged for food. Maybe if she ate something the answer would become clear. Yet she feared swallowing a single morsel of food while under duress.

Her appetite could careen out of control easily enough without the added stress-related triggers she now possessed. Memories of eating an entire box of cereal surged through her.

A handful of granola might satisfy the gnawing that tore at her gut. But she wouldn't stop at a handful, and she knew that. As long as there were clusters of oats and almonds left in the bag, she would retrieve them, one by one, knowing that just one more wouldn't make much of a difference.

Twelve handfuls however, would. And when the last kernel of sweet crunchiness was gone, her belly distended, the urge to eat gone, the feelings numbed, the blurry headache would make thinking and feeling impossible.

That might have sated a child, but not an adult.

She kicked off the sidewall she had treaded over to, and swam around the pool like an Olympian—face down in the water, coming up with every third stroke, legs propelling her forward—until exhaustion overcame her.

The pool was adjacent to the sauna, and though she had seen two people slip inside as she rounded the last corner, she pulled herself out of the water and made her way inside of the steamer for adults.

Amanda drew the door open with a pronounced squeak. The couple jumped away from each other, obviously fearing being caught in an embrace, or worse. After mumbling an apology, she spread her towel across the redwood planks and splashed a ladle of water onto the coals.

Steam billowed upward, filling the small space with heated air. The warmth seemed to seep through to the bones beneath her thin skin. She enjoyed sweating; reveled in the sensation of melting away layers of excess salt, fat, and calories.

Finally, sufficiently tired and sweaty, she grabbed up her towel and wrapped it around her, retreating to her room. She showered and went straight to bed. Her mind reeled from the recent revelations. There seemed to be so many strange coincidences. Yet she was too tired to think about them rationally.

In a fit, she sat up in bed. She had forgotten to check for messages. But it was Sunday night. Who would have left a message today? She gave in to the tiredness and fell asleep.

Chapter 22

Monday morning came quickly. Had all these events really happened to her in the course of one weekend? Amanda couldn't think about it.

She hurriedly dressed, packed her laptop in its case, and headed downstairs for coffee. The smell of frying batter hit her as soon as she exited the elevator. *Waffles.*

Fresh doughnuts and other pastries lined the breakfast bar. Under the kind of duress she was experiencing, it seemed inviting to sit down with a plate of them and chow away. It would momentarily make her feel calmer, less stressed.

She stood in front of the sweets and contemplated it while her brain engaged. *No, I will not make these bad choices. The sugar will restart cravings and the energy will fade before mid-morning. I'm having yogurt and berries and maybe a boiled egg.*

Amanda grabbed a cup of coffee and a container of plain yogurt from the ice-lined case—skipping the berries as they looked heavily sweetened—and sat down at a table with a newspaper spread out before her. She didn't intend to read it, but it worked to keep other people from making benign conversation.

She glanced at her watch and knew it was time to head out. Taking a long swig of her remaining coffee and exhaling a deep breath, she set off for Charlotte-

Douglas Airport.

The airport was always busy. Early morning, late night, it didn't matter. Flights took off and landed all hours of the day and night. She parked and headed for the domestic terminal, checking her phone for a message confirming the flight number.

"Shit," she exclaimed when she read the phone message and then looked around her to see if anyone had heard the derogative language. Seeing no one within immediate earshot she added, "Double shit!"

When had this happened? When did Judson decide to come along? They would be in his private plane, to ensure no delays. He wouldn't stand for the same stalling tactics the others would have likely sustained.

She sent a text to Judson. *"Am at airport. Which terminal are you arriving at?"* She paced as she waited.

Slipping into a quiet area, she phoned Reece. He didn't answer, and she feared he might not retrieve the message in a timely manner, if she left one. She would just have to try him again in a minute.

Amanda decided to ask someone where the incoming private flights would land and deplane. At that moment she caught a glimpse of Judson, in his usual black attire, headed directly for her. Her phone pinged, signaling a message. She clicked on it as she headed toward Judson. *"Have landed and am in security. Meet us in domestic arrivals."*

Judson extended one hand for a quick shake. "Good to see you, Lassiter. I was beginning to get worried."

"Worried, sir? Why?" She immediately fell into step with him, nearly ignoring the rest of the team. All they received from her was a slight nod.

"I didn't hear back from you last night. I'm used to having a quick response to messages and receiving none at all made me fear for your safety." He raised one eyebrow.

"I'm sorry, sir. There are a few things you should know. I'll fill you in on the way to Dixie." She wondered how much to tell him. She hadn't even thought about it or how she would explain being with Reece in the garage of his apartment building. But how could she disclose what he needed to know about Pamela and the stolen funds if she didn't?

"Will it change the outcome of this deal?" he asked bluntly.

"No, sir, but—"

"Then I don't need to know about it today," he interrupted.

"But you do, I'm afraid," she continued.

"No, Lassiter. I don't." He turned away from her. "Sloan, when we get to Dixie, debrief Lassiter while I pay the Jordans a personal visit."

Amanda could hear the glee in his voice. It was ego on steroids. If what Roger had told her was true, Judson had waited for this moment for a long time. And today—thanks to her—he was going to get the chance to do what he had tried to so many years ago but, thanks to her father, couldn't.

Her phone buzzed, and she saw it was Reece's number. Hitting the silence button, she continued walking, ignoring the call. Judson didn't even react, obviously used to people hitting the silencer in his presence.

She felt the sweat beading on her forehead. Her entire face felt like it had been seared between the golden hot plates of a hair iron.

"Mr. Matheney," she said trying to recapture his attention. "We'll need to get another car. I'm afraid my rental isn't big enough to accommodate all of us and the luggage."

He gave her a look that made her feel idiotic and dangled a key in front of her. His tone was chastising. "I hadn't assumed it would. Mary took care of it when I called her yesterday with the news I had decided to come along."

Amanda had learned to decipher his meanings and moods through his communication style. He was sending her the message that she had let him down by not receiving and promptly answering his message the instant it was left.

And his assistant Mary, one of the few people he routinely called by their first names, had swooped in and saved the day. Amanda wished, in that moment, she could have choked her.

"Great," she answered, chewing her bottom lip. Her stomach growled and ached. She felt as if she might get sick any minute.

If she didn't get in touch with Reece, he wouldn't have a chance to get his money back. "Shall we stop for coffee?"

"No, Lassiter. We had coffee on the flight." Judson looked at her with a glint of suspicion.

"Great," she repeated, knowing after the singular word came out that it made her sound nervous.

Amanda saw the sign for the restrooms pointing ahead and knew it was her last chance to call Reece before the team swarmed on him and his company. "I need to use the restroom—it's just ahead—and then we'll get started."

Judson shuffled his feet to a halt. He dropped his chin, and Amanda didn't wait for the scowl she knew would be following. She raced off to the restroom, leaving the others staring a hole in her back.

As soon as she cleared the door she began to dial. It rang only once before Reece answered.

"Good morning, beautiful. Sorry I—"

"No time for that. Listen. Judson is here. He came with the team. I won't be able to stall."

"What? You're breaking up. Can you find a better signal?"

"No. Listen." Her heart was beating louder than her own voice in her ears. "Get out of there now. Go to the bank and wait at the drive-through."

"Yeah. I'm going to the bank in about an hour," he said too loudly into the phone. Apparently his inability to hear her made him think he also needed to speak up.

"No! Listen..." A creak as the door opened caused Amanda to peek under the stall doors. The shoes didn't resemble those of Lilly, the other woman in her group. "Go now."

"Go now? Why would I...?"

"For God's sake, don't argue. Just do it. Judson Matheney is here and I have to go."

"Did I hear you correctly? It sounded like you said Judson Matheney was there with you." His voice had lost its happy edge and now sounded drab.

"Yes! Go!" The door creaked open again, and she snapped the phone shut, ran her hand across the motion detector that would flush the toilet automatically, and pushed through the stall door. She washed her hands and splashed a little cool water on her face.

Amanda rejoined the annoyed group who had managed to rise in the middle of the night, board a plane with their luggage, and get through the airport security with professional aplomb, while she was thrown together like an old dish rag, wrung out and past its prime.

She forced a confident smile. "Ready?" she asked.

"More than," Judson answered.

Amanda retrieved her rental and managed to get to the curb at almost the same time as her colleagues. The team divided their luggage among the two trunks and then they chose vehicles before pulling away in the two-car convoy to Dixie Millwork.

She tried to think of a more roundabout way to get to Dixie from the airport but didn't know the area well enough. And as she was the lead driver she needed to be able to give signals far enough in advance to alert the second car. Could she lose them on purpose; then circle back?

Judson was riding in her car.

He had said something and she hadn't heard it. *Damnation!* "Would you mind repeating?" she asked.

He raised one eyebrow and frowned.

"I was watching for the other vehicle," she explained. "I don't want to lose Sloan. And since I have spent all of my time at the millwork, well, I haven't learned the roads terribly well should we get lost."

Judson's memory was, unfortunately, excellent. "What happened to the job site outing? And where were you this weekend? If you were in your hotel, you certainly weren't answering your phone."

"Well, sir, that brings us to the subject I need to discuss with you."

"Be quick about it. If my memory serves we are not very far from Dixie."

His warning shot through her, reverberating inside like sound waves. "Yes. Right." She chewed her lip.

"I find its best to just spit it out when I have something to say."

Lilly had chosen to ride with them. She sat perfectly quiet in the back seat. In fact, it was easy to just forget she was even there.

"There is a problem at Dixie. There are missing funds in a subsidiary owned by the company." She took a deep breath and looked at him.

He gave a half-smile. "Go on."

"Well…" *Why is he smiling?* "A large amount of money was missing from J & S Consulting and the wife of the father, Roger Jordan, appears to be the culprit."

"Is that what is bothering you? Did you think I wouldn't know about that?" He turned his palms over and surveyed his fingernails, grinning largely. "But I believe it is his son who signed the withdrawals."

"No. It wasn't Reece," she said too quickly.

Judson leaned back in the seat and tilted his chin forward. "Reece? Just 'Reece'? Already on a first name basis? And *in his court*?"

"I…I…" She what? How would she answer that?

"And now stammering and defensive. I see."

Amanda glanced up into the rearview mirror. Two eyeballs, the size of the lollipops she remembered chewing on all day as a child, glared at her from the back seat. When their gazes locked Lilly immediately lowered hers and pretended to be engrossed in a document from a file.

Amanda looked further back and caught sight of

Mark Sloan's vehicle being stopped by a red light. "We've got to slow up for Mark," she said in a shaky voice. Other vehicles zoomed around them.

"Come on...out with it, Lassiter," Judson demanded. "Exactly what have you been up to down here?"

Chapter 23

Reece stood for a moment longer than he should have waiting for more conversation with Amanda. He was stunned by her strange comments. Did she say Judson Matheney had decided to join the team? If so, that meant stalling wouldn't be possible. Amanda might have the confidence to push around a team of pencil pushers on the same payroll as she, but would never be able to pull off that kind of antic with the master bluffer Judson Matheney.

And if what he thought he heard was correct, it meant he had no time and she had sacrificed her position to make the call to him. No wonder she hadn't answered when he called her. She was probably standing next to Matheney.

There was one thing for sure. He had to get out of the office and to the bank. If he made the transfer early enough, maybe he could beat the clock. Only one way to know. He raced out of the office and headed for the bank.

There was a coffee shop next door, the ubiquitous kind with the green swirly logo. He didn't care for the coffee—it always tasted a little burnt to him—but he could see the bank and knew the drive-through window opened half an hour earlier. He ordered a coffee straight up, refusing to use the terminology coffee-holics accepted as cute, and a cinnamon roll.

Reece sat down at a table in full view of the bank. The next hour clicked by as slowly as cold butter going through a sieve. He nibbled at the cinnamon roll, swigged the coffee, and resisted the urge to make a face. Reece got a refill, looked at his watch, and frowned.

He wasn't used to waiting. People usually did the waiting for him, people like Vernella. *Oh God,* he thought, *I have to warn her.*

Hurriedly, he clicked her on speed dial number four. Only his dad, his dad's wife, and the shop manager ranked higher than Vernie.

"Yeah, Vernie here," she said in a gruff early-morning voice.

"Vernie, I need you," he said.

"Where and when?"

He smiled. Maybe the stunt that hadn't worked with Amanda would actually stall Matheney long enough for him to get his proceeds back.

****

"Up to? That's a little strong? I've been up to the task you sent me to complete," Amanda said, surprised at her sudden surge of courage. Eyeballs popped back up from the back seat in her rearview mirror.

Judson shook his head. "Don't try to bullshit the master steer keeper." A sneer drew his lip toward his nose.

"I would never try to 'bullshit' you, sir. I have always been a company woman. Only this time, there is more going on than meets the eye." She grasped the steering wheel with shaking hands, thankful to be driving since they kept the tremble from showing.

"This time?" He narrowed his eyes, focusing on

her face.

She looked behind her. There was no sign of Sloan's car.

"I've lost Sloan."

Judson hit the dash with the palm of his hand. "I don't give a damn about Sloan! I care about this acquisition. You have no idea how important it is to me."

"No sir. I believe I know *exactly* how important it is." She had lost the desire to care about her job. She was tired. She was confused. And the more he talked, the more certain she was that he had known about her family's ties to the Jordans and Dixie Millwork, had known and purposefully kept it from her.

"I don't think I appreciate your attitude," he said, grinding his teeth.

"I'm sorry, but I can't do anything about that." She pulled over to the edge of the tree-lined street, looking back for the lost car. "I can tell you that a lot of strange things are going on down here, and they all lead back to some long-ago feud between you and Roger Jordan. And I can also tell you that I've never seen happier employees in my life, so obviously the Jordans are doing something right."

"I can see you have been brain-washed. I sent you down here to see what you were made of, and you have shown me."

"No, sir. You sent me down here to accomplish what my father prevented you from doing many years ago!" *Did I just shout at Judson?*

He turned red from the top of his head to the tips of his fingers, one of which he pointed at her. "You knew? You knew about the Simmons connection and didn't tell me?"

"You knew about my father and didn't tell me!"

The door to the back seat opened. "I think I'm going to be sick," Lilly said as she jumped out of the vehicle and ran for the shrubs beneath the willowy trees.

Amanda's phone buzzed indicating an incoming text. She glanced down. "It's Sloan. He says he has us in his sights, and we can merge back into traffic."

"We can't leave her here," Judson said, motioning to the bushes as if Amanda would have even considered it.

Though, for a moment, she thought he might have in his overwhelming desire to feed his ego at the Jordans' expense.

She gave him a quick questioning glance before texting back: *sick passenger in bushes, stay behind me.* A set of flashers flickered behind her as Sloan pulled the car to the side of the road.

"How did you find out about Roger Jordan's wife being behind the embezzlement?" Judson asked, suspicion and surprise coloring his question.

"She's been arrested," Amanda answered simply, wondering how many details to share.

Judson's eyes popped, a rare expression. She couldn't remember if she had ever seen him surprised before. He always seemed to be one step ahead of everybody, as he had demonstrated when he dangled the key to the extra rental car in front of her.

"Arrested?" he shouted. "When?"

"This weekend. If you had given me a chance, I would have explained. I was attacked in a parking garage, and taken to the police station as a witness to her confession."

"She admitted it? And you were there?"

Amanda's mouth flew open. He had totally disregarded the part where she was assaulted in the garage. He had just skipped over it—another mundane detail—not even bothering to ask if she had sustained injuries. Anger built. It boiled and rolled and gathered energy as she glared at her boss.

"Well," he asked, "yes or no?"

She gripped the steering wheel with both hands, dropping her head to her chest to take deep breaths. Rage threatened to overtake her sensibilities.

The car door opened and Amanda's head shot up as Lilly, looking pale, quietly resumed her seat in the back. "Sorry," she whispered. "The flight must have aggravated my inner ear problems." Her voice faded away.

Amanda cranked the car and gave a signal before pulling back into traffic. "Are you all right now?" she asked the sick woman. "Do I need to find a drug store for you?" She glanced into the rearview mirror to make eye contact with her.

"No. I'm fine. Thank you for asking."

"It's only right that the people you work with, *and for*, should care about your well-being," she said in a biting tone. "It wouldn't occur to me *not* to ask." She looked at Judson.

"Are you trying to imply something, Lassiter?" he asked harshly.

"I'm fine too. Thank you for asking about me after I told you I had been pounced on in a garage."

"I don't like your tone. If it weren't evident you were okay, I might have asked. Seeing as you are perfectly fine, there seemed no need to waste time on the obvious."

"You faced physical danger?" Lilly asked. "When? Who? What happened? Did you get hurt?"

Amanda raised a hand and then pointed it at Judson. "See? *That* is the natural reaction."

Judson jerked his jaw and set his mouth into a thin line. It was an indication of a bad mood. Yet, for the first time since she had come into his employment, Amanda didn't care. She glanced back into the rearview mirror catching the look of surprise in Lilly's eyes.

"My assailant intended to steal from me the purse of a woman who had been embezzling funds from the subsidiary company Mr. Matheney has just acquired. I managed to thwart the mugging attempt, and he was badly injured by his own gun."

"He had a gun?" Lilly's eyes got even wider. "I'm not sure I like it down here."

Amanda smiled in spite of herself. "Yeah, it is a little different."

Judson appeared to be fuming in the seat beside of her. Obviously, this wasn't turning out as he had imagined. Amanda glanced at the dashboard clock. It was eight thirty-seven. Great! Reece should be at the bank retrieving his money. She relaxed a little.

"So is this going to interfere with my plans for Dixie?" Judson spat.

"Most likely. I'd say accounts are being frozen as we speak, while the police investigate."

"Luckily, I have already taken care of that." A sinister grin played on his face.

"What? How?" Panic built again, the reprieve short-lived.

"As of close of business Friday evening, all accounts associated with Dixie Millwork have been transferred into a new account under Builders Tech. And I was happy with the balances. So *if* there was embezzlement, it was reversed."

Check-mate. Her heart sank. Reece was probably getting the bad news right now. Judson knew about Pamela, and he had watched the account, assuming the signature she had forged would force Reece into replenishing the account with the funds paid to him by Judson. Roger and Reece would be ruined. All of their employees would be jobless.

"And I have *you* to thank," Judson said suddenly. "Your wisdom on this project has proved to be brilliant, in spite of your sudden sullenness and grumpy attitude. I'll attribute it to the aftermath of the little scuffle in the garage and will overlook it, just this once," he warned.

"That's very magnanimous of you," she retorted.

"Yes, I thought so too."

They were nearing Dixie, and Amanda's heart felt like it was breaking. Her father was probably looking down on her and shaking his head. It was soul-wrenching.

"Why *did* you send me on this project?" she asked.

"What?" Judson asked, clearly not paying attention to her. She repeated the question and he grinned.

"Poetic justice," he whispered, his words barely audible. He turned toward her, his black eyes sparkling with renewed vigor. "And you learned a lot, didn't you?"

"Yes sir, I did." It wasn't a lie. She had learned more than she could have ever imagined, and she would never be the same. "But did I hear you say 'poetic justice'?"

"A slip, I assure you."

"You knew before you hired me, didn't you? You planned for this day during my entire employment with your company."

Dixie Millwork loomed ahead. She felt like she was marching toward doom—the kind that left destruction in its wake and people behind to mourn their shattered lives. And she was the weapon that had been used against them.

Judson's grin looked sinister, growing as a cancer across his face. "Have you never played chess?" he asked.

Chapter 24

Amanda's mind raced back to the chessboard in Judson's office. It always looked as if a game was in progress, yet she had never seen a single person at the small table upon which it rested. "Yes sir, I have."

"Then you understand that the king can be fallen by a pawn if properly placed."

"I was just a pawn," she answered, feeling as sick as the quiet woman in the back seat. Amanda merged into the turning lane, still driving to her doom.

"Business is a game of chess, Lassiter. Don't forget that. It isn't philanthropy. It isn't charity, or a community of people who care about each other."

"Yet you built us a gym and a daycare and…"

She heard Roger's voice in her head. "It wasn't because you had a desire to keep your employees happy; it was to prevent us from networking with anybody outside of Builders Tech and to keep us at the office for longer hours."

"I knew you would understand, Lassiter. I'm proud of your work on this case, prouder than you can ever know." He rubbed his hands together as they pulled into the parking lot. "Park there." He motioned toward the space reserved for Reece.

She did as he asked, though she felt her heart drop. At least Reece would see the car and know Judson Matheney had arrived.

Judson stretched after exiting the car. Amanda helped Lilly from the rear of the vehicle. She still looked a little pale and shaky.

"I'm sorry," Amanda whispered, knowing her aggressiveness with Judson had instigated much of the woman's attack of nerves.

The second car wheeled in and parked. Well-dressed bodies emerged. They could have been posing for a photo shoot for a business chronicle, expensive dark suits, budget-breaking shoes—even on the men— gelled and tamed hair, soft hands, starched white shirts with collars that stood up by themselves.

Amanda heard Reece's truck even before she saw it. She gathered the team and suggested they all start with an introduction to the company's receptionist. She held the front door as they invaded the small office, but she didn't enter with them.

****

Reece started to wheel into the space he had been parking in for thirty years. He saw the small rental just in time, and his tires barked as he hit the brakes. *They're here. Thank God my father isn't. This would kill him.*

Anger coursed through his veins. He knew he had to try to control it or else he might end up in the cell next to Pamela's. That son-of-a-bitch Matheney had already closed the accounts and transferred them to another under his own name. Reece had just forfeited every dime of the funds he might have lived on, might have used as seed money to start another company. Now where would he go—and more importantly— where would his employees go?

He saw her then. Amanda stood alone at the

entrance. He wondered why she wasn't with the rest of her colleagues. Part of him was glad to see her there, another part worried about why she was alone at the door. And another tiny part, a part Reece refused to acknowledge, wanted to assign a bit of blame to her.

If she had just waited…if she hadn't been so quick…No! He wouldn't let himself go there. He couldn't. She held his heart. She intrigued and excited him. And if she wasn't with the rest of the goons, then it signaled that maybe he meant something to her as well.

He walked quickly to her, watching as her hands grasped onto themselves, the left swallowing the right. The pain of what was about to happen showed on her face. Reece didn't even stop to think. He grabbed her into his arms and embraced her as tightly as he could.

"He knew," she whispered in a shaky voice. "He knew who I was all along. That reprehensible jackass had the gall to call it 'poetic justice.'"

"It's okay," he assured her.

"And he took your money already." She started trembling, and he ran his hands along her back, stroking her spine.

"I know that, too."

"You must…hate me." She heaved against him, crying.

"Shh…please don't. I feel bad enough already for what I've put you through."

She pulled back, the tears stopping. "What *you've* put me through?"

"This is all my fault. I should have been on top of it. I should have—"

She interrupted. "No, don't you see? He planned

this from the first moment I was hired. This is my fault. If it hadn't been for me then maybe…"

"Maybe what? Maybe he would have given up? I thought you said you knew Judson Matheny. He would have found someone else and some other way, and you know it." He peeled her off of his chest. "Look at me."

She looked up with sorrowful eyes.

"None of this is your fault." He kissed her on the forehead and she grabbed him tightly.

"What the hell?" Judson appeared in the doorway. "Get your hands off my employee!" he demanded of Reece. "Or I'll have you arrested this instant."

"I am no longer your employee," Amanda said. "I quit."

"Are you sure you want to do that?" Reece asked.

Her tears turned to certainty and self-confidence. "I've never been surer of anything."

"Then you are making the biggest mistake of your life," Judson sneered.

"Maybe. Maybe not. We'll see, won't we?"

Vernella appeared in the doorway. "He's ordered us all out of the building," she said to Reece.

"That's okay, Vernie. Initiate plan B immediately," Reece said. She broke into the Cheshire grin that sparked a bit of hope in Amanda's heart.

Judson glared at Amanda. "And you?"

She ripped the lanyard from her neck and handed it to Judson. "There is something I want from Reece's office."

"Get it now. There won't be another chance," he glowered.

"Come on," she said to Reece.

"No, he stays here. This man is not permitted back

on the premises."

"I have personal belongings in there," Reece snarled, his jaw clenching.

"We'll box them up and send them out to you."

Amanda raced off to Reece's office while the two men faced off on the front stoop. She returned with the scrapbook which Judson insisted on inspecting before he would release it. He stopped at the picture of her father and smiled.

"Checkmate," he whispered before snapping the album shut and handing it to Amanda. "You'll be paid through today. Just so you know; I was done with you after this job anyway. You served your purpose well, though"—he winked—"and are saving me the nice severance package I would have awarded you when I fired you." He stalked off through the door.

Reece burned with fury. His fist clenched and opened and clenched again. He wanted to knock the cockiness out of the man who was ruining the lives of everyone he cared about.

"Come on," he said. "We've got to get to the valley."

"Jordan's Valley?" she asked.

He nodded. "Yes, they'll be arriving shortly."

Chapter 25

The cars and trucks wheeled into the tree-lined driveway that ended in the valley—Jordan's Valley—and up to the perch where Reece's shell of a lodge stood as strong and fierce as its owner.

The bales of straw intended to cover the areas where he would have the lawn reseeded were being lined up across the room and covered in tarps for use as benches. Sawhorses formed the framework with a solid wooden door laid across to become a table.

"Welcome, welcome all," Reece greeted them cheerfully, calling them by name as they entered the house that few had seen the inside of.

Reece asked Amanda to watch from the alcove, hidden from view so as not to alarm the others. He didn't know how receptive they would be to her presence at their short meeting. They had been through a rough day, each receiving a slip they would take to the local unemployment office in order to begin the meager draw that would hopefully last long enough for Reece's plan to materialize.

"Thank you for coming, especially on such short notice. I just figure it's time to start something new. I'm hoping you will feel free to add any of your ideas to mine."

They cheered, sending a clear message they would go with him into whatever adventure he could imagine.

The millwork manager spoke up. "I think I speak for everyone when I say we are with you, Reece. You have always been a good boss and treated us fairly and with respect. I'm not even sure this Builders Tech conglomerate even sees us as human beings."

Reece looked about the room, doing a mental inventory on who was present and who was yet to arrive. When he was satisfied the majority was accounted for, he gave a short announcement. "I'm sure you know this isn't how I expected this to go. There is a non-compete order in the buy-out contract, so I can't put a new millwork company in my name or have anything official to do with it for at least seven years. But, I want you to know that if I can find the backing and the building, I'll make something happen."

Energy sparked among the group. Reece knew they could expect him to be up to something and he was confident they would desire to be part of it.

"You should draw unemployment while I try to get another venture going. And for those of you who find employment elsewhere, accept it. I don't know how long it will take me to acquire enough loans and investors to get this thing off the ground."

His eyes misted over as he said, "And I wish to apologize. You trusted me, and I let you down. I'm truly sorry."

Choruses of "it's not your fault," and "we don't blame you," and "count me in whatever you start," began to waft around the cavernous room.

"You will hear from me through Vernie. It wouldn't surprise me if my phone lines have been bugged, and I'm being followed." He pointed to Vernie and she gave a little wave. "So I'll get information to her, and she will relay it to you. Any messages you wish to get to me, should also go through her."

Vernie's joy at her newfound importance caused him to smile. Reece grinned one of the few smiles he had found in the course of the day. She would be the sole source of information flowing to and from him to the rest of the group, and she couldn't hide the happiness it brought her.

"Okay?"

They cheered.

"Get some snacks and try not to worry. We'll network and see if we can find some temporary jobs for you. One or two of our contacts often has summer employment available for extra hands since it's the peak building season. Getting a crack at my best hands would delight them."

****

Amanda watched the positively medieval-looking meeting going on. Reece could have been a general in the army or a knight in King Arthur's court. *No,* she corrected, *he would have been the King himself.*

She had never seen a man more attuned to the needs of his employees. They needed a pep talk after their abrupt firing. They needed to know there was hope for their families and that someone still had their best interest at heart.

Reece had given them all of that. He had provided optimism, peace, reassurance, and confidence in their fine skills. He made them out to be the most desired work force in the south.

Her heart ached as she felt the sting of how she had treated them. She had never had the privilege to work for someone like Reece. She didn't know employers could lead without being taskmasters. Reece's employees *wanted* to work for him. They would follow him anywhere.

Amanda couldn't help comparing him to Judson, who cared about nothing outside of his own ego and pride. The words he had spoken to her had been humiliating. The fact that he had known about her father and kept that information from her just to use as a weapon against the very people Bill Simmons had worked to protect made her nauseous.

It dawned on her that she was in the same shoes as all of the people from Dixie. She had no job either. She began to shake. What on earth was she going to do? Who would hire her after hearing of her traitorous behavior? And they *would* hear of it. Judson would eke revenge on her, she could be sure of it.

Oh God, what have I done to us all?

Chapter 26

When the tail lights from the last car to leave—Vernie's, of course—disappeared into the wooded drive, Reece called out for Amanda. He respected and understood her need to keep out of view. His former employees likely attributed her arrival last week to their occupation's demise.

Once enough time had passed and they realized she was no longer in Judson's employment, he felt sure he could convince them she'd meant no harm and could be trusted. Until then, having her lie low was the best approach.

"Amanda," he called, waiting for a response. "Amanda, where are you?"

Lights were sparse in the house. The ones in existence were temporary and more or less bare bulbs dangling from sockets. Fixtures were more of a decorative issue and he hadn't reached that stage yet.

"Amanda, they're all gone. You can come out."

He listened. Sniffling. Was she crying? *Of course she is, idiot,* he chastised himself. He felt a bit like crying himself. He followed the sounds around the corner wall that would eventually lead to a bathroom. The linen closet had been roughed in, and he could see her shoes sticking out of the recess in the wall.

She had her head buried in her knees, sobbing.

"Oh, Amanda," he sighed, feeling his heart

breaking. "Come here."

She didn't respond, and he couldn't take it. How much pain had he caused everyone? He straddled her feet and reached into the opening. Clamping his hands onto her waist, he lifted her out and into his arms.

"I'm...so...sorry..." She hiccoughed.

"You have nothing to be sorry for," he soothed.

"It's all...my...fault."

"You stop that. It isn't your fault. It's Matheney's and Pamela's faults. At least she will be paying for her part in this."

"You've...lost your company, your...employees, your...proceeds...everything."

"Not everything. I still have you." Reece took her tear-stained face in his hands. He kissed her eyes, her nose, her cheeks. The fire that caught in his belly tore through him as she responded to his kisses in spite of the carnage that had become their lives.

"I don't...have...anything...either," she said.

"You have me," he responded. He lifted her up and carried her to the room with the straw bales. He sat her down upon one as he slid the others around the room until they met, forming a makeshift bed of sorts.

"Do I *have* you?" she asked.

"If you want me. Although I must admit, I'm not much of a catch right now—middle-aged, jobless, broke."

"Sounds a bit like me," she said wistfully.

"You're not broke," he said. "Remember the bonds."

She leapt up from the straw bale, swiping at her face. "Oh my God, Reece! Do you know what this means?"

"That you are too good for me? I suspected it from the start." He was teasing, but her eyes had grown large and the tears had ceased.

"No silly. *I* can fund the new company. I can be your backer. It's perfect really, when you think about it."

"Partners? You and me?"

"Why not? We'd make a pretty good team, don't you think?" She was grinning from ear to ear. "Now *there's* some poetic justice!"

His answer was to take her back into his arms and shower her with more kisses. How could he think when his veins pulsed with the desire to melt into her?

She responded, pressing her body into him. She no longer resisted his affection. In fact, she seemed to crave him as much as he craved her, returning his kisses with full abandon. Amanda dropped her suit coat to the floor, and he wondered if it had ever been treated so shabbily before.

A thunderous rush interrupted his thoughts as her hand dipped into his jeans. With deft agility she sent him reeling while she offered smooth strokes over him. Reece fumbled with her skirt, unbuttoning the waistband and letting it join the jacket. Her touch seemed to slice all the way through his flesh and into his heart.

She was light as air, and he lifted her up, putting her gently upon one of the bales before tugging his shirt over his head. Forgetting the buttons, he nearly got his head stuck.

Though she giggled at his eagerness, she seemed to match his desire, removing her blouse and bra in one yank.

Reece loved the sight of her, naked and ready for him. He especially enjoyed the expression of lust in her eyes and the smokiness of her voice. He wanted to stoke it and slipped his fingertips along her thigh and upward into the cleft that arched to meet his touch.

She trembled and shook from his gentle strokes. A series of breath intakes and a shudder allowed him to know he had achieved the desired effect. He pushed her to the center of the bale and climbed atop with her.

Amanda looked into his eyes while dropping her legs apart, making it easy for him to find her and sink inside. She hooked her legs around his waist and arched upward to meet his thrusts. He couldn't stop the sudden eruption that tore through him and into her. It was the quickest he had ever released, and if she hadn't already achieved satisfaction before he entered her, he would have been embarrassed. Yet, as he pressed against her for the final pulse, she began to quiver and shake and push upward into his hips. He met her action with a smile.

"Twice?" he asked.

"Shut up." She laughed as she went limp beneath him.

****

Amanda's telephone buzzed. She reached for the jacket on the floor and fished the phone from its pocket.

"Judson changed his mind?" Reece asked.

"No, it's the hotel. They need a different credit card if I intend to stay past tomorrow at eleven a.m."

"Judson's having you evicted?"

"Appears to be the case." She glanced over at him with none of the anger over the situation she would have expected to feel under those circumstances.

"You can stay with me," he said, running a hand along her arm.

"Have you forgotten? I have my own house." She smiled. It was true. She could go to Wilkesboro and stay at her grandparents' house.

"That's too far," he exclaimed.

"You could come with me. Now more than ever it is imperative we find every bond, stock, and wad of cash those two wonderful, crazy old people left for me to discover."

"That's tempting," he teased. "You and me, all alone, working side by side. Do you think you could handle that?" His bright eyes shone with merriment.

"Better than I can handle these straw bales." Even covered in a canvas drop cloth the occasional blunt hay end worked through to irritate her flesh.

Amanda heard dread creep into his voice. "First we need to talk to my dad. I haven't told him yet about the J & S account."

"He's going to be devastated." She shook her head.

Reece reached for her chin, pulling it up from its downward descent. "You have nothing to hang your head about. In fact, he's going to jump with joy when he finds out another Simmons is on board with our latest project."

"You think so?"

"I *know* so. Besides"—he tossed her clothes over to her—"he's best at *starting* new ventures. Maintaining them is where he gets a bit side-tracked."

****

It was late when they left the city limits. Reece noticed the closer they got to Simmons Point, the more withdrawn Amanda became.

"Penny for your thoughts," he offered quietly in the darkness of the car. The only light apart from the stars was that of the dashboard's glow and the headlights against the street reflectors.

She sounded dreamy, her voice soft and wistful. "This all seems so odd. I feel as though I am going to wake up and find out it was all a dream."

"Do you want it to be a dream?"

"Yes."

"You do?"

"Parts of it. The parts I could undo."

"Life doesn't work that way. If you like where you are, you have to appreciate how you got there."

She thought about it; at least, he thought she was thinking about it. She could have been regretting their time together and wishing she had joined Judson in throwing everyone out of Dixie. *No...stop it,* he commanded himself. *You're being totally irrational.*

"Do you wish you had chosen Judson and stayed on board with his company?" He asked it softly, aware he might not like the answer.

She turned toward him, staring at his profile. His peripheral vision could see her eyes on him. Reece kept his eyes firmly on the street ahead.

"How can you ask me that, Reece? I know you lost your company and your money, but I have just found out the employer I trusted and gave one hundred percent of my life to, admitted to using me as a pawn on his damned chess board. I was the weapon he used to hurt you."

He could see her head shaking back and forth. Reece took a deep breath. He reached over and lifted her hand to his lips.

They were almost to his dad's. "No regrets, Mandy," he whispered.

Her hand slipped slowly from his, as though the life had just been drained out of it. "What did you call me?"

"It just slipped out. I'm sorry if you don't want to be called Mandy...I won't..."

"No. That's not it."

He whipped the car through the gate and down along the driveway. When he had pulled to a stop, he reached for her.

"Tell me what it is that is bothering you. Or we'll sit here all night."

She was looking at him oddly, as though she had seen a ghost. "I don't have many memories of words of wisdom from my father. But he *always* called me Mandy. The way you said that reminded me of him so much it could have been his voice talking to me across the boundary where life meets death."

Reece felt a little shaky too. He wasn't at all sure why he had called her Mandy instead of Amanda, nor why he had used that phrase. His dad had referred to her that way, but Reece never had.

They sat there, each in awe of what might have just happened. Both jumped at the sound of knocking on the window.

"You two just gonna sit out here all night?" Roger asked.

"Come on," Reece said, coming to his senses. "Let's go inside."

Chapter 27

Roger didn't take the news well. He hated being bested by Judson Matheney. "So he won after all," he said with defeat in his voice.

"No, not yet. Although, it is a temporary setback." Amanda felt she was the right one to speak for Judson. She knew him better than anyone else in the room. "Judson will crow for a while, and he may be a little cocky for a few days, but another deal will come along and a new chessboard will replace this one."

"Chessboard?" Roger pointed to her while speaking to Reece. "What the hell is she talkin' about?"

Amanda filled him in on the chessboard Judson had mentally labeled "Dixie" and how she had been one of his pawns from the first day she was hired. When she told him what Judson had said about being finished with her anyway, Roger ground his teeth and reached for the bourbon.

"Better make it three glasses," Reece said and rolled two more along the table toward his father.

After swigging back a few sips, Amanda punched Reece. "Now…tell him the good news."

"About the new company?" Reece asked.

"And the new partner," she answered.

"Have you two lost your minds? What in hell are you talkin' 'bout?" Roger looked from one to the other of them.

"Dad, you had better get ready. This little spitfire is funding our next operation. We're going to be partners in a new business. I've already met with our old employees. Now we just need a building and some trucks."

Roger thought for a minute and then grinned hugely. "What's wrong with using the building we had?"

"Well, we can't, Dad. It belongs to Builders Tech."

"Didn't you say he was going to sell it?"

Amanda slapped the table. "I see where you're going with this. We can buy it from them. We just need a phantom buyer to make the purchase under a different identity."

Roger pointed his thumb at Amanda. "Son, this one's a keeper!"

"You two amaze me," Reece chuckled.

"But who can we get to make the purchase?"

****

"You're kidding," Reece responded when Amanda made the best suggestion she could think of.

"Think about it before you say no," she begged. "What does he have to lose and if he cooperates, what can he gain?"

"Are you suddenly feeling bad for the man with one leg?" Roger asked.

"Yeah. What makes you think he can be trusted?" Reece asked. "He's already taken one crack at my skull." He rubbed the knot that still popped from his head.

"He's rolled over on Pamela and Randall for immunity against our charges. And losing a limb is punishment enough I suspect. But mainly he admitted to his part in all of this for money. He's broke." Roger sounded sure of himself.

"So he should be willing to take the job we're offering?" Amanda asked, not knowing him as the two Jordans did.

"What's he got to lose? I doubt anyone else will be offering him employment any time soon."

"It does sound good when you say it like that," Reece agreed. "But what would he say he wanted the building for? Judson would be suspicious of someone without a purpose. And that is one big warehouse with lots of docks and tall ceilings for forklifts and the like. Dad, do you know anything about his past? What did he used to do before he ran through with his family's inheritance?"

"I think he might have done some kind of mechanical work. I got him to spruce up that old boat and make a few repairs. John and Timothy both said he'd done work for the Yacht Club." Roger rubbed his chin.

"Well, that's it then, isn't it?" Reece said brightly.

"What's *it*?" Roger and Amanda shot him a look simultaneously.

"Boats!" He burst into laughter. "This crazy plan just might work. Ted Logan can say he's using an inheritance to start a boat repair and storage business. He might even talk old Judson into selling him the forklifts, air guns, and some of the other tools."

"It's brilliant!" Amanda laughed, joining in the gaiety of the moment.

Roger poured three shots of bourbon in the glasses and they raised them to toast. "Here's to Jordan & Simmons," he declared.

"That name belongs to Judson now," Reece reminded him, sending a pall over the happy threesome.

"Well then, Simmons & Jordan," Roger said. All three laughed, clacking thick whiskey glasses together over the center of the table.

"I'm actually excited about this," Amanda admitted.

Roger turned serious. He took her hand and stared intently into her eyes. "I couldn't be prouder of a daughter of my own. You've really come through for us, Mandy." Tears welled up in his eyes. "Finding out about Pamela, nearly losing my son to her scheming, losing my life's work..." He faltered for a moment, choking back tears.

Reece rubbed Amanda's back as she sat with her hand in Roger's.

After a minute his dad swallowed hard and patted her hand with his other one. "Well, you've made it bearable. Your generosity will never be forgotten. I needed this. I needed something to be hopeful for once again." He patted her hand and then released it.

"I think we all needed something to cheer us and throw our energy into," she replied. "I know I do."

"Come on, let's head upstairs. We've got a lot to do tomorrow." Reece stood and held a hand out to her.

"Yes, starting with collecting my things from the hotel and returning the rental car."

"I've got to get to bed, too," Roger said. "I'll need to get my attorney on the phone bright and early. I'll get him to handle the legally binding contracts for our dear boat repairer. That way, they'll be ready the instant we get him to agree, assuming my lawyer doesn't think the District Attorney will have an issue with this." He winked and shuffled off in what Amanda imagined was the direction of his bedroom.

****

Roger was already gone when Amanda and Reece padded down to the kitchen the following morning. Of course they had lingered in bed a little longer than they should have, touching, whetting appetites, and then setting about satiating those hungers that only each other could satisfy.

Reece took the note off of the refrigerator. "Gone to see Mitch. Breakfast in the microwave," he read from the slip of paper.

Amanda opened the microwave's door and pulled out a plate with wax paper-wrapped biscuits with thick slices of country ham layered between the soft fluffy centers. The aromas took Amanda right back to her childhood.

"All I need is a bowl of cooked apples and I'm yours," she crooned.

"Cooked apples?" He fished through the refrigerator, pulling out a bowl of partially firm apple slices that had been fried in butter. "How did you know that was one of Dad's favorites? A minute in the microwave and they'll be perfect," he said.

"I think I'm in love." Amanda leaned over the bowl of warm apples with their scent of cinnamon and brown sugar.

"If only I could turn myself into a bowl of apples," Reece said, eyeing the subject of her desire. He flipped on the coffee, and they settled in for a fabulous country breakfast before their drive into the city.

It didn't take long to clear out the hotel room and even less time to return the car.

"You can drive the convertible," Reece said.

"Are you sure? I mean, you just got it back from Pamela."

"Which shows you how often I drive it. Besides, I've seen your driving. I totally trust you."

"All right. But as soon as my Chicago condo sells, I'll purchase something for myself."

"You don't have a car there?" He said it with such surprise that it astounded her.

"Why would I need one? I can get a cab every day for less than I would pay for parking. It's just an expense I chose not to make."

"Have you listed your place already?"

"Of course not. I only knew yesterday that I wasn't going back."

They laughed and turned the car north, heading for Wilkesboro and her grandparent's house. "Do you think there might be more bonds?"

"According to your father there are. Otherwise, a lot of money is missing for no obvious reason. You know, we need to get some fresh towels, sheets, and laundry supplies if we're going to stay out there for a few days."

"And food and maybe some nice wine." He winked.

"I'm not much of a cook," Amanda warned.

"That's okay because I am an excellent cook. Just leave it to me."

"If those biscuits and apples are any indication of where you learned to cook, I'm totally buying it. There's so much we don't know about each other. Do you realize we haven't been on an official date?"

Reece thought about it for a minute. "You know,

you're right. We've been thrown into the strangest and most dangerous situations but haven't had a simple moment to just talk and share a meal and get to know each other."

"Well, that's about to change. I get the feeling we're about to spend a lot of time together."

Chapter 28

"You want me to *what*?" Ted Logan was hooked up to IVs and monitors and the remainder of his recently amputated leg was heavily bandaged.

Roger and Reece stood silently by as the attorney went over the particulars once again.

"It's an offer of employment. You would be wise to recognize what an opportunity you have been presented. If you succeed in convincing the new owner that this piece of property you are interested in is solely for your own purposes, and then sign that property over to my client, a tidy sum will go into your bank account to help you over the hump as you adjust to life with a prosthetic limb."

"And if I don't agree?"

"You have many choices. It just seems that one is rather attractive and the others less so. You've made a few ill-advised decisions up to this point. Perhaps you are wiser now."

"I didn't choose to forfeit my leg," Ted said, anger tingeing every word.

"Don't expect sympathy from your victims. You might have cost my client a relationship with his son. You are now being offered a way to obtain a prosthetic limb. Have you priced them? I doubt your insurance company will want to be on the hook for it, especially as you obtained it by your own hand in your attempted—albeit thwarted—robbery and murder."

Even Reece winced when the lawyer said that. It seemed a little harsh. But as soon as he started to feel something akin to sympathy, it dissolved with the memory of how Ted had attacked Amanda.

"I wasn't trying to kill anybody. I just wanted the purse." He looked down, obviously ashamed.

"We know you were acting out of your need for a little cash. With that scheme having backfired, perhaps a more legal one would appeal to you? Of course, it's your decision." The attorney started to close his briefcase, the unsigned contracts inside.

Panic spread across Ted's face. "And if he won't sell to me?"

Mitch grinned. "Failure to obtain the property we desire is failure to fulfill the contract. You either deliver it to my client, or no deal."

"That's hardly fair. Maybe he won't part with it."

"He'll be quite eager to part with it. It's your job to make sure it is to you."

"Okay. Where do I sign?"

The attorney pointed to the lines requiring Ted's signatures.

After each party had agreed on fees and conditions, they all signed the binding agreement. Though it was the normal custom at the end of a deal, Reece refused to shake hands on it. He kept thinking of Amanda on the night of the attack in the garage and the thump on his own head.

"You don't know how lucky you really are," Reece pointed out, shutting the door behind him.

On the way back to his office, Mitch slapped Roger on the back. "There you go. He's in."

"But still, Judson Matheney might not sell to him."

"We just needed to get Logan motivated. A motivated buyer will be successful. I wouldn't worry. That building is as good as yours."

"I sure hope so," Roger said. "Can I buy you some lunch?"

"I'll take a rain check if you don't mind. Other appointments." He waved and hurried off behind the courthouse doors.

"How about you?"

Reece shook his head. "I had a fantastic breakfast with a lovely lady, and I just want to get back to her."

"I don't blame you. I might disown you if you let this one get away."

"Not a chance."

****

Amanda phoned the real estate agent she had used to find her condo in Chicago. Elizabeth Graham sounded excited about the prospect of having a property for sale within that particular complex.

"Okay, I'll be hiring professional movers to clear out my belongings." Amanda had no desire to return to Chicago which now came as a surprise to her. She had felt equally reluctant about coming south on that first day of the project. "And you can fax the contract to me."

"Absolutely. Great." Elizabeth's smooth voice went up an octave. Clearly she was making it easy for her to do her job and make a nice fat commission.

"I'll mail you a key." She added that to her list of things to do—make a spare key and mail it to Elizabeth.

Reece was stirring up something that smelled good in the kitchen.

Heady scents of garlic, oregano, basil, onion, and olive oil wafted through the house, giving it the aroma of a fine Italian restaurant. He greeted her with a smile and a glass of wine, turning back to the stove to stir his sauce.

"So what got you interested in learning to cook?" she asked.

"Necessity. Living alone requires a man to develop a few skills he might not otherwise."

She laughed, and he shot her a confused look. "Now why is that funny?" he asked.

"Because I've been living alone for a long time too, and I didn't learn to cook. What does that say about me?"

"That you rarely eat. What's the deal with that? Are you one of those women who just don't find food attractive?" He opened the oven door, checking something she couldn't see—something that smelled heavenly and gave a sizzle as the door opened—and then shut it back.

For a moment she hesitated answering. *How much should I tell him?* Would he still find her attractive if he knew the truth, that beneath her shell lay fat cells just waiting to plump up again? She had read enough to know the cells are never lost unless you have liposuction.

"Hello!" He waved an oven-proof mitt in front of her face. "Where did you go just now? Was that such a hard question?"

She took a deep breath. Her whole life had recently turned into one thorough cleanse, might as well make it complete. "The truth is…I mean…what I want to tell you…" The words brought tangles of emotions. She couldn't even say it.

Reece dropped the mitt and wrapped his arms around her. "We've been through more in the past few days than some people ever experience: a search for your past, the muggings, the hunt for buried treasure between the walls of this place, quitting a job, starting a new company, finding—"

"Okay, I get it," she interrupted with a laugh.

"Yeah, so what is it you're having such a tough time telling me? I think I've proved I can take it." He raised an eyebrow and cocked his head to one side.

"I'm fat," she said quickly before she changed her mind and chickened out.

He laughed. "You are nuts." He picked up her wrist and wrapped his thumb and little finger around it. "You are so thin I can reach around your wrist with two fingers. I can reach around your waist with my hands and my fingers touch. Is this attitude because I've been feeding you some good southern-style food?"

"No, you don't get it. Underneath this exterior is a fat woman. I can't eat like you. I have seen what it can do to me and it is not attractive."

"I can't imagine not being attracted to you, regardless of your size. If you gained some weight, it wouldn't bother me. It bothers me more that you never seem to eat and that you guard against every morsel as if it were an enemy about to attack."

"I know you mean that sincerely, and I appreciate it. But the truth is I used to be really fat, and I fear returning to that place."

"Is that what all the calorie- and fat-counting is about? You think you'll get fat?"

"I know it."

"How do you know this?" He grabbed a bag of pre-washed salad from the refrigerator and doled out two portions into small salad bowls.

Amanda reached for the cucumber and began to slice it into thin rounds, adding them to the two bowls. "I know it. I've done it. I'm like an alcoholic where food it concerned. Yet I must eat something every day, whereas the alcoholic can make a choice to never drink again. I can't ever *stop* eating."

"You almost have." Reece said this so matter-of-factly that she had difficulty arguing the observation.

"But if I get the cravings again...if the weight returns..." She looked away, dropping the sentence. Amanda knew she couldn't go through that again. It was too hard to take off the excess pounds. Once they were glued to her body, they didn't seem to want to let go.

Reece took hold of her shoulders giving them a small shake. "Stop tormenting yourself. There's got to be another way...a healthier way."

She looked into his eyes and wanted to believe him. She wanted it more than she had ever wanted anything in her life.

"Dining is considered a pleasure to most people. To deny yourself a good meal seems torturous. And you exercise a lot, too, don't you?"

She nodded.

"Well, we're going to be getting lots of exercise starting and running this new company. And if you need more to keep your sanity, we'll swim, jog, walk, lift weights, whatever it takes. But please, I'm begging you, stop seeing food as the enemy. Besides"—he ran his hands along her hips—"I know a really great exercise we can enjoy together."

Amanda was instantly turned on. His hands on her body always made her ache for him. Even when his hands *weren't* traveling the length of her, she craved them. "I don't think I've ever met a man who could make me desire him as much as you do."

"Good." He winked. "I like it that way. But I've got to check the chicken."

"Chicken?"

He released her and returned to the oven. "Aha. Just as I suspected." He pulled out a pan that had two large and lovely flattened, battered, and browned chicken breasts.

"Oven-fried chicken?" Her mouth began to water. She watched him sprinkle cheese over the two portions and slip them back into the oven.

"Chicken parmesan. Just wait 'til you taste it." He kissed his fingertips and then splayed them apart to indicate the deliciousness that was his fancy dish.

She watched as he tossed a handful of spaghetti noodles into a pot of boiling water before removing the chicken from the oven once again, this time with a bubbly golden cheese topping. He gave the noodles a jiggle and then declared them "perfectly al dente."

"I have to say," she admitted, "I'm impressed."

He placed a dollop of noodles onto each plate, topped it with the tomato sauce he had been stirring, and then placed a chicken breast with the oozing cheese atop the sauce. It looked divine as he carried the plates to the table. Amanda brought the salads and returned for the wine.

"Eat what you want. You don't have to finish it, but making a decent-sized dent is required." He gave her a smile, and she relaxed.

"Only if you allow me to cut this portion in half." She crossed her arms to make her point.

Reece grabbed another plate and pointed to it. "Guess that makes sense. You *are* about half my size, if that."

Amanda put the untouched portion to the side and inhaled the Italian seasonings and herbs that made the tomato sauce smell so rich and homey. She cut a bit of the cheesy chicken, crusted in panko crumbs and parmesan. As she chewed she made noises that reminded her of the sounds she made in the throes of passion.

Reece chuckled, watching her with his mouth half-open.

"Oh my, this is the best I've ever tasted. I'm more impressed than ever. But still…how?…the panko crumbs—"

"Okay, I'll come clean too. My ex-wife was a chef in one of Charlotte's finest restaurants. I paid attention."

"And yet you let her slip through your fingers?" Amanda mused.

"Well, once I had all of her secrets, what was the point?"

"That's why you'll never know all of mine," she teased, between bites of salad and swirls of spaghetti drenched in rich sauce and sticking together with cheese.

"There's more? I thought the chubby kid phase was it."

"Keep on thinking."

Their playfulness had made her forget how scared

she was to actually eat a few tasty morsels of real food. Lettuce with lemon, steamed vegetables with balsamic vinegar, raw fruit, black coffee—those were the things she normally ate—pasta, fried anything, meat and potatoes, cheeseburgers, milk shakes were not on her menu. Still she was eating with relish and enjoying every bite.

Reece turned serious. "I love having someone to have dinner with."

"Why is it I have trouble imagining that you find dinner dates hard to come by?" Amanda sipped her wine.

"Dates are not hard. Dates *with interesting women* are nearly impossible to get. Smarter men than I get them to commit. The dating pool becomes younger and younger and suddenly I'm looking across the table at a girl half my age, barely out of college, with no real life experience and a vernacular that is pretty much a foreign language."

"Sounds hideous," she teased.

"Then *you* show up. I have to confess, I'm caught in your net, Amanda. It's been a long time since I felt this connected to someone." He reached across the table and took her hand in his, rubbing his thumb along the back of her fingers.

The show of emotion made her uncomfortable, yet she couldn't bring herself to pull away. Amanda looked up and caught his eyes intently focused on her. Her heart started pounding in her chest. Hot blood rushed her veins and caused her face to break into a sweat. She swiped at it with her other hand.

He shook his head, and let his hand fall away. "Expressions of tenderness and affection make you nervous, don't they?"

"Please try to remember that after I lost my parents, the easy displays of love were also gone. My grandparents weren't demonstrative with their feelings. They were pragmatic, and soothed all of my hurts with a chocolate pie or a bowl of fried squash—whatever was on hand—hence my strange, forbidden love affair with food, and also my tragic inability to sustain a relationship." She shrugged, flexing her hand to rid it of the goose bumps caused by his caress.

"I knew you would be complicated. I could sense it from the start. But I've always enjoyed a challenge, and I believe I am the right man to love you enough to break through the wall you've built around you to keep people at bay."

Reece pushed his plate away and walked around the table. Lifting her, he carried her to the room they had prepared to use as theirs, laid her gently upon the bed, and removed every piece of clothing slowly. He tortured her with nibbles that started on her ankle and continued to the crest of her cleft. His tongue found the spot that pulsed with desire and flicked over it, flattening and circling, causing her to writhe with pleasure.

Amanda reached for him, but he refused to stop his tantalizing tease. He grasped her hands and pulled them behind and underneath her, lifting her buttocks to make his luxurious licks easier to maneuver.

"This is all about you," he said, as his other hand slipped alongside of his lips and joined in on the seduction.

The building up of anticipation caused her to forget herself. She became the moment, the feel of the hot blood pulsing from the one tiny button, fanning outward and upward in waves that built on themselves until she shook and quivered and contracted around his fingers.

Then he slipped his clothes off and eased inside the warm moist spot he had just teased to elation. She lifted her hips to allow the deepest penetration, and he buried his head in her neck as he burrowed himself against her innermost spot. She felt him tense and then thrust as he joined her in ecstasy and bliss.

Chapter 29

The next couple of weeks were a blur of similar days and similar activities. Reece and Amanda searched every corner of the house, every piece of clothing, every drawer. They found another $50,000 in bonds while uncovering several issues with the house that would need to be addressed.

Reece knew the right people to hire to correct the leaning chimney and service the heat pump so they could have a little air conditioning before the weather got too steamy. Amanda scanned decorating websites, trolling for wall colors and patterns for the furniture—a few pieces she had decided to throw out, the rest could be tweaked to fit into her developing taste for a more casual country house.

In Chicago her sleek, modern condo was exactly that—clean lines, straight backs, neutral colors. She had loved the crisp feeling that rose up to meet her at the end of a long, hard day. It would have to go with the condo as none of it would work in this old cottage. She made a note to tell Elizabeth if the buyer didn't wish to keep it, she should send it to a consignment shop.

Amanda also made note of the things she wished the movers to pack up and ship down to her. It didn't take long. Reece looked over her shoulder at the screen.

"Is that all?" he asked. "No art work, no pots and pans, no dishes and silver, no vases or lamps or books?"

"I hate to disappoint you but I lived cleanly and sparsely. And I believe we have already covered my lack of culinary skill, so there wasn't a need for fancy cookware. As for artwork, I have one great impressionist piece over the fireplace—Paris in the rain, mostly in gray and black tones with simple shimmering light and one red awning. Can you imagine it here among the florals and checks?"

Reece sounded surprised at her parsimony. "What did you do with your free time in Chicago?"

"That's what I've been trying to tell you. I didn't *have* free time. I stayed at the office complex. I exercised. I worked. I gave my life to Builders Tech…"

She looked away. It was still shocking to recall the cavalier manner in which Judson had just dismissed her dedication. And it was worse to remember that the entirety of her employment with him had been something besides what she had assumed it was.

A pawn. He had used her as easily as a pawn on that wretched chessboard she saw every day, not realizing she was being maneuvered in Judson's game. How could she have been so blind?

She had thought she was building a career with Builders Tech when all Judson had wanted from her was the one perfect moment of using her lineage to *correct* the one career loss he had suffered. What kind of an unprincipled, soulless carpetbagger sought vengeance on the subsequent generation of that single defeater?

Reece nudged her. He quietly asked, "What's on your mind?"

"Umm…what? Oh. The condo," she lied. "I've got to call Elizabeth." She quickly dialed the number and left a message for her real estate agent to give her a call.

Elizabeth Graham returned her call promptly. She was excited about the appraisal and had confirmation on a suggested asking price for the condo. Amanda was thrilled. Despite the bad market and the shrinking values of most real estate, her condo, in a desirable section of town, had doubled in value since Amanda had purchased it. She was going to make a nice profit. Elizabeth already had three people in mind to show it to.

****

Roger kept his eye on the building that had housed Dixie and when the For Sale sign went up, he called Reece and Amanda, giving them the news.

Ted Logan had gotten out the hospital. With his medical bills piling up, the stakes couldn't have been higher. His nonchalance about the scheme while lying in bed with tubes sticking into and out of him appeared to have turned into a strong desire to put those unfortunate events behind him and move forward.

Ted stayed in contact with Roger, and Roger with Reece and Amanda. Amanda answered the phone on the afternoon that Roger called with the news that Ted had put in an offer and Judson had arranged a teleconference so he could vet the prospective buyer.

Ted used the conference room of the club house at Simmons Point. Roger, Reece, and Amanda looked on from a spot beyond that which the webcam could capture. Hearing Judson's voice sent a chill down Amanda's spine. How could she not have noticed how cold and calculating he was before that iciness sent her plunging beneath the frigidness of his demeanor?

Reece circled his thumb over the back of her hand,

a habit he had that was growing on her. It was comforting, reassuring. She liked the contact with another human being. And she believed he was sincere. They were both too old and had too much hanging in the balance to playact at emotions.

"So what is it you plan on doing with this enormous warehouse, Mr. Logan?" Judson asked. The image on the overhead screen was that of cool confidence as he reclined slightly, fingers steepled in front of him.

"Does it matter?" Ted asked, showing the right amount of self-assurance. He too looked amazingly collected.

"Actually it does to me." Judson picked up a pen and tapped it on the legal pad in front of him as if he was about to jot a note.

"He's getting frustrated," Amanda whispered to Reece.

Reece nodded at Ted to keep the act up.

"Why?" he asked, turning the tables on Judson.

His face suddenly grew enormous on the screen. Judson had leaned very close to the computer's webcam. "I don't have to sell this jewel."

"Jewel?" Ted asked. "The place is an eyesore. Everybody in the whole city of Charlotte is glad to be rid of the palette-stacking building supply that kept the air polluted with its constant stream of exhaust from their trucks and machinery. I'd think you'd be glad to see someone willing to take it off your hands."

"Sir, I've got a dozen calls to return on this prized piece of property."

Amanda saw his eyes cut to the left of the screen. "He's lying," she said.

Ted raised an eyebrow. "It is slightly further from the lake than suits me, but I thought a deal might make the extra distance worthwhile."

"Building houses on the lake, are you?" Judson sounded annoyed.

Ted laughed. "Never built a house in my life, and don't intend to. But I got a thing for boats. I figured..." He stopped, appearing to think he had said too much.

"Go on," Judson said, leaning back in his chair.

"He's buying Ted's story," Amanda said to Reece.

Once again he nodded to Ted.

"I've made you an offer. The why of it is my business. Yours is to decide whether or not you can make it happen. That's really all I have to say on the matter."

"I've got a few more people to vet and offers to take. I'll get back to you by the week's end."

The screen went green, and the conference ended. Roger, Reece and Amanda all exhaled the breaths they had been holding. Ted closed the computer and they all congratulated each other.

"He's got nothing else," Amanda said, a sly smile curling the edges of her lips.

"Do I get my money now?" Ted asked.

"Right after you sign the building over to us," Reece answered.

"Hey, I think I've done a good job for you so far," Ted bargained.

Reece rubbed his head. "Don't rush me," he warned.

Amanda and the Jordans left the club house.
****

A truck arrived at Amanda's late the next day.

Reece raised the blind and watched three men exit the cab. One held a clipboard out in front of him and approached the front door. Reece was on the phone with a supplier, Gilbert Hayworth, getting another informal commitment on behalf of the embryonic new business.

Amanda scribbled across the clipboard's pad and followed the man to the back of the truck.

"Right," Reece said, "it's all still in development. My name will not be involved due to the conditions of the buyout contract, but you can be assured the people you will be dealing with will be the same as before.

"Builder's Tech is looking at your window line? Guess that kind of contract would be hard to turn down." His head throbbed as he heard the news from his best window supplier. Hayworth Windows had been released from the contract the Jordans had with them and could now court the giant *box store* suppliers with their line.

He listened as Gilbert apologized and offered his best wishes for whatever Reece managed to get off the ground. Hayworth assured him that he would keep Reece's business plan under wraps, and hoped he would reconsider their product should the Builder's Tech proposal fall through.

That was the comment that allowed Reece to feel comfortable that Gilbert would not divulge his intentions to Builder's Tech. A bit of courting was probably occurring between several suppliers. Keeping Reece's plans secret would assure good faith in approaching him should Hayworth Windows not make the final cut.

Reece doubted Gilbert's willingness to take the

slim profit margin that Builder's Tech would give him. His operation would have to multiply by considerable measures. Though the numbers would be larger, the profits would shrink per window unit until it would be hard to make the same as he likely would by keeping the plant small, overhead manageable, and the profits decent.

It was a story Reece was hearing over and over again. Builder's Tech now owned the contracts Dixie had earned. With the close of DMBS, Matheny could hold the contracts until they ran out, transfer them to larger ones with Builder's Tech, or release them. The contract holders were a little nervous.

Reece had seen this coming and Amanda would sign new contracts—since Reece was still under the non-compete order—with several of the smallest ones. These were the ones he knew Builder's Tech would never consider re-signing. They were all firmly behind Reece and the new venture.

He made it to the front door as the last of several large boxes were being unloaded from the cavernous back end of the truck.

"Just in time," Amanda said to him with a smile.

It had taken the three men less than fifteen minutes to unload all her worldly possessions into the corner of the dining room. "So we're done?" one of the workmen asked.

"Yes, thank you," she said, taking the receipt being offered to her.

"Not much, is it? And yet I dread the unpacking."

"Let's go into town for dinner."

"Sounds like a plan," she said as they bounced off together to get changed.

Chapter 30

The boxes haunted Amanda. How could her entire cache of worthwhile belongings fit into a single corner of a small room? It made her sick to look at them. In fact, she had felt nauseated since the delivery truck had dropped them off.

"It's stress," Reece said, rubbing the back of her neck. "You've had an enormous amount of lifestyle changes in a very short period of time."

"It's staggering to think about," she confessed. "You know, one thing I keep wondering is whether Judson would have ever mentioned my father to me had we not figured this out for ourselves? Would he have just fired me one day?"

"His plans don't matter anymore," Reece assured her. "And he'll soon regret letting you go."

Amanda glanced back at the stack of boxes. She opened one. A picture of her mother and father wrapped in protective bubble-swollen plastic stared up at her. Her grandfather had sent it to her after her grandmother's death.

The note attached to it had broken her heart. "Your grandmother wouldn't want something to happen to me and you not have this picture of your family. Know we are all with you always. We have left you everything we can in this world. With my love. Always, Grandpa."

She had looked upon it every day in Chicago. She

tore at the wrapping and ran a hand over the photograph, the stickiness of a piece of tape clung to the glass The offending goo left behind was right across her mother's eyes. Amanda couldn't bear that. She took the frame to the sink, and started the water running to get it hot.

"Reece," she called out.

He appeared almost instantly. "You call?"

"Do we have something to remove this residue from the glass?" She ran her finger along the edge.

"I think so." He immediately began to search through the cleaning supplies from beneath the sink. "Here we go."

She released the back from the frame and began to disassemble the entire picture. Along with the matting and the photograph popped out an envelope with her name on the outside.

Although he was right beside her, she squealed out. "Oh my gosh! Reece!"

"What is it?

"That's my grandfather's handwriting." She stood still, shocked.

"Well, don't just stand there. Open it up."

Her heart began to palpitate. Excitement and anticipation competed in her psyche until she could barely move her fingers.

Reece handed her a knife from the silverware drawer and she slid its tip beneath the seal of the envelope. In a flash of blade against paper she opened one end. A folded letter—two pages thick—dropped out.

Amanda unfolded the letter. Her grandfather's scribble made her instantly want to cry. It was if he was standing right there in the room with them.

"What does it say?" Reece didn't try to look over her shoulder, but he couldn't keep his curiosity at bay either.

"My dear granddaughter..." Tears immediately choked her. She swallowed hard three times and blinked furiously. "There are many things your grandmother and I should have told you. It never seemed like the right time. But if something should happen to me, you need to know there are some valuables here in your name. We intended to give them to you when you got married, but we never trusted Lassiter. Seems we might have been right about the no-account. Anyway, no point on going on about rubbish."

She laughed and Reece grinned. "They never liked Adam, my ex-husband," she explained.

"So it would seem. I think I would have gotten along with Grandpa." Reece winked.

Amanda nodded and continued to read. "Then we thought we'd give them to you when you came back home. But you didn't visit often, and we dreaded the explanations. So here I am, alone, and at the end of my life. I need you to know where to find these things. I wouldn't want them to be discarded by accident. There's a map enclosed of every place you should look. I know this picture is one thing you will never part with."

She gasped. Tears had turned to sobs.

"What's wrong?" Reece rubbed her back, attempting to soothe her.

"I threw them away. I did...and he felt it. Here, this says it all. The only thing he knew I valued from all of this"—she motioned around the house—"was this picture of my parents."

"I don't think that's what he meant. I think he just meant you could keep the picture with you. A sofa won't fit in your luggage."

She tried to smile at his attempt of humor. "I was awful, just awful."

"You were simply a human being trying to make her way alone in the world. Your mother left Wilkesboro and went to Mooresville. Why *shouldn't* you move to Chicago?"

She separated the pages. The second one had a listing of all of the items and where she could find them.

Her head spun and her stomach rolled. She pushed Reece out of her way and raced to the bathroom, emptying the contents of her stomach into the porcelain bowl. Amanda stayed on the floor for a few minutes, waiting for the wave of sickness to pass.

Reece knocked at the door and opened it slightly. "Are you okay? Can I get you anything? A cold cloth maybe?"

She could hear the concern in his voice. He was the kind of man who did everything with passion, protecting his company, his employees, his father, and showing love in every form to the intimate partner in his life.

That same level of passion rose to the surface if you found yourself on the opposite side of his good graces, as she well-remembered from the first day she had laid eyes on him.

He ran cool water over a wash cloth and knelt beside of her, pulling her hair back and laying the moist cloth gently across the bend of her neck. His strong sinewy hands caressed her with soft strokes along her shoulders.

The episode passed, and she collected herself as best she could while letting Reece help her from the cold tile floor. He held onto her, steadying her as she swayed.

"I'm okay now," she reassured him.

He helped her to bed, leaving her to rest while he made more phone calls. "That's a lot to absorb. Just rest."

She heard him puttering about, trying to be quiet and failing. Amanda started to get back up but decided against it, feeling as tired as she ever had in her life.

All of the stresses since arriving in North Carolina, including the betrayal of a man she had thought of as mentor and finding the emotion-laden letter in the picture frame, had all culminated into an exhaustion that left her so weary the effort to lift her hand seemed to take all of the strength in her body.

****

The jangle of the telephone jarred Amanda from her sleep. She looked at the clock and saw it was nearly midnight. Running her hand over the sheets next to her and finding only empty space she wondered, *Where is Reece? And who is calling at midnight?*

She pulled herself up and snatched a robe off the door, getting dizzy as she made her way to the hallway. Light seemed to pour from every opening not covered with a blind. It couldn't be midnight. She steadied herself and walked slowly in the direction of Reece's voice.

He broke into a smile as soon as he saw her. "I'll tell her right now," he said into the receiver. "She'll be delighted."

"Feeling better?" he asked, pulling her into his arms.

"I'm still a little lightheaded and weak, but better I suppose. What time is it?"

"It's half past noon." He kissed her on top of the head.

She pulled away. "It's after noon! Does that mean I slept fifteen hours?"

"Yes, and you obviously needed it."

"I haven't done that since I was in college."

He offered her his cup of coffee, but she pushed it away. "My stomach is not up to coffee yet."

"I'll drink it myself then," he said.

She realized he was very cheerful. "So what's going on? You seem terribly happy."

"I *am* happy. We've just received some wonderful news."

Amanda watched joy light up Reece's face. It shone from his eyes and radiated from him as though a production crew had back-lit him.

"I've just heard from my attorney. It seems we *can* file a claim on the money Pamela stole from J & S since we replaced it. Plus that case will keep Matheny very busy because it will be heard in North Carolina."

She smiled. "He won't like that. He wants things clean and neat and all loose ends tied up in a sailor's knot."

"And it gets better. Logan just sealed the deal for the warehouse and shop along with some of the equipment. He's even working on getting the trucks, too, at least a few of them."

"That's fan…" She had meant to say fantastic, but

the word got caught behind a wave of nausea. She ran to the bathroom with Reece on her heels.

"Enough," he insisted. "I'm taking you to the doctor."

****

Amanda did her best to convince Reece she was probably experiencing food allergies. She had eaten so many things lately she normally didn't. But she could tell he was concerned.

"You're the most important thing in my life. I won't risk your health with these hypothetical allergies. Let's get a medical opinion. If the doctor agrees with your diagnosis, we'll get you tested and then we'll know what to avoid so you don't have these attacks."

It made sense.

Reece didn't know who to call, but Vernella did. Strangely enough, Amanda was beginning to warm to Vernie. Once the feisty redhead realized the sacrifices Amanda was making, she had become friendlier.

Reece drove Amanda to the appointment, even though it seemed unnecessary. She had been taking care of herself since college, even through her brief, and albeit dissatisfying, marriage to Adam Lassiter.

Amanda liked Reece's concern for her. It made her feel special, loved in a way she hadn't for many, many years. He even insisted on going into the waiting room, just in case she needed him.

It wasn't until her medical history forms were being reviewed that she realized a possible cause of her problem, though it still seemed incredibly improbable. "Yes, my period is late, but I am forty-six. Who gets pregnant at this age? Isn't it more likely I'm just having perimenopausal symptoms?"

"Could be. But let's not chance it." Her physician's assistant—the woman she was seeing at the late notice—handed her a cup. "We'll know soon enough. If it comes back negative, we'll look for other causes for your symptoms. Here's the restroom. I'll be back in a few minutes with your results."

Amanda waited in the examining room in a stupor. It was crazy.

She had read about women trying to get pregnant at advanced ages. After forty-five, the experts said, there was only about a ten percent chance of naturally conceiving. She didn't dare get her hopes up.

Amanda had often thought she had missed the gene that would have given her family ties of any sort. She had lost her parents so young, married right out of college and divorced within three years, and afterwards was such a workaholic that she had even managed to lose contact with most of her close friends.

She had come to accept that love wasn't meant for her, not from a husband or significant other, not from children, not from anybody. And now…no…she couldn't dare contemplate it.

But what if? The possibility played tricks on her mind. It sucked her into a vortex of daydreams—imagining a child as a baby in her arms, going off to school, learning to ride a bicycle—and then the concept turned into a nightmare.

Reece might not want to have a child. His hands were pretty full starting up another business, and he was in his fifties. This would not be the ideal time to bring a child into his world.

She began to pace the office, chewing her lip. And then she started laughing at herself. She was nuts.

Clearly it wasn't a pregnancy. It was a food allergy.

Yes, that had to be it. She had been eating so much lately, consuming real food while getting lots of exercise. Reece had been making sure she ate well-prepared meals. Her body was rebelling. She was getting herself worked up over nothing. She settled down and searched through her phone for messages she hadn't responded to.

"Ms. Lassiter?" The PA rapped twice on the door.

She looked up and saw the grin spreading across the woman's face. Amanda couldn't speak. Her heart raced, forcing the blood through her hot veins. Her forehead flushed and she felt her cheeks warm.

The PA crossed her arms. "Looks as if we have a pregnancy to deal with. What would you like to do?"

"Do? Pregnancy? Are you sure?" Even after considering and letting herself imagine it, Amanda couldn't digest the thought as fact.

"Let's talk, shall we?" The woman pulled up a chair and began to give Amanda the sad facts about the dangers and risks to mother and child of advanced-age pregnancies, especially when the eggs were her own.

Amanda was still processing the reality of being pregnant. "Are you sure? Isn't it more likely my body isn't functioning properly with the sudden extra calories?"

"It's the opposite really. A body teetering close to starvation resists added stress. I'd bet the extra calories have made your pregnancy possible." She adjusted the laptop.

Amanda saw the medical professional's lips moving, heard bits of words fading in and out as if someone had a hand on the volume button and was turning it up and down. "...to be sure...blood test...lab to take...risk for birth defects...heart and lung..."

All she could think about was how having starved herself for so long she had nearly stolen the opportunity from herself to have a child. Maybe food *didn't* have to be an enemy any longer.

"Sure," Amanda said, meaning to respond to the blood test question. "Of course we should make sure first. Let's get the blood test."

The next few minutes passed in a swirl of pandemonium. A nurse teetered in with a small basket and drew a vial of blood. The PA returned, grinning still.

"It's a definite pregnancy. We should send you to the hospital for tests, a sonogram—"

Amanda held up her hands. "I'm lightheaded and nauseous. Is that normal?"

"Well, yes, but—"

She held up her hand again. "Can I have the information in a brochure or something...a website...a printout...I just can't process...I mean...I need time to think."

"Of course. Think it over. It's likely not too late for any choice you might wish to make. I'll get you some printouts for ways to deal with the early symptoms."

Reece leapt up when he saw Amanda walking through the door. She folded the fistful of papers in half and stuffed them into her handbag.

"So what did they say? What's wrong? Did you have some tests run?" Worry and concern underlined every word.

It had been a long time since anyone had been so caring. Amanda wanted to cry. Again. She had been crying a lot lately and suddenly realized why. She never cried. She had stopped crying when the last person of importance in her life had slipped into the afterlife. Even for some time before that, tears had been rare.

"Come on," she tugged Reece by the arm. "I'm going to be fine. But I need you to take me someplace."

"Anywhere," he agreed, looking confused. "Pharmacy maybe?"

"No, Jordan's Valley. I have a strong urge to see the view from your dream house."

Reece furrowed his brows, but he agreed. "I probably need to check on it anyway," he said.

He took her by the waist to lift her off the truck's runner as he had done on the day when the hawk had disturbed their near-kiss. Amanda felt his strong hands on her stomach and wanted to blurt it out, but waited.

She followed him to the large glass windows looking over the valley and the lake below, trying to form the words that would be the best way of telling him.

Chapter 31

"Reece, have you ever wondered what is going to happen to all of this after we're gone?"

He shrugged. "I'll donate it all, I suppose."

"No children?" she asked, as if there might have been one lurking in the bushes he had forgotten to mention.

"None." He chucked her underneath her chin. "Have you got an idea in mind? A pet charity or something?"

She turned away from him, suddenly fearing a negative reaction. "Did you ever think about having a child?"

"Why the talk about children? Do you have one I should know about?"

Her heart raced. Her breath stuck in her throat. The air didn't seem to want to flow in and out the way it normally did. She braced against a stud in the wall. "I might."

She looked away. It would devastate her to lose Reece now. What if he didn't want the child?

"Okay. I think we'll be able to support it once the company gets off the ground. How old is he? Or is it a she?"

"I don't know." She laughed, liking the *no-problem attitude* he possessed so far.

"If you have a child, you must know which sex it

is," he reasoned.

"It isn't here yet." She looked up at him. His face went blank, then it seemed to come alive.

"Oh, I see. You've put in for an adoption."

She grabbed his hand and held it to her heart. *Please want this child. Please want our baby*, she prayed silently. Then she slid it down to her stomach. "No, that's not it either. As strange as it seems, I've conceived a child. *We're* going to have a baby."

"We're going to do what?" The color drained from his face. He appeared shocked.

She closed her eyes. She couldn't bear to look. *He's not happy. He doesn't want the child. Oh God!*

He grabbed her up, embracing her as he spun her around the room. "You're carrying my child—our child—we're going to have a baby?"

She pulled her eyes opened and saw the excitement there. "You're happy?"

"Happy? I'm beyond happy. Oh Mandy!" Reece spun her around and she was reminded of the way her father had done the same thing with her. "Is that what is wrong with you?" He set her down. "You're going to be okay, right?"

"Yeah, if I don't throw up after all of that spinning."

He kissed her eyes, her nose, her cheeks. "I can't believe this. I hadn't thought…I didn't imagine…" He pushed her back from him. Suddenly serious, he dropped to one knee. "Amanda Simmons Lassiter, would you do me the very great honor of becoming my wife?"

She wanted to scream "yes," but her memory clicked back to something he'd said before and she hesitated.

She didn't want to marry anybody because of a sense of duty or responsibility. And no matter how she felt about him, she wouldn't agree to become his wife unless she knew beyond a shadow of a doubt that he wasn't responding to their predicament.

"You told me the first night we made love that if I conceived you'd make an *honest woman* out of me. You're only asking me because I'm pregnant."

"Want to bet? Just wait right here." He walked out to his truck and came back with something in his hand. He snapped open the box and a large emerald-cut diamond winked at her. "I've had it for over a week. I've been waiting for the right time and the right place, and the right moment. I'm not asking you to marry me because of some sense of duty. I love you. And I'm asking you to marry me if you love me too. It's that simple."

"I do love you, too," she said, reaching out for the box.

He snapped the lid closed. "You haven't said 'yes.' You must say, 'yes, Reece, I'd love nothing more than to be your wife.'"

She laughed and then cut her eyes at him. "You know I'm never going to say it that way, don't you?"

"Well, it'll be a pity to have to take this back to the jeweler. But…"

"Okay. Yes, Reece. I'd love nothing more than to be your wife."

"That's better," he said, grabbing her into his arms for another spin around the room.

"I'm going to throw up," she yelled, laughing at his exuberance.

****

March 13th Charlotte-Mecklenburg Spectator, Birth Announcements

"Mr. Roger Jordan proudly announces the birth of his first grandchild, William Simmons Jordan, born to Reece Jordan and his wife, the former Amanda Simmons Lassiter. Reece continues construction on their home in Jordan's Valley, while Amanda is owner/operator of Simmons-Jordan Building Supply."

A word about the author...

Renee Johnson has contributed to Bonjour Paris, an online travel website; Storyhouse—where she won second place for travel story of the year two years in a row; and received an honorable mention in a travel essay contest from Study Abroad. Only then did she begin to pursue her true passion for fiction, one which started when she was only nine years old. After placing third in Indiana's Golden Opportunity Contest for romantic/suspense in 2013, she signed with The Wild Rose Press for *ACQUISITION*, a sassy southern novel full of intrigue and secrets.

Renee lives in North Carolina with her husband Tony, son Caleb, and a very spoiled German shepherd named Gretel.

She is a member of Romance Writers of America and She Writes.

~*~

You can follow Renee online at:
http://writingfeemail.com
(for personal observations and photography)
http://reneejohnsonwrites.com
http://twitter.com/@writingfeemail
http://www.facebook.com/renee.johnson.549436